MW01131754

For Moonie Kay,
Thank you for teaching me that stories, however fantastical they might be, are invaluable.

Fear comes from the pit of your soul,
bringing forth emotions the Devil would extol,
Nothing but a growing urgency
coming from within
It makes you shudder,
your heart eerily flutter.

EDGAR ALLAN POE, *THE RAVEN*

CONSUMED

A NOVEL

AARON MAHNKE

PRELUDE

EDITH POWELL HAD TAKEN her dog for a walk, but now she was running for her life.

She staggered to her feet, pulled forward by the frightened pet at the end of the leash, and then continued running toward the gray light still visible through the trees.

The sounds of snapping branches and crushed leaves seemed to surround her, but she kept her eyes on the small patch of sky between the narrow tree trunks about a hundred yards ahead. The light that was visible through them was heavy with the approaching dusk, but she could still see enough to understand that it was her best way out.

Something scratched the back of her leg, cutting the flesh and causing her to miss a step. She stumbled and then caught her right shoulder against a small tree, bending it enough to cause an audible break in the trunk. Or maybe that had been her arm.

Blood trickled down her brow and into her left eye. She had somehow avoided blinding herself on the bare limb of a pine a few yards back, but it had still connected with her skull, knocking her down and tearing a gash in her forehead. She wiped the back of her free hand across the wound absently, never taking her eyes off the edge of the forest.

Behind her, another limb exploded as the thing that pursued her collided with a tree. Sammy, her terrier, did not stop running ahead of her, but Edith could hear a loud whimper. Even the dog was afraid.

A thicket appeared in her path, and she veered to the left, hoping Sammy would do the same. The little terrier did, thankfully, and Edith remained on her feet. The crashing sounds behind her continued unchecked, and her heart beat more urgently in response.

Movement to the left caught her eye, and she risked a glance back into the woods she was so desperately trying to escape. She still couldn't see it, whatever *it* was, but she was certain there was a shadow a few yards back. A shadow that moved. And that shadow was big.

Leaves covered the forest floor, concealing roots and fallen branches, but Edith watched Sammy and tried to follow his path. When the dog leapt over a lump dressed in brown and yellow leaves, she did the same. Her shoes had not been made for sprints through dense forest, though, and as she landed she felt her left ankle twist slightly. The pain shot up her leg like lightning, and she cried out into the quickly dimming light.

She managed to stay on her feet, though, running through the pain, refusing to allow herself to limp. Limping would slow her down, and she mustn't do that. Even still, the sounds seemed to be louder and closer.

Another sharp pain, this time across her back. It was as if someone had slashed out at her with a knife. She could feel the burning pain, and then the cool autumn air on the exposed flesh. Panic rose in her throat, but the scream she wanted so desperately to let out would not come. She was too winded, too stretched. And the deep gray sky beyond the trees still seemed miles away.

More movement caught her eye, and this time it came from behind her and to the right. She turned but didn't see the dark shape she had expected. Was it still there? Was it still following her? She didn't know for sure.

What she was certain of, though, was that her ankle throbbed. A cramp was also growing in her side, but she tried her best to ignore it. Sammy was still far ahead, and Edith knew that if she loosened her grip, the dog would be gone in a heartbeat.

That was when she tripped. It was hard to see in the dimming light, and she must have caught her foot on a fallen branch. Her momentum carried her over the obstacle and forward more than six feet. She brought her arms up to shield her face as she landed, hoping to protect her eyes from whatever debris might be waiting for her beneath the leaves.

Edith refused to allow her legs to stop moving. Even as she lay on the ground, they kicked and bicycled through the leaves and small branches, pushing her forward slowly. She needed to get up. She needed to move. Her mind was on fire with fear, but everything seemed to be moving too slowly.

Then, everything became quiet.

At first she thought she might have cracked her head on a rock, damaging her hearing somehow. There was no pain, though. Just the absence of noise, and the rhythmic thud of her heart beneath her breast.

Edith rolled over to look back into the dark forest. She was sure that she would find something dark and savage hovering over her, ready to pounce, but there was nothing. Even so, the feeling of being watched was still pervasive.

A tug on her arm caused her to shriek with fear before she realized that it was Sammy, still a few feet ahead of her, tugging at the leash. Suddenly she wanted the dog close; Sammy's tiny frame offered no hope of protection, but comfort might serve as an adequate substitute.

She opened her mouth to call out to the dog and then stopped cold. She could hear wind, like a distant gale howling through the trees. A shiver climbed up her spine, and then her mind rejected the sound.

There *was* no wind. She felt no breeze against her sweaty skin, and the leaves lay still around her. The branches overhead were as motionless as photographs, yet the sound of the wind continued.

Edith panicked and quickly struggled to regain her feet, stumbling forward as she did. In her rush to get moving again she allowed the leash to slip from her grasp and Sammy, the dog she had rescued as a puppy nearly thirteen years before, vanished into the darkness without hesitation.

She caught hold of a tree to steady herself and then tried to chase after the dog with one final burst of panicked exertion. The strain on her foot was too much, though, and she felt the bone bend at an unnatural angle. As if the pain itself had reached up and tripped her, she toppled forward again and crashed into a pile of fallen limbs.

This time she could feel her pursuer approaching. It was nearly on top of her, though it no longer made the noises that had frightened her off the path and toward the light. She could smell the fallen leaves and the musty soil beneath them, and something else. It was the smell of rot and decay.

Shaking with fear, Edith glanced one last time over her shoulder. She wanted to see whatever it was that had chased her down. She could no longer run; she could barely *stand*. If she was going to die, she wanted at the very least to *see* the thing that would end her life. She leveraged herself, twisted, and glanced backward to see...

Nothing.

The woods were completely empty.

A sudden thought occurred to her, as if someone had tossed a thin rope to her as she drowned in fear. What if she had simply imagined all of this? What if a random noise had set her off, and she had been chased off the path, not by some kind of monstrous creature, but by her overactive imagination?

That notion died with the sound of a snapping twig behind her, somewhere between the edge of the forest and the place where she now lay exhausted and broken. It was as if that thin thread of hope had snapped. And then she felt her head gripped from behind by something cold and savage.

The woods seemed to fill with the sound of the phantom wind as her body was lifted high off the ground. The creature's grip on her skull was tight, and she could feel the pressure that her body weight had on her neck and spine. The fetid scent of decay was almost unbearable, filling her nostrils with a rancid sweetness that made her stomach clench.

For a brief, horrible moment, she felt a second hand —impossibly large and powerful—grip her thrashing legs. Then she began to feel an uncomfortable tension, followed by intense pain.

In the end, just when she thought she could not bear the pressure any longer, she heard the sound of popping bone and cartilage, and then her world went black.

CHAPTER ONE

BEN SIMMONS WAS EXHAUSTED even before he got behind the wheel of his aged Passat, but his eagerness to get home and start writing proved stronger. Months of research had culminated in his trip to Rhode Island, and although he had arrived with little hope of finding anything useful, his week of research had been a success.

Less than ten minutes into his return drive north, however, all of that had changed.

He hadn't planned to take a detour. Getting home quickly was a priority for many reasons, the most important of which was a very hungry cat waiting for him in his condo. He had left out just enough food to cover his absence, but if he didn't get home by nightfall Mr. Perkins would be one distraught feline.

It was Rob Marshall's fault, really. He was the Deputy Manager at the Great Swamp Wildlife Refuge who had been assisting in Ben's final research project, and as Ben was leaving, the man said something. It was just a passing comment, but it had sparked an idea.

"Don't head over to I-95 just yet," Rob had said as he lowered the box of Ben's paperwork into the trunk. "If you love history as much as you say you do, you owe it to yourself to swing through Exeter."

"Oh?" he had replied. "Why's that?"

"Vampires," Rob said, as if it was completely normal to say such a thing in public.

"I'm sorry?" Ben replied. "You're kidding, right?"

Rob laughed—the kind of deep laugh that a stage actor might bellow in hopes that those in the back row might hear it—and flashed a broad smile at him.

"Don't worry, it's nothing real. Truth be told, New England has a long tradition of vampire lore that dates back more than two centuries. They say the last of them was a girl named Mercy, back at the turn of the century. She's buried up there, in Exeter."

Ben closed the trunk and brushed off his hands. "Well now, nineteenth-century American vampires might be just the excuse I need to avoid I-95 on a Friday afternoon." He extended a hand and the other man accepted it. "I couldn't have done any of this without your help, Rob. Thanks again."

The older man smiled again. "It was my pleasure, Ben. I hope the words flow when you get home. Sounds like you've got quite the book to write."

"Indeed I do," Ben agreed as he opened his car door and climbed in. "North on Route 2, right?"

"For a few minutes, yeah," Rob replied. "But I'd recommend you take the left onto 138 when you see it. Route 2 might get you there faster, but it's half as scenic. This is prime foliage season, after all. Just follow the signs."

"Noted," he said with a nod. "Thanks again."

Rob waved one last time as Ben pulled off the shoulder of the small road and headed north. There was no place for vampires in the historical fiction he was writing, American or not, but who knew. Maybe he could mine that lore for a future novel.

Ben saw the sign about a mile and a half after taking the left onto Route 138. The road was of the almost-paved, mostly-gravel variety, and he followed its rough curves for about a mile. After crossing a bridge, his road merged with another that approached from the left, changing names in the process—a classic New England strategy for confusing outsiders, his mother used to tell him—to Exeter Road. He followed it north.

The picturesque New England countryside lived up to Rob's praise. The road stayed pretty well hidden in the trees, and ancient stone walls lined each side, broken here and there by driveways. Mailboxes were infrequent, but Ben could see the occasional porch light from some of the homes that were set back and out of the way.

In a few places, the road cut straight through enormous granite boulders, most likely the same granite that had supplied stone for many of the low walls in the area. Some of those walls were tall and proud, while others looked as though an earthquake had rattled them to pieces a century before. Each of them, though, appeared permanent, almost monumental.

The wooded land to the left of the road fell away, and open pastureland stretched out to the west. Ben could see a farm house in the distance at the top of a rise, flanked by a pair of large barn-like structures. The small shape of a white pickup sat between the house and the other buildings.

He wondered if the people who lived there were long-time Rhode Islanders, or if they were part of the Great Hipster Exodus from the big cities, seeking a more simple life. If they were of the latter, he assumed their organic garden and free-range chicken coops were located on the portion of the property he couldn't see from the road.

As if triggered by his gaze, the white truck began to travel at a leisurely pace down the long drive toward the road. It was in that moment, while studying the plume of pale dust that rose in the truck's wake, that a deer stepped out from the trees to his right and walked into the road.

"Shit!" Ben shouted as the movement in the corner of his eye brought his full attention back to the narrow strip of pavement. The deer, no more than twenty yards ahead, stopped and turned its head toward him.

Ben cranked at the steering wheel, turning the nose of the car away from the animal and toward a stretch of stoney New England wall. His tires squealed and he felt gravity pulling him forward and to the right. Whether it was the sound of his spinning tires or the sight of the approaching vehicle, the startled deer finally gathered its wits and bolted back the way it had come.

Immediately, Ben reversed the turn and forced the car back into his lane, hoping to avoid a collision. The old Passat's tires cried out again as he tried to prevent the fishtail that he knew was going to happen, but it wasn't enough. The back left tire of the car skidded off the road, and there was a low thump as something—a stone or piece of wood—connected with the undercarriage.

He braked hard and brought the car to a stop on the shoulder of the wrong side of the road. His heart was in his throat, and he killed the engine for a sense of relief. When he looked up, he was surprised to see the white truck from the farm slowly approaching.

The late afternoon sun reflected off the windshield, making it hard for Ben to make out the driver, but he managed to see a person wave. He returned the gesture and then exited his own car. The white truck's headlights lit up, most likely to alert oncoming traffic of their presence, and then the driver door creaked open.

"Afternoon," Ben said as he walked toward the man who had stepped out. He looked to be about Ben's age —somewhere near forty—and well-built. The man's face was kind, but there was a hard edge to it.

"That was a close call," the stranger said. He motioned back down the road in the direction the deer had vanished as he stepped onto the gravel at the side of the road. "You alright?"

"Yeah, thanks," Ben said with a nod. "That was completely my fault. I wasn't looking at the road. Foolish, and damn-near deadly. Sorry you had to see that."

The stranger smiled. "Hey, I'm just glad you're alive. And you managed to avoid knocking down my wall, so you get bonus points."

Ben paused for a moment, and then laughed. It felt good, and he could feel the tension begin to drain from his neck and arms. The stranger standing on the shoulder of the road beside him laughed along with him.

"I'm Jack," the man said, extending his hand in greeting. "Jack Brooder."

"Good to meet you, Jack," he replied, gripping the offered hand. "I'm Ben Simmons. I'm also, apparently, the luckiest man in the world. That could have ended very badly."

Jack nodded. "You bet. But hey, you're still here, and that's a good thing. You're sure you're feeling alright? That gave me quite a scare, and I wan't even in the car with you."

Ben nodded again. "Yeah, I'll be fine. A bit shook up, but that'll go away."

"I'm sure it will," the man said.

Jack was clearly a confident man, and that was reassuring. The last big car accident Ben had been in, just a few years back, had involved a psychotic soccer mom and an oversized SUV full of screaming kids. She had turned left from the outer lane of a two-lane highway and Ben's car had slammed right into the back fender.

Everyone in the suburban tank escaped injury, but you wouldn't have known that by the way the woman exploded from her vehicle. She came out shouting, her arms waving about as if she were being attacked by a swarm of bees, and headed straight for Ben's car. He had started to open his door but quickly reconsidered that choice, opting instead to remain inside where she couldn't touch him.

Ben was a level-headed man by most accounts, and he understood that the woman's behavior was just a result of the accident. If he had joined her outside on the side of the road, the only thing that would have happened was a lot more shouting from her, and that wasn't going to help anyone. It had been better to wait for the police and let them sort it out.

The shock from that accident made this little event seem like the minor leagues, and he was glad for that. He smiled at the man, thankful for someone with whom he could verbally process what had happened.

"Sorry to trouble you," he finally said. "And I'll admit that I'm more embarrassed than shaken up. I think I'd rather avoid having an audience the next time I need to swerve around a deer."

The other man laughed. "Well, just be sure to do it in front of someone else's wall. That one's been in my family for seven generations." He gestured to the long, even pile of granite stones that stretched into the distance in both directions.

"Seven?" he replied. Clearly, Jack wasn't one of those urban hipsters living out here in self-imposed exile. "That's quite a legacy. Color me impressed."

"I like it," Jack replied. "Helps me feel anchored to the past. I've lived outside the area—all over the world, actually—but there's something about this farm, wrapped up in these ancient walls, that makes me feel grounded." Then, motioning to Ben's little Passat, "Does it still run?"

Ben glanced back at the car. "I think so. I mean, I only shut it off to let myself calm down, so I don't see why it wouldn't. I did hit something back there, though."

"Let's give it a try, then," Jack said, walking toward the car. "Just to be sure."

Ben complied, climbing back into his seat. He worked the ignition, confident that the little engine would turn over and start up, but it didn't. He tried it again but the result was the same.

Jack leaned in and tapped at the dashboard. Ben followed the man's finger. "You're out of gas," the man pointed out.

"Damn," Ben muttered. "It was half-full a few moments ago. Whatever I hit back there must have damaged my gas line."

He sniffed at the air and, sure enough, he caught the unmistakable scent of gasoline. He guessed that there was a dark patch in the gravel underneath his car to go along with it.

Jack straightened back up and glanced up the road. "Well, it's a long walk to town. Care for a ride? We can see if the auto shop is available to help out."

"Really?" Ben asked. "I mean, that would be great, sure. Thanks so much."

"It's the least I can do. You saved my wall, after all." Jack grinned, and the two men walked back toward the white truck.

It was more than white, though. Ben was amazed he hadn't noticed it before, but Jack's truck was a beauty. The generous curves and ample chrome hinted at a mid-century make and model.

"Oh, my," he said as he set his hands on the sill of the open passenger window. "What is this? Chevy?"

Jack nodded. "You bet. A 1952 five-window, to be precise. It was my grandfather's, like most of the things I own. Hop in."

Ben did, and grinned at the sound the engine made as Jack started it up. The rumble was deep and strong, and he could tell that the truck had been well maintained over the years.

The ride into town took no more than a few minutes. Jack turned right at an intersection, passed a cemetery, and then downtown began to appear around them. Before Ben knew it they were pulling off of Main Street and into a cramped parking lot. The sign on the front of the building announced that they had arrived at *Buster's Garage.*

"Welcome to Kettering," Jack said, gesturing down the main street.

It was clear that the town had seen better days, but it was far from dead. To the east, Ben could see the town center. The red brick buildings typical of every late nineteenth-century American downtown lined both sides of the street.

Back the way they had come was the only intersection in town that had a traffic light, the place where Main Street crossed Exeter Road. A left turn would lead south to Ben's broken Passat, still waiting near Jack's home. A right turn would eventually lead travelers to Exeter, where the road earned its name, after a short trip through the thickly wooded land to the north of town. Heading straight through the traffic light, Ben assumed, would lead to I-95.

The biggest clue that the town had seen better days was the vacant movie theater next door to *Buster's*. Posters no longer hung in the windows and the glass of the ticket booth was opaque with a film of soap, but the title of the last film to play there, *The Great Outdoors*, was still proudly spelled out in plastic letters on the marquee above.

"Seems like a nice place," he said.

Jack glanced down the road. "Oh, it's not that bad. We've got a town library a couple of blocks that way. There's a nice upscale restaurant nearby—the Old Dog, I believe—that seems to be all the rage with the young couples who live here and work in Providence or Newport. Angela's is the local bar and hangout, and their food is passable if you're not too picky. Our lone school is solid enough, and the city government doesn't screw things up for us *too* often."

"It's the little things in life, right?" Ben suggested with a smile. "Thanks for the ride." He extended his hand again to Jack, but the man shook his head.

"Nope, I'll wait right here," he explained. "There's no guarantee that Buster will be free to help you out. Last I checked, I'm your only ride, so I'll just wait here and see what happens."

"Are you sure?" Ben asked, feeling horrible for taking up so much of the man's time. "You've been awfully kind to me so far. I don't want to wear out my welcome."

Jack smiled as Ben climbed out of the truck. "I'm happy to help."

Buster's Garage was a collection of twenty-year old sedans in various states of disrepair, the remnants of a gas pump island, and a large boat still on its trailer and backed into a corner. The pavement looked as if it hadn't been swept in years, and every footstep seemed to create a crunching sound.

The door was open and Ben stepped inside. The room was small, consisting of a filthy aluminum desk, a pair of metal folding chairs, and a rubber floor mat. There was another door on the far wall, and through it Ben could see the dark, cavernous space that looked like every auto repair garage in the world.

He paused for a moment before deciding to open the second door and go searching for the man Jack had called Buster. Some mechanics didn't like people to enter their domain. They typically gripe about how unsafe it is, or how they 'can't take no responsibility' for what might happen around all those tools and holes in the floor.

Ben wasn't one to rock the boat, but his circumstances required taking a risk, even if that risk involved angering a mechanic. As he opened the door, the gritty sounds of Bob Seger belting out *Night Moves* came pouring out. Ben walked in just as good old Bob was apparently waiting on the thunder, and glanced around for someone to speak with.

"Can I help ya?" came the sound of a voice so gruff even Bob Seger would be jealous.

Ben turned to see a man standing at a workbench far to his right, cleaning something with a tattered rag. He was built like a mountain and as bristly as a pine, and Ben knew at once that this man must be Buster.

"Um...hello," he replied. His voice came out weak and far less masculine than he wanted. "Jack Brooder said you might be able to help me. My car broke down."

"Jack, eh?" The big man turned and set the part down on the bench and then walked toward him. He was quite possibly the largest man Ben had ever seen, topping him by more than a foot and at least a hundred pounds. "Anything for Jack. What's the trouble?"

Ben explained, and Buster gave it some thought. "Well, if it won't start, you need a tow. I can do that before the day is over, but I'm not going to be able to even take a look at it until morning. I hope that's alright, mister. I mean, it better be alright, 'cause it's the best I can do."

Ben wasn't sure if the man was kidding or serious, but he forced a smile and nodded. "So, you can help?"

"I'm happy to try," Buster said. "Jack bring you here?"

He nodded and the large man grunted in response. It might have been a laugh, but Ben wasn't sure.

"Let's go chat with him," the giant said before walking out the way Ben had come in.

Ben followed and soon the two men were outside. Buster approached Jack's truck and then leaned down—it seemed as if he bent himself in half—to talk to the other man. When he rested his forearms on the sill of the truck's window, Ben could see the vehicle lean.

"Hey there, Jack," the big man said. "So, where's it at?"

Jack motioned with his hand. "Back on Exeter, just south of town," he said. "Not more than a hundred yards from my driveway. You can't miss it."

"Good enough," Buster replied. When he stood back up, the truck's suspension groaned and the driver's side rose a couple of inches. Turning to Ben he held out a hand that looked like it could be used to paddle a small water craft. "Keys."

Ben pulled out his keyring and removed the spare. It seemed to vanish when he dropped it into the man's open palm.

"Stop in tomorrow, late morning. I'll have her inside, at least, and we can talk about getting her running again."

Ben nodded, and then the mountain turned and walked away to return to his rags and Bob Seger.

"Sounds like you're going to need a place to stay, then," Jacked said, leaning out his window. "Hop in. I'll have Lori make up the spare room."

Ben shook his head. "Oh, no. You've done more than enough, Jack. I'm not about to impose myself on your family. I'm sure I can find a motel or something around here."

Jack smiled. "That's not likely," he said. "The *Colonial* was the last of them, but they shut her down a couple of years ago. Nope, the *Brooder Motel* is the closest you're going to get, my friend. Now get in, I mean it."

Ben did as he was told, but reluctantly. He hated inconveniencing others. Self-reliance was something he strived for, and he usually got his way. It helped that he lived alone and worked from home. But in those rare instances when he couldn't avoid putting someone out, he had a tendency to go into it kicking and screaming.

Maybe it was because his parents divorced when he was young. He was sure a therapist would blame it on those dark days of fourth grade, but who really knew.

So much of a person's behavior was just a bunch of indicator lights responding to genetic prompts. Ben cared less about *why* he was this way, and just focused his resources on managing the results.

So I'm independent, he thought. *Fine. But I'm not going to become a burden. No one likes a freeloader.*

"Alright," he said to Jack. "You won me over. On the way there, though, do you mind if we stop at the car to get my things?"

"You bet," Jack said, turning the ignition. The truck thundered to life, and they were quickly on their way.

CHAPTER TWO

JACK CARRIED THE BOX of papers up the short walk to the house while Ben managed his wrinkled old duffle bag. This meant that Ben was the one to open the door for his host, and immediately those feelings of being an inconvenience resurfaced.

"Hey, Lori?" Jack called as he stepped inside.

A woman stepped into the hallway from another room and smiled. She had a youthful face, but there were lines at the corners of her mouth and around her eyes that hinted at an age closer to Jack's.

"Hey, honey," she said with a cheerful tone. Then, when she noticed the box, "Got something for me?"

"Nope," he replied with a grin. "I need a favor, though."

One of her eyebrows twitched up. "Really? Well, then, that'll cost you." She grinned, but then stopped when Jack stepped aside and Ben came into view. "Oh, hello there," she said. "Are you the favor?"

Ben sighed and nodded. "Yep, that's me."

He stepped through the door and set his bag down on the floor. Waving at her, he introduced himself. "Ben Simmons."

She returned the wave and smiled. "I'm Lori," she said. Turning to her husband, she asked, "What's going on?"

Jack set the box down on the floor beside Ben's bag and then straightened up. "Ben here had a close call with a deer out on the road. He made it through just fine, and so did the deer, but his car needs some work now. Buster's going to help him out, but can't get to it until tomorrow."

"Oh," she said, as if that was a logical answer she had been looking for. "Well, let me get the spare room fixed up. I think the bed needs fresh linens. I'll get some towels out, too."

"I really don't want to put you folks out," Ben said. "I really appreciate the hospitality, though."

Lori smiled warmly. "I'm happy to help, and glad you're alright. The deer have been extra brave this fall, stepping out onto the roads more and more often. It's not as bad here as it's been out north of town, but unusual just the same."

"Well," Ben said with a shrug, "it would have helped if I'd been driving with my eyes on the road. It's easy to surprise a man who's not looking, right?"

"On the bright side," Jack added, "he didn't hit the wall."

Lori rolled her eyes and headed back down the hall. "You and your walls, Jack."

Once Lori had vanished around a corner, Ben turned to his host. "She doesn't share your romantic attachment to the stones of your forefathers?" he asked.

"She didn't grow up here," he replied. "Me, I spent my childhood walking on those walls, and a good portion of my teens helping my grandfather repair them. You could blindfold me and drop me off at any point along that wall, and I'd be able to tell you where I am just by the feel of them."

Ben raised an eyebrow. "Impressive. Are you the same way with the rest of the property?"

"Yep," Jack nodded. "Every inch of her. Like the back of my hand, as they say."

To Ben, who had moved more than a dozen times since his parents' divorce, the thought of spending years getting to know one home sounded too good to be true. He and his mom had rarely spent more than a year in one place, the longest stretch being the eighteen months they lived outside of Hartford, Connecticut during his freshman and sophomore years of high school.

His mother had worked hard to keep a roof over their heads and food on the table. Sure, that roof was often nothing more than an apartment most of the time —it was hard to pay for anything more luxurious on the tips she pulled in as a waitress—but he hadn't expected more from her. Her sacrifice only made him wish he could contribute somehow.

He eventually did, once he was old enough to get a job and earn some cash, but she never came right out and asked. Ben was pretty sure that his mother was the most selfless person he had ever known. When she eventually did settle down—right about the time his friends were all moving off to college—he had already moved out and was doing the wandering on his own.

"My childhood was a little different," he said, "but then again, I didn't have to repair stone walls."

"You don't know what you missed," Jack said. "Well, let's get your things up to the room, and you can make yourself at home."

They carried Ben's few belongings up the stairs to a wide landing. The room that had been set up for him was across the hall from the bathroom, on the south side of the house. He could see his Passat from the window, its dirty green paint glinting dully in the dying light of the afternoon.

Lori was still getting the last of the linens on the bed, and Ben helped by stuffing the pillow into the fresh slip case. She thanked him, and then told him how he should be prepared to fight with their son Tyler for time in the bathroom.

"Do all teenagers spend hours in the shower?" she asked with exaggerated frustration. "I swear we're going to have to sink a new well just for him. It's a wonder he makes it to school on time."

"I don't have kids of my own, I'm afraid," he replied. "But looking back on my own teen years with a bit of honesty, I'm sure it's common."

"Grab that corner, would you?" She motioned toward the flap of fitted sheet that was sticking up near his knees. "Can you tug that down tight?"

"Gladly," he said, pulling it into place. "Jack says you didn't grow up around here. Do I hear a bit of California in your voice?"

Lori grinned. "Wow, very good," she said with a bit of surprise. "Yep, I spent most of my life there, in the Monterey area. Until I married Jack, that is. The military took us around the world for a few years, and then fate dumped us off here when his tour was done."

"Dumped, eh?" Ben said. "That's not the most enthusiastic choice of words."

"It's a long story," she replied, "but yeah, it wasn't my top choice at the time. Looking back, I think it was a good one, but I didn't accept it willingly."

When they were finished with the bedding, Lori invited him back downstairs to join the family for dinner. "It's not a gourmet spread," she added, "but my teenage boy never complains."

"Thanks," Ben replied, "I'd be honored."

On this particular Friday night, though, their son Tyler wasn't home. That left Ben to become the focus of the dinner conversation. Jack started the discussion by asking him what he meant when he said his childhood had been very different. Ben did his best to cover all the traveling that he and his mother had done after the divorce, but eventually ran out of cities to tell them about.

"So, where's home now?" Lori asked.

"Hollesley," he replied. "A little town a few miles north of Boston. I've actually been there for a few years now. It's nice."

"What brought you down to our part of New England, then?" Jack asked. "I don't know many people who take large boxes of paper on vacation, so I'm guessing this was a work-related trip?"

Ben nodded while he chewed a bite of food. "Yeah, this was a research trip. I spent a week down at the Great Swamp and the South Kingstown area."

"Researching what?" Lori asked.

"The Great Swamp Fight," he replied. "Some people call it a massacre, not a fight, but that's just semantics. It was a battle fought during King Phillip's War back in 1675 between the colonial forces and the local Native Americans."

Jack raised an eyebrow. "So you're a historian?" he asked.

"Oh, no," Ben shook his head, "Worse: I'm a novelist. Historical fiction is my passion. Though, yes, I did major in American history during the three semesters I spent in college."

"Fantastic," Lori said. "I love to read. Can I find your books in the store?"

"Not yet," Ben replied. "I'm still shopping my first manuscript around. I have some interest from a publisher in Woburn, but nothing solid yet. In the meantime, I'm getting the details ready for another book, and that led me down here."

"What were you looking to discover in person that you couldn't find on the internet or a library?" Jack asked.

"There's something to be said for actually standing in the place where something happened centuries ago. It adds perspective, you know? I've managed to uncover some little details that will add texture and nuance to the story. Ultimately, though, I just wanted to get a feel for the place."

Jack was quiet for a moment, and then he spoke up. "If this question is too nosey, just tell me, but why were you driving up this way? Isn't I-95 nice and close to the Wildlife Reserve?"

"Vampires," Ben said with a shrug. "At least, that's what I was told, but I don't know the story behind it."

Jack gave Ben a confused look, and then both of them laughed. "Ah, I see. You were headed up to Exeter, weren't you?"

Lori's face took on a perplexed expression. "What in the world are you two talking about?"

"It's a long story," Jack replied, "but Exeter is said to be the resting place of the last New England vampire, a young woman named Mercy Brown. I heard about it all the time as a kid, especially around Halloween. I even knew a kid from high school who tried stealing the headstone from the girl's grave."

Lori pushed her empty plate away. "That seems a bit creepy to me."

"It's a cautionary tale about the power of folklore," Jack continued. "The people in Exeter overreacted to a tuberculosis outbreak and blamed it on supernatural powers. They thought that one of the people who'd died was actually still alive and sucking the life out of the people in town. From what I've heard, they thought that if they could destroy the corpse responsible, they could break the curse."

"Wow, that's horrible," Ben said. "They actually did this?"

"Yep," Jack nodded. "Dug her up and cut out her heart. They burned it right there in the cemetery."

"That's barbaric," Lori muttered. "Why would they do that?"

Jack shrugged. "People a lot smarter than us have wondered that for a long time. But when folk in Europe heard about it, they thought it sounded like their old vampires stories. Some say the Mercy Brown events inspired Bram Stoker to write *Dracula*. A newspaper clipping of the story was found among his papers after he died. At least, that's what I've heard."

Lori stood up and gathered the dishes from the table. "Sometimes I wonder who the real monsters are. Humans are pretty capable of some nasty things."

"Here, let me help you," Ben said, standing up with her. "Dinner was fabulous, Lori. Thanks for feeding me."

"Glad to help," she replied, heading toward the sink. "With Tyler spending the night over at Gavin's house, I was worried I'd made too much food."

"Shoot," Ben said suddenly. "I almost forgot about my cat. He's probably run out of food. I hadn't actually planned on spending the night down here."

"Do you have a neighbor who could check in on him?" Jack suggested.

"Yeah," Ben replied. "Mrs. Eckerton from next door has a key. Nice grandmotherly type."

"The phone is on the wall over there" Lori said, gesturing toward the home unit that hung on the wall by the backdoor. "You're welcome to it."

"Thanks," he replied. "I'm bad with numbers, though. I'll just use my cell. She's programmed in it someplace. Mind if I step outside?"

"Have at it," Jack replied.

Ben pulled his cell phone out—an old flip-phone that had the well-worn look of an antique—and located Mrs. Eckerton's number on his list of contacts. He pushed the screen door open and felt the cool evening air. As he stepped outside he was struck by how bright and piercing the stars were overhead, and he couldn't help but smile.

Well, this turned out to be a pleasant detour, he thought as he dialed the number. *Unexpected, sure, but pleasant.*

Alfonso Quezada carried the last trash bag out to the dumpster in the back corner of the parking lot. They were heavy with scraps of food and melting ice, the typical leavings of a busy Friday night at Angela's. His right arm strained under the weight of the swollen bag and he wondered what the limit was. At some point, he assumed, one of these things will just rip open and dump its contents all over the blacktop.

The stars were crystalline in the sky overhead, and the air was crisp. The year was creeping into Autumn, a season that was bittersweet for him. It was a refreshing alternative to the sweltering heat and humidity of summer in New England, but it also intoned the approach of winter. Daytime temps that rarely broke 70° were a welcome treat; shoveling three feet of heavy snow before logging ten hours behind the bar was not.

Al's parents were immigrants who crossed the border between Mexico and Texas on foot in 1985. There were fewer patrols back then, and the Rio Bravo had a tendency to get pretty shallow around the Granjeno area, which made their journey into the promised land possible. Al was born less than a year later—a true American—and the family wandered north and east during the following years.

Rhode Island was a far cry from Matamoros, but something in his blood held on to that dislike for snow and freezing cold. Nights like this, with its cool breezes that carried the scent of the ocean from the east, were what made the winters worth it. Al took a deep breath and closed his eyes to soak it in.

This time he smelled something different, something rotten that caused him to wrinkle his nose. Nothing like being downwind from the trash at the end of a long night. Trash pickup wasn't until Tuesday morning, either, so he guessed the smell was only going to get worse as the weekend went on.

The dumpster sat crooked and dented in the far corner of the lot, like some sort of metal whale that had been beached on the edge of the property. Behind it, trees and undergrowth filled the edge of the street light's reach. It was Al's fourth trip out tonight—and thankfully his last—so he headed toward the open plastic lid on the left side.

This one was heavy, though. He strained to get the bag high enough to fall in, but his arm gave out and he had to set it down. The long day of work had robbed him of his vigor, apparently. He stood up straight, ran his hands over the small of his back, and then grabbed the bag again, this time with both hands. He heaved the bag with a grunt and finally managed to get it onto the lip of the open dumpster, from where it toppled inside like a body being tossed off a bridge.

A sound like wind came from the darkness behind the dumpster, and he turned toward the trees. The leaves were still and he couldn't feel the cool air on his skin as he had on the way out. Yet the sound repeated itself.

It had a dry, almost rasp-like quality to it, like steel wool being dragged over a piece of metal. Al's stomach knotted up at the sound and he could feel the hair on the back of his neck stand up.

"Mark?" he called out.

Mark Royer was one of the cooks that staffed the kitchen of Angela's on the weekends. He had a love for rum in his Coke while he worked, lewd comments about blondes, and practical jokes on the people who worked with him. Al was sure that if someone was trying to frighten him from the bushes, it would be Mark.

He reached up and pulled the plastic lid shut. After wiping his hands on the white apron that was still tied around his waist he walked around to the backside of the dumpster. The rancid smell was even worse back there, and he held the back of one hand up to his mouth.

Some lazy busboy ditched a trash bag behind here, he thought as he scanned the pavement at the edge of the grass. *No wonder it smells so ripe.*

The trouble was, he couldn't seem to find the bag. He checked along the full length of the dumpster but found nothing more than a used condom and one red stiletto-heeled shoe. *Someone had a fun night,* he thought.

Rasssp...

Al turned and glanced into the trees. This time he was almost positive that the sound had come from somewhere in the shadows. If his nose could be trusted, that's where the rotten smell was coming from as well.

He sighed. He was sure he could explain it to the manager on duty, but trash was usually his responsibility, and if someone else found a rotting bag of garbage in the woods behind the dumpster, the first person to be accused of being lazy would be Al. That's not something he wanted.

He took a deep breath through his mouth, doing his best to avoid using his nose at all, and stepped into the thin trees. The ground was littered with the first leaves of autumn and each step seemed loud and careless. Al pushed the low branch of a sapling aside and stepped deeper into the darkness. But still, no bag of trash.

Rasssp...

Al spun around this time, thinking he might be able to catch the source of the noise. The faint glow of the parking lot was there, broken up by the dark slashes of tree limbs, but nothing else. The smell had gotten worse, and even without breathing through his nose it seemed overpowering, as if it were hovering over him.

He heard the crackle of a lone, dry leaf just a few steps behind him and decided that he'd had enough. *They can blame me for whatever they want,* he thought, *but I'm getting out of here.*

He took a step toward the pale, flickering glow of the street lamp, but stopped when the dry, harsh sound of that imaginary wind filled the world around him. It was as if someone had slapped headphones on his ears and turned the volume up. He blinked at the suddenness of it, and then turned to look back over his shoulder.

He saw darkness, deep and black, where the gray of the woods should be, and then a wave of fetid air washed over him. It was as if death itself were breathing on him. He tried to scream, but his voice caught in his throat and all he managed was a weak sigh.

His world went black before a brief moment of intense pain, and then it was over.

CHAPTER THREE

BEN COULDN'T REMEMBER THE last time he slept in so late. The sun was already a good distance over the tops of the trees when he looked out the window from the bathroom while emptying his bladder. Considering it was early October, that meant he had really overdone it.

He headed back to his room and grabbed his cell phone. It was half-past nine, according to the display. *Shit,* he thought. *That's no way to avoid looking like a freeloader.*

Once he was dressed, he pulled his laptop out of his bag and tried to check his email. It had only been a couple of months since he had started shopping his first novel around to the handful of publishers who put out his type of fiction. He hadn't given up hope yet, maintaining a daily ritual of checking for a response of any kind. Even a rejection would be helpful.

He opened his laptop, but within seconds it became clear that this had been a pointless effort; the house, it seemed, had no wireless network that he could find. Closing the lid of the computer he returned it to the slim black bag and slung it over his shoulder.

When he finally went downstairs, Lori was in the kitchen. She made a friendly joke about teenagers and sleeping late, and then offered to make him some breakfast. Ben refused, feeling guilty enough as it was about not coming downstairs at a respectable time, and instead headed outside to see what Jack was up to.

It was warm compared to the previous day, and the blue sky was clear of clouds. From the driveway Ben could see the road, now empty thanks to Buster. To the south a wide spread of woodland swallowed up the highway that had brought him into town. Off to the north, in the direction of downtown Kettering and the auto repair shop, the dark haze of yet more trees ran along the horizon.

"Morning."

Ben turned to see Jack standing a few yards away, just outside the large shed that was across the gravel driveway from the house.

"Get enough sleep?" he asked.

Ben walked toward the shed and gave Jack an exasperated look that was mostly real, but accented with sarcasm. "I'm pretty ashamed of myself," he said. "Sorry about that."

"Nothing to apologize for," the man replied. "You had a rough afternoon yesterday. Maybe you just needed a good night of sleep. Thinking of getting some work done?" Jack asked, pointing at the bag on Ben's shoulder.

He nodded. "Yeah, I figured I would head into town and check on the car. See if Buster has made any headway with it. I never thought to ask yesterday, but he's open on Saturdays, right?"

"You bet," Jack answered. "Buster seems to work most days. The man's got no family as far as I've been able to figure out, so he must just pour himself into his job."

"Well, I'm glad for that today. I really need to get home, as glad as I've been for all the hospitality here, of course."

Jack pulled off his work gloves and set them on the ground beside the shed. "Well, let me give you a lift into town."

"Oh no, not this time," Ben said with a shake of his head. "You've done enough already, and I have a feeling you've got more than a little work to take care of today. No, I'll walk into town. Can't be more than half a mile, and my legs could use the stretch."

"Are you sure?" Jack asked.

"Absolutely," he replied, "but I appreciate the offer all the same. Hopefully, I'll be back within the hour and out of your hair shortly after that."

"Well," Jack began, "you're not a burden, so don't go thinking you are. But I can understand the need to get on back home. You know the way?"

"Sure do," he replied. "North to the traffic light, then right, and Buster's place is down on the right."

"You've got it," Jack said. "Walk safe, and let me know if you need anything."

"Will do," Ben said, adjusting the bag's strap on his shoulder before walking down the driveway and then onto the narrow road.

—◆◆◆—

The stretch of Exeter Road between the Brooder residence and the traffic light in town was uneventful and quiet, something that Ben welcomed after the excitement of the day before. The time alone provided a great opportunity to think through the discoveries that his research trip to South Kingstown had uncovered, and how he might work those bits into his work in progress.

Very few cars passed him on the way, and those that did all seemed to be coming from the north. He wondered where the people of Kettering spent their weekends, if they went anywhere at all. With the big sprawl of Providence near by, he assumed many headed that direction if they could manage it. Not Ben, though. He was walking into the heart of a town that didn't have a lot happening on the best of days, with hopes that the sole auto repair garage was open and available.

When he reached the traffic light, he turned right and headed down Main Street. Across the road was the small cemetery that he had noticed while riding in Jack's truck. It appeared, like many similar burial sites in New England, ancient and tired. Many of the dark gray headstones leaned slightly to one side, as if they had long ago given up and slumped over the graves that were tasked with marking.

Ben could see the trees that ran along the back side of the cemetery, and noticed how they crept toward the road along the side facing downtown. It was thin, but the band of trees that grew toward the road acted as a wall between the rows of tombstones and the more consumer-oriented businesses beyond.

Just past the graveyard was the parking lot of a restaurant. The sign atop the tall pole near the road identified the place as Angela's. It was clearly of the dine-and-drink variety, but at a quarter to nine in the morning it was understandably deserted. At least, that's what Ben thought when he first glanced at it, before he saw the small crowd.

Toward the back of the parking lot stood a cluster of perhaps a half-dozen or so people standing with their backs to the road. They weren't shouting or moving around much at all, but every now and then one of them would turn and glance over their shoulder. This was enough to pique Ben's interest, and after glancing both ways down the road, he crossed and walked toward them.

As Ben drew closer, he counted seven people standing at the back of the lot. A large metal dumpster stood beyond them, the kind you find behind just about any retail establishment in the country. But everyone seemed to be gathered around an area of pavement to the left of the trash.

One person, a man in wrinkled khakis and a sweat-stained t-shirt, was squatting low to the ground. A woman in a pink track suit stood beside him, pointing at something. There was something about everyone's body language that gave Ben a bad feeling.

"Morning," he said as he approached the crowd. "You'll have to forgive my—" he began, but stopped. One of the others, a teenage boy clearly dressed for a run, stepped aside to turn toward him, and when he did

Ben was able to catch a glimpse of what was on the ground.

A shape lay in the weeds at the edge of the pavement. Parts of it were still covered in clothing, but much of the skin was exposed and smeared with blood. Ben could make out an arm, though some of the fingers appeared to be missing. Of the legs, though, he could find no sign.

He could hear the sound of dozens of flies buzzing around the bloody remains. Bones protruded from the body, giving it the appearance of a macabre pincushion. The neck was bent at a sharp angle and though the face was turned away from him, he could tell that the head had an unnatural shape to it, like a lumpy pillow.

"Oh, God," he muttered before losing a grip on what he had been thinking. "Is that…?"

"Careful, Mister," said the woman in the pink track suit. "It's not a pretty sight, that's for sure. Sheriff's on his way over."

"What…why," he tried to ask, but couldn't manage to find the words through the nausea that was building in his stomach. He brought a hand to his mouth and fought a strong retching sensation. "What the hell is going on?"

Squatting Man stood up and stepped over to him. "I found it a little while ago. It's Alfonso, man." The way he said 'man' reminded Ben of movies about surfing.

Ben stared blankly back at the man. "Who's Alfonso?" he asked. "Who are you?"

"I'm Mark, man." It was said as if Ben should already have known it. "Mark Royer? Come on, man. Everyone in town knows who I am. I cook here at the restaurant."

Ben shook his head. "I'm from out of town. Just passing through, sorry."

He braved another step closer and glanced at the corpse again. There was much less of it than there should have been. He didn't have to be a medical expert to understand that. What was there, on the parking lot pavement, was *part* of a man, but certainly not *all* of a man. Not even *most*.

"Al works here, too," said Track Suit Lady. She looked at the body again. "Worked, I guess. He made the best margaritas. Kindest man you'd ever meet."

Others moved away from the body now. One of the men was thin and tall, and his face was covered in a matted beard. His dirty coveralls made him look like a hobo from some kind of political caricature.

The woman beside him looked like a tired mother, young but exhausted, and she was flanked by an older man. He wore neatly-pressed slacks along with a shirt and tie, and appeared to be approaching retirement age if the graying hair was any indication. He broke away from the others and pointed back toward the remains.

"I was here just last night," he declared. "He was alive then. Who in their right mind would do this to someone?"

Everyone glanced back at the road as the flash of red and blue lights caught their attention, and Ben watched a police cruiser slow down and turn into the lot. Like a swarm of flies being waved off of a piece of raw meat, everyone near the body stepped away.

Teenage Runner actually left at that moment, walking toward the road before waving to the officer in the car and then jogging off. Track Suit Lady and Mark Royer stayed beside Ben, and the others began to walk in their direction as well.

The man who got out of the police cruiser was tall and broad-shouldered. *What a mess*, Ben thought. *I hope he's ready for this.*

"Folks," the officer said, "I sure hope none of you have touched anything." It was more of a statement than a question, driven home by the stern glare he gave them.

"No, sir," said Mark Royer. "We've done nothing. Just looking, is all."

A younger officer exited the passenger side of the cruiser, dressed in the same uniform as the sheriff. He made his way over to the body, and then back to the truck of the car, where he began to fish around for supplies.

"Who found the body?" the sheriff asked, scanning the small group of bystanders.

"I did," said Track Suit Lady. "I was out on my morning walk—"

"Don't leave," the officer said, cutting her off. "I'll have some questions for you in a moment. The rest of you should get going to where ever it is you need to be. Deputy Cranston needs some room to work."

Everyone dispersed, heading back toward the street in a slow shuffle across the cracked parking lot. Ben was about to follow along when the sheriff saw him. The man held out a hand like an experienced traffic cop.

"I don't know you," the man declared. "That makes me nervous. So, who are you, and why are you here?"

Ben stopped, feeling a strange new anxiety. He was fairly certain that this officer was willing to consider any person to be a suspect if they weren't part of the normal flow of life in Kettering. Ben, as it happened, fit that description perfectly.

"Ben Simmons," he replied. "I'm from out of town. My car broke down yesterday afternoon, and I'm just on my way to see if it's ready to go."

The officer didn't say anything for a moment. Instead, he seemed to be studying him, soaking in the details, both spoken and unsaid. Finally, the man looked away.

"I'm Sheriff Roberts," he said while he watched Deputy Cranston run a length of crime scene tape between a tree and the dumpster. "Can anyone verify your whereabouts from last night until this morning?"

"Are you serious?" Ben replied. "I mean, you can't think I could do anything like that?" He waved his hand toward what remained of the body. "Hell, I don't even know if *anyone* is capable of that."

Sheriff Roberts didn't reply, but simply stared back, like a parent waiting for a disobedient child to wise up and change their behavior.

"Yes," Ben finally said. "I stayed out at the Brooder's last night. Jack has been very helpful. He and his wife both saw me last night, and again this morning. They can vouch for me."

"The Brooders?" echoed the sheriff. "Figures." It was more of a mutter than anything, but Ben heard it all the same. "I'll assume you're on your way to Buster's, then?"

"Yes, sir," he replied.

"Then why would you be standing here, in the back of an abandoned parking lot? Buster's garage is down the street."

"I got curious," he replied, this time with a bit more frustration in his voice. "Look, just because I'm not from town doesn't give you the right to harass me. I wasn't the first person to arrive here. Hell, I was the last of them, I think. I was walking by on my way to Buster's and saw the crowd. I just wanted to know what they were doing. That's all there is to it."

"You'll have to believe me, Mr. Simmons, when I tell you that I'm not harassing you." Sheriff Roberts leaned a bit closer. "I'm not, but I can if you give me reason to. Right now, I'm going to have a chat with Mrs. Brooks, and then I'll check on your alibi. I recommend staying in town until I've done that."

"You've got to be kidding me." Ben was astonished at the man's audacity. "Sheriff, I need to get home. If my car is repaired and ready, I'm leaving today. If you need to check my story, do it. The Brooders are home right now and I'm sure they'd be happy to answer your questions."

"Mr. Simmons," the sheriff began, "I would strongly urge you to avoid doing anything stupid. You'll hear from me later today, I promise. But don't leave this town until you do."

With his warning issued, the sheriff walked over to Track Suit Lady, who was whispering with panicked tones into her phone. Ben wanted to say more, but he was wise enough to understand what that might do to his odds of getting home by this afternoon.

No, he wanted to go home more than anything. He had work to do, and a cat that was probably very eager to sleep on his lap. Ben liked taking care of problems when they were alive and fresh, and he had a book that needed to be pushed out of his head, like a newborn in the birth canal. The longer he waited, the more often his thoughts were going to be focused on that problem.

Even being unable to take care of his email was becoming a tiny ball of tension in the back of his mind. As he walked down the street and aimed for Buster's garage, he was beginning to wonder how long he was going to have to fight that feeling. He had fought the transition to a smart phone that could send and receive email, but that was a decision he was learning to regret now.

A town this small also wasn't likely to have the typical chain coffee shops that made staying connected to the internet so easy. Even the Brooder's didn't seem to have an internet connection, at least not one that was wireless. He felt stuck.

When he arrived at Buster's, the garage seemed deserted. Ben knew where to look this time, though, and headed straight through the office and into the repair area. Buster was there, bent over a small Asian car that looked even more minuscule with him beside it. He spotted his own car in the far bay, hood up and slightly raised from the floor.

"There you are," Buster said as he looked up from his work. "Didn't think to get a phone number from you yesterday, and wasn't sure how to get ahold of you."

Ben smiled as he approached. "I'm glad I hoofed it over, then. Any news on the car?"

"Yep," the big man replied. He stood up and walked toward Ben's Passat. "I can fix her, for sure."

"Wait, you haven't started on it yet?" Ben was shocked.

"Let me finish," Buster said over his shoulder. "I can fix her, but the part that I need isn't easy to come by. Volkswagens are notoriously hard to repair, and this place ain't Providence, my friend."

Ben sighed. "Yeah, I've been told that before. That's the price I pay for all that fancy German engineering, I guess. So, you've ordered the part, then?"

"Tried to," Buster replied. "It's Saturday, man. Shops aren't as good at getting back to me on the weekend. I'm going to be honest with you: I don't think I'll have the part in here until Monday. I know that's not what you want to hear, but it's the best I can do, given the situation."

"Crap," Ben muttered. *Well, I guess I won't be leaving town after all. At least the* sheriff *is going to be pleased.*

"I'm sorry…er…I never got your name, either." The large man scratched his head.

"Ben," he replied. "Ben Simmons. And don't apologize. Like you said, I'm not in the big city right now, and parts are hard to find for an old German car like mine. I brought this on myself."

"I'll keep trying," Buster said. "I'm sure I'll track down a replacement part today, but getting it here before Monday is going to be tricky. I wouldn't put money on it, if I were a betting man."

"I understand," Ben replied.

"Here," Buster said. He reached into his pocket and brought out a pen and a scrap of paper. "Put your number on there. I'll call you first thing when I get news."

Ben did as the big man asked, and was handing back the pen when it occurred to him that Buster might know where he could find a free wifi network to connect to. That is, of course, if Buster knew what wifi was.

"Oh sure," the man said to him with a smile. "I go to the library whenever I need to get online. I'm barely ever home, so it makes no sense to pay for it at the house. Stop over at the library and they'll get you set up."

Ben thanked the man and then headed outside. He might not be able to get home as soon as he'd like, but at least there was a ray of hope now. He had email to take care of, and he wasn't about to let anything get in the way of that.

CHAPTER FOUR

THE KETTERING PUBLIC LIBRARY was a large, beautiful structure that evoked feelings of mid-American architecture. It was a Carnegie library, one of close to 1,700 such facilities built using funds granted to cities across the country. All this was thanks to Andrew Carnegie, one of the wealthiest men of the nineteenth Century, a man who believed in giving it all away rather than taking it with him to the grave.

Ben mounted the wide, shallow steps to the front door and then stepped inside. The foyer was just as wide as the stairs had been, but was flanked on either side by twin staircases with spindled balusters that curved upward and into the library space, accessing the upper level.

Past the foyer, though, the ceiling opened up and revealed a massive dome, painted with scenes and figures dressed in clothing that would have been common a century before. Large windows topped with stained glass let in a generous amount of light, illuminating much of the space.

It reminded him of his childhood. Money was always in short supply for his mother, and so rather than buying Ben books, she took him on frequent trips to the public library. Their nomadic life afforded him a tour of many Carnegie libraries. Many seemed cut from a similar cloth, whether it was the layout or the building materials, but it was the dome that always caught his attention.

Beneath this dome and directly ahead from the entrance, as it was in many other libraries, sat the wide wooden reception desk. Each end of the desk held tall lamps that resembled miniature street lights, and they both acted as bookends with a few volumes leaning against each. Behind the desk sat a woman, though Ben could see little more of her than the top of her head.

His footsteps echoed on the cold marble floor and caught the woman's attention. As he arrived at the desk, she stood up and gave him a friendly smile.

"Hello," she said in that soft tone that librarians have been the custodians of for centuries. "Can I help you?"

Ben shifted the bag on his shoulder and stepped up to the desk. "Hi," he replied. "Yes, I was wondering if I could borrow your internet."

The woman grinned. "Oh, do you plan to take it anywhere in particular?"

For a moment her words didn't make sense to him, and then the true meaning of what he had asked became clear. It was the type of moment that his mother would have followed up with the phrase 'Light dawns on Marblehead,' referring to thick-headed people and their slow understanding of things.

"I stand corrected," he replied with a smile. "It would be rude of me to take the internet right out of here and leave everyone else wondering what happened."

They both laughed, Ben a little more loudly than the woman. It drew a glance from the only other person visible from the lobby, an elderly woman hunched over a newspaper at a long, polished oak table. Ben shrugged at the woman apologetically and then turned back to the librarian.

Her face was smooth and fine-lined, with auburn hair spilling down past her shoulders. The smile on her lips was genuine and warm, and for a moment Ben thought that he would give anything to keep that smile there. Then, reality broke through and he remembered his errand.

"So," he tried again, "I'm in need of access to the internet. Buster, down at the auto garage, sent me here." He gestured to some unseen object in the corner of the room as if it helped clarify what he meant. Despite his vagueness, the woman nodded in understanding.

"Sure," she said. "Buster's a frequent visitor here. He's an avid collector of salt and pepper shakers. That man sure knows his way around an online auction site, believe it or not."

"Really?" he asked in disbelief. "Somehow he doesn't strike me as a collector, but that could just be me jumping to conclusions. I probably shouldn't judge people based on appearance."

"Nor a book by its cover, right?" she replied. "Are you from out of town, then? I mean, we've never met, and you've obviously had some car trouble, so I'm guessing you're not from around here."

"Good guess," he replied. "And yes, that's my situation. It's a long story, but I think I'm stuck in town for the next couple of days. I knew I had a lot of email to take care of even before I arrived yesterday, and I'm sure it's just begging for attention by now, so I was hoping I could sit at a table and get some work done."

"Of course," she replied. She turned and reached for a card on the desk a couple of feet away, and then slid it across the desk. "Here, this has all the information on it that you will need. Network name and password, really. And if you need anything else, feel free to ask. My name is Ellen Hornsby; I'm the head librarian here."

She extended her hand in greeting, and Ben took it. Her grip was firm and her hand was warm.

"Ben Simmons," he replied. "A pleasure to meet you."

<hr />

To say that he had a bit of email waiting for him when his laptop finally connected to the internet would be a gross understatement. Like a parched man stumbling out of the desert into an oasis, his computer took deep gulps of the wifi network until its belly—his email inbox, that is—was full to bursting.

It was a full hour before he had managed to trim the list of messages down to the few important ones that required his immediate attention, and another hour before those were squared away. All the while, sitting at one end of the long wooden table that the elderly woman had been at earlier, he had his notebook out and was jotting down story ideas and notes as they occurred to him.

His research into the Great Swamp Fight, with its political and cultural inner-workings, had finally reached a point where the novel was ready to flow onto the page. There was a richness to the historical records, the personal stories of individuals such as the Native American leader Metacom, also known as King Philip, and Joshua Tefft. He could see the intertwining lives and stories weaving themselves into a novel that would captivate readers, and he couldn't wait to share that tale.

"Can I interrupt you?" The familiar voice belonged to his new friend, the librarian. She had walked over to his table without a sound, and Ben wondered briefly if stealth was a skill they were born with or one they were taught in school.

"Absolutely," he replied, gesturing to the chair across the table.

She took the seat, resting her arms on the smooth, glossy surface. Her face wore an apologetic expression.

"You look very busy with all that typing and clicking away, but I thought this was important enough to tell you now," she said. "I just got off the phone with Jack Brooder. He said that Sheriff Roberts called a little while ago looking for you."

Ben sighed. "You're going to think I'm a criminal now, aren't you?" He extended both of his arms toward her, hands balled into fists and wrists close together. "I'll go quietly, I promise."

Ellen laughed softly. "No, I'm sure you're alright. Gil—that is, Sheriff Roberts—has a reputation for being a bit judgmental and quick with his accusations."

"I noticed," Ben replied, frowning. "So what did Jack have to say? And how in the world did he find me?"

"Well, he said that he knew you were looking for a place to work, and the library was the first place he thought of. Maybe he got lucky. Anyway, he said that Sheriff Roberts wanted to let you know you were free to leave town. He said that if he needed anything else from you, he would get in touch with you."

Ben exhaled with relief. "That's good news," he said. "Though, a bit premature. Turns out, I'm going to be sticking around for a couple more days, whether or not your fine Sheriff says I'm free to go. According to Buster, that is."

"He can't fix your car?" she asked. "That's very unusual for Buster. I once took him a blender and he managed to get it working again. The man is amazing."

"No, it's not that," he replied. "He needs a replacement part that's hard to get, and the weekend is causing a delay. My guess is that I'll be driving away Monday afternoon at the latest."

"Well, that's good to hear," she said. "I'd hate to think Buster was losing his touch." She then leaned forward and whispered even more quietly than before. "Can I ask what the call was about from Sheriff Roberts?"

Ben looked around. It wasn't that he was afraid to talk about what he saw, just that he didn't want to frighten anyone who might overhear him. When he was sure there was no one close enough to eavesdrop on their conversation, he nodded.

"It's not a fun story," he said. "I'm not sure I can express that seriously enough. If you have a weak stomach, you might not want to know."

Ellen shook her head. "No, you'd be surprised what I've heard before, Ben. I have a feeling I already know what you're going to tell me. It doesn't make me enjoy the topic, but at least I'm prepared."

"Fair enough," he said. "Bear with me, though. I don't know anyone else in town besides you and Jack, and the fantastic Mr. Roberts, of course."

"I understand," Ellen replied. "It's not a big town. I'll fill in the blanks if I need to."

Ben nodded in agreement, and then began with his walk into town. "When I came to the stoplight down the street, I turned and made my way toward Buster's shop. I hadn't walked very far when I noticed a small crowd of people standing toward the back of the parking lot of a restaurant. I forget the name, though."

"Angela's, most likely," she said.

"Yes, that was it," he replied. "I'm not really sure why I did this—maybe because I'm naturally curious, or that I have a tendency to do stupid things—but I decided to walk across the street and see what everyone was doing. I mean, it was odd, all those people congregating in the corner of a parking lot on a Saturday morning. It just didn't seem normal, I guess."

"Well," she interrupted, "Kettering isn't the most normal of towns, by most standards. Some of that is because it's insular and slowly withering away. But I also think some of it has to do with the past. Please, though, continue."

"As someone who studies the past for a living, I might have to ask you later what you meant by that." Ben shrugged and glanced over toward the main desk. "Anyway, what I found was a small group of people standing around something. They were in shock; most of them seemed badly shaken by what they had found, but a couple of them were more talkative than the others. And it was an odd bunch; I think they had all just randomly stumbled upon each other at the same moment."

"What did they find, Ben?" she asked. Her voice was gentle but firm. There was a hard look in her eyes.

"A body," he managed to whisper with a shaking voice. "Someone said it was a man named Alfonso."

Ellen brought a hand up to her mouth. "Oh, no," she whispered with a sigh. "I know just who you mean. Alfonso was a sweetheart. God, are you sure?"

"I honestly don't know," Ben replied. "Not knowing anyone in town outside of a handful of people—well, I just assumed what the guy said was true. But I do know that what I saw was barely a body. Maybe they're wrong about who it was."

Ellen dropped her hand and stared at him with wide eyes. "The body was," she struggled for the right word, "badly mangled?"

"Oh yes," Ben replied. "Of course, I didn't look at it for long. It was horrible, really. But I do remember that much of the lower body was gone. I don't want to say more, but I think you get the picture."

"Poor Alfonso," she sighed. "It's so much harder to accept it when you knew the victim personally."

That didn't sit right with Ben. "Wait," he said. "What do you mean?"

Ellen looked back at him with fear in her eyes. "Oh, it might be better if you didn't know," she replied. "That way it will be a whole lot easier for you to leave town on Monday and forget all about this little part of Rhode Island."

"Oh, no," Ben said, shaking his head. "You won't throw me off the scent so easily. Tell me, please. I get the feeling that this isn't the first time something like this has happened. I'm right, aren't I?"

Slowly, Ellen nodded. "It was all people were talking about a few days ago. The body of a local woman, Edith Powell, was found in the woods north of town near the walking trail. Not far from Angela's, actually."

"You say *body*, but it was a far cry from intact, wasn't it?"

Ellen nodded. "They say she was badly mangled, yes. Parts of her were," she paused to collect her emotions, "missing."

Ben had a hard time accepting the idea that what he had witnessed this morning was somehow not unique. *How could something like that be anything other than unique?* he thought. He was no detective, but two similar deaths would certainly be a lot more significant than one.

One might be random; two starts to look like a pattern. And a problem. That would certainly explain why the Sheriff had gotten so worked up at the sight of a stranger near the crime scene earlier.

Surely there had to be a logical explanation for both deaths. What he saw had been so brutal and animalistic that the first idea that came to mind was that there was some kind of wild animal in the area.

"Ellen, if you think this is something that's happened before, that they're somehow related, what are you suggesting it could be? Some kind of rabid animal roaming the streets at night?"

Ellen forced a smile. "I honestly don't know what to think," she said with a sigh. "When I heard about Edith Powell, I honestly thought it was just a tragic accident. Maybe a wild animal, sure. But that was when it was just one random instance. Now…" she held both palms upward and shrugged.

"I'm sure there are smart people in Kettering who are working on it," Ben offered. "It's sad, but I've heard wild animal attacks are common all over the country. They just don't get as much press as school shootings or the conflict in the Middle East."

"Yeah, you're probably right," she replied. "Let's move on to happier topics, then. You mentioned you're a lover of history. What do you do for a living?"

Ben smiled. It wasn't a beautiful segue, but it got them off the macabre topic of this morning's discovery, and he was thankful for that. "I am what people today refer to as an *aspiring novelist*," he said. "Specifically, I write historical fiction. You know, dramatic stories of my own invention, set within documented historical places and events."

"Fascinating," she said with a grin. "As you'd imagine, I do a fair share of reading, myself." She waved one of her hands toward the rows and rows of shelves as a demonstration of the truthfulness of this statement. "And history, believe it or not, is one of my favorite subjects."

"Any particular point in history?" he asked.

"Early American, mostly," she replied. "Having been born and raised in New England, I think I have a deeper appreciation for the local history that's all around us. And of course, most people expect the local librarian to know a thing or two about local tradition and events."

"There's a lot of depth and richness there, for sure," he said. "I have a thing for the very early American stuff. Late fifteenth-Century and early sixteenth, really. In fact, that's why I was down here. I spent a week near Great Swamp doing some research."

The soft sound of the door caught her attention and Ellen glanced backward over her shoulder. A mother had walked in with two small children and a large bag full of books. She waved at them, and then turned back to Ben.

"Alright, duty calls," she declared, standing up. "It was really good to chat with you, Ben. Sorry for the morbid events of this morning. And thanks for letting me interrupt you."

"Oh, yeah," Ben said, "this inbox isn't going to empty itself, so I better get back to it. I mean, you didn't interrupt me from anything too important, so don't worry about it. Thanks for the conversation."

"My pleasure," she replied with a smile, and then turned to go.

"Wait," Ben called after her a bit too loudly. He flinched and glanced around as Ellen turned back to him. "Say, you wouldn't want to get dinner with me tonight, would you? I mean, I know it's last minute and all, and you probably have other commitments, but hey, it couldn't hurt to ask, right?"

There was a moment of quiet, and Ben began to think that she was searching her mind for a believable excuse—something about washing her hair or changing the oil in her car—to let him down politely. Then suddenly she blushed and nodded.

"I'd be delighted," she said with a smile. "That's really kind of you. I'm here rather late, though. Would half-past seven be alright with you?"

Ben smiled. "I think that would be perfect. Where could we eat?"

"There's a nice place down the street from here called the Old Dog. Sound good?"

"I'll be there with bells on," Ben said, and then added, "You don't know where I can buy some bells, do you?"

Ellen laughed softly. "Ok, time to get back to work, but I'll see you tonight."

When she was gone, Ben packed up his notebook and computer. He had writing to do, but that could be done back at Jack's house. Right now, though, he really wanted to find the library's archive of old newspapers. There was something he wanted to look into.

Most libraries have one or two microfiche machines tucked away in a corner of the reading area, and they are hard to miss. Ben found one hidden behind the card catalog and set his bag down on the desk. It was a beast; the casing was crafted from thin sheets of steel that had been painted with the same gray enamel that could be found on just about every metal book shelf in the building.

The library in Hollesley had a nearly identical machine—three of them, in fact—and Ben had spent countless hours sitting in front of those large, angular displays while scrolling through films of old newspapers. While the technology found its roots in the 1930's, the wealth of ancient New England publications was a deep rabbit-hole that spanned centuries.

He hoped that he wouldn't have to use the machine today, though. It was the tall wooden rack beside it that

Ben was actually interested in. Hanging from each of the dozen or more metal rods mounted horizontally across the rack were recent editions of the local paper. He hoped to be able to find what he was looking for among them.

He started with the prior day's paper and quickly scanned the headlines. When he found nothing, he moved on to the day before that. He finally found what he was looking for in the paper printed Tuesday. The story had been big enough to warrant placement on the front page, just below the fold and to the right of a photo of County Sheriff Gil Roberts.

BODY OF LOCAL WOMAN DISCOVERED was spelled out in large type that spanned two lines. Below the headline was a handful of paragraphs, which Ben scanned quickly for anything helpful. It didn't take long, and much of what the article had to say was a repeating of Ellen's comments. One portion, though, jumped out at him, and he had to read it three times before the implications fully resonated.

Because of the location where Mrs. Powell's badly injured body was discovered, local authorities have said they suspect she may have fallen victim to a wild animal. One person who witnessed the scene, however, stated that he did not know of any animal capable of the type of damage that Mrs. Powell's body sustained.

CHAPTER FIVE

AN AFTERNOON OF WRITING gave way to an early evening of nervousness for Ben Simmons. It's not that he hadn't ever been on a date before. Hell, he wasn't even sure if he *should* be thinking of tonight's dinner with Ellen as a date. They had only just met that morning, so he was pretty sure they hadn't reached that invisible threshold that separated acquaintances from friends. *Can strangers date?*, he wondered.

Of course, this would be a brief interlude, however unexpected and pleasant. Hollesley was nearly two hours north of Kettering, and even in the digital age, that felt like too large of a gulf for two people to bridge after only a couple of days together. Monday would soon be here, and he would be back in the car driving north.

Still, he felt like there was quite a connection between them today. Whether or not that justified his nervousness was up to him to decide. He was just amazed at how easily he had let his mind run away with notions that he knew were not possible. That would need to stop.

If Ben was an expert at anything, it was managing his own expectations. When a person allows their conjectures to get out of hand, they make stupid decisions. Sometimes those decisions lead to imposing on others. It was all about control for Ben. Control the emotions, control the expectations, and he could control how others perceived him.

There were days when Ben worried that his attitude belied a manipulative streak that ran through his core like a ribbon of fat in a thick cut of meat. People who enjoyed order and process ran the risk of drifting into obsessive behavior. He worried about what could happen if his desire to control things were to become tainted and broken.

Words, though, were things he had no qualms about controlling, and he had spent the majority of his afternoon making them up and writing them down on his laptop. His first novel had been an experiment in process, and he had simply pushed himself through while inventing his own tools and techniques along the way. This new book, though, was different.

This time he felt at home. He had walked the journey already, and knew his mind could take him all the way. He had the endurance and skills, and they had been tested in the fire. Now, here he was at the start of a new book, a new adventure. He felt ready and confident.

The first task he undertook was to build an outline of the new novel's plot. Having his newly acquired research at hand made that easy to push through. He began with a sentence that wrapped up the story he wanted to tell, and then doubled it. He repeated this process over and over, expanding on the theme and details, until he had a good long list of paragraphs that each described the events of a unique scene.

Ben loved this part of the process because, in many ways, he was able to write the book in one sitting. Sure, it wasn't complete, but the core was there, like the metal armatures that are used to guide a sculptor's work with clay. The completed figure might look bare and thin, but the curves were there, and the form was evident. Days spent writing like this were rewarding.

Within five hours he had worked through each and every one of the problems that had reared their heads during the outline process. Details were changed, characters morphed to fit the setting better, and the climax of the book evolved from something he had liked in theory to an ending he couldn't wait to write.

As he clicked the *Save* button one last time and closed his laptop, Ben knew he was off to a fantastic start.

All I want to do now is drive home and start, he thought. *Turn on my favorite writing music, sit myself down in front of the window that overlooks the Hollesley River, and wait for the Muse to come and dance. Monday,* he thought. *That will have to do.*

He checked the time on his phone and smiled. He would have enough time to clean up and then set off on the walk back into town. If he walked fast, he might even beat her to the restaurant; he would hate to cause her to wait for him.

Ben grabbed his overnight kit and headed to the bathroom across the hall. When he was ready, he went downstairs to check in with Jack and Lori, but he found the kitchen empty. Outside, the truck was absent as well.

He quickly wrote a note to let them know where he had run off to, and then left it on the table with the salt shaker on top as a paperweight. Then, pulling the door closed behind him, Ben set off for town.

When he arrived at the Old Dog about ten minutes early, he requested a table near the front window. He sat facing the direction of the library in the hope that Ellen would notice him as she approached, and then took stock of the rest of the room.

It was a small restaurant, holding no more than a dozen small tables within the dining area. A bar lined one wall, and beyond it extended a short hallway that led to the kitchen and, he assumed, the restrooms.

The atmosphere was intimate, with lights that were tuned to a setting that barely allowed the menu to be visible, and music that never intruded on conversation. Ben didn't care for the wall colors; he couldn't help but imagine that the human brain was a similar shade of taupe. The rest of the details, though—the exposed brick, the ancient wood beams that ran along the high ceiling, and the stainless steel accents—were attractive and full of character.

The sound of the door opening brought him back around. Ellen was standing just inside the entrance and she smiled warmly when she saw him. Ben wasn't sure why, but he found himself standing up as she approached. It felt old-fashioned, but somehow appropriate.

"Welcome," he said, and then sat back down as she took her seat.

"You didn't wait long for me, did you?"

Ben shook his head. "Not at all. I sat down maybe five minutes ago. So, is your job the type that's easy to bring home with you?"

Ellen laughed. "Unless you consider dragging piles of books home that I want to read, no. I imagine writing is an occupation that's a lot more slippery."

"It can be," Ben agreed. "The trick is to set limits. I have a goal for each day's writing session, so I strive to hit that. But if it gets out of hand, there's usually a reason, and I've learned to just walk away when I've spent too much time. That's not easy, but it's important."

"It sounds like you have a good handle on it, then," she replied. "You mentioned that you were an aspiring novelist. How aspiring?" she asked with a grin.

Ben chuckled. "Very," he replied. "I have one novel in the hands of an agent who's shopping it around for me at the moment, but no bites yet. So, my plan is to fill the wait by starting the next one."

They paused for a moment when their waiter approached. After he introduced himself and the evening's special—James was apparently in love with the salmon and highly recommended it—they each ordered a glass of wine. James wandered off to get their drinks and Ellen continued.

"Have you published anything before?" she asked, and then added: "Please don't take that the wrong way."

"Not at all," he said with a wave of his hand. "I've managed to get a handful of short stories published over the last couple of years. Nothing that's paid well, but they make for a great list on a query letter. And they certainly don't hurt my chances at getting the novel published. I take it as a sign that people like my stuff, and because that includes editors as well as readers, I have a good feeling about the book."

Ben glanced down at the menu and then motioned to Ellen's. "Do you recommend anything?"

"I haven't been here many times," she confessed, "but I've never been disappointed with the sirloin. They put gorgonzola cheese on it, and use a wonderful balsamic reduction as well."

"Sold," he said, closing the menu. As if on cue, James approached their table with their glasses of wine. He quickly took their orders before vanishing again down the hall beyond the bar.

"So, this will sound like a deeply personal question, so feel free to ignore it or decline to entertain it, but how do you support yourself? Do you have a job somewhere?"

"Ah," Ben sighed, "yeah, that's a personal one, alright. I don't might answering it, but it means that I get to open up a lot more of my life to you than I had expected. Not that I mind, trust me."

"Don't feel obligated to—" she began.

"No," he interrupted her, "this is completely fine." He smiled reassuringly. "It's complicated. My mother passed away three years ago. She had spent most of my childhood moving us from city to city, following jobs as they came up. After I moved out, she decided to root herself in one spot, and a good job offer led her to Hollesley, just north of Boston.

"For the first time, she was able to work toward owning a home. When she did buy something, it was at the bottom of a hard housing market dip, and she landed a nice condo that she could afford. Small, but nice. That job turned out to be different from every other job she had worked before, for two reasons. First, it paid well; she was able to pay off her condo within eighteen years. And the job offered great benefits, one of which was an employer-matched life insurance policy."

"I think I see where this is going," Ellen commented.

"Indeed," he replied. "The cancer that killed her three years ago did its job quickly, I'm thankful for that. But I miss her. She was a very giving person, always trying to take care of me, even long after I had struck out on my own and was managing to get by."

Ben paused. His throat felt tight, and he tried swallowing the emotions. He glanced out the window at the pale dusk sky and the yellow glow of the street light across the road. *Get it together*, he thought. *It's a universal law: never cry on the first date.*

Ellen reached across the table and set one of her hands on his. The soft touch helped him return to the conversation. "Thanks," he said.

"Where were you living when she passed away?" she asked.

"Boston," he replied. "I had found a job working as a research assistant in Boston University's American History department. I was basically an indentured servant, doing all the dirty work for the grad students in the doctoral program. It paid minimum wage, but it gave me a crash-course in historical research—the educational equivalent of second-hand smoke—without the burden of a degree. Or the loans, I guess."

"Ouch," Ellen winced. "Let's not talk about student loans."

Ben smiled. "Well, when mom died, she left everything to me. And that included her condo in Hollesley, and a life insurance policy that I hadn't been expecting. She had never talked about it. Maybe that was good. If I had inherited it ten years earlier, I would have blown it all. But I had matured enough to see the opportunity that it offered me."

"What a blessing," Ellen said. "Did your mother know you wanted to be a writer?"

"Oh yes," he said. "She saw that in me even as a child, and she nurtured it. We practically lived at the library on Saturdays when I was growing up. Everything about books was a drug to me—their shape, the way they were constructed, the words on the pages and the writers who put them there. I was reading novels like *The Hobbit* and *Lord of the Flies* before I entered middle school."

"Impressive," Ellen said, raising one of her eyebrows.

"It wasn't like I had a choice," Ben replied. "The stories called to me. I just wanted to soak them all in. And when you read enough, you start to drip story from your pores. At some point, I just started to write them down."

"I read a lot," she said, "but I don't write. I don't think every binge-reader ends up writing novels or poetry. Some of us just end up reading all the time."

Ben smiled. "I still do that, too. Mostly thanks to my mom. I've managed to trim my expenses to a very tight budget, and I live in the condo she left me. If I can keep my footprint as small as possible, I should be able to write full-time for another three years. If I haven't landed a publishing contract by then, I suppose I'll just look for another research job."

"Well, here's to hoping you make it, and sooner rather than later." Ellen held up her glass of wine and Ben did the same, taking a drink of the Merlot and then setting it aside.

Ben glanced out the window. It was almost completely dark now, but the street lamp illuminated most of the pavement outside the restaurant. There were very few people outside from what he could tell, but the figure that was approaching from the east caught his attention.

At first, he wasn't sure why. There was something about the man—perhaps his filthy coveralls—that seemed familiar, but he couldn't put his finger on it. The man was thin, almost frail, and he shuffled along the sidewalk with the elegance of a sleep-walker. His face was covered with a full, greasy beard the color of steel.

"I feel like I should know that man," Ben said, nodding toward the stranger. Ellen turned and glanced out the window. "I can't seem to place him."

"That's Jasper Levett," she said with a whisper. "Town drunk, as you might be able to tell. He's the caretaker over at Maple Hill Cemetery. I've only ever seen him mowing the grass there, but I'm sure he does more than that."

Levett shuffled past their window, but it wasn't until he was past them that Ben suddenly realized why the man seemed so familiar.

"I think he was one of the people in the parking lot at Angela's this morning," he said. "In fact, I'm sure of it. He has on the same clothes that he was wearing then, and it's hard to forget that crazy beard."

"He wanders around town when he's not working," Ellen said. "It's sad. I've heard that he was once married, but his wife died young. Maybe that's why he drinks. It certainly explains why he's alone all the time; no one else to look after him, I suppose."

They were interrupted by the arrival of their meals. James set each plate on the table with expertise and asked them if they needed anything else. Ellen shook her head, and Ben did the same, sending the waiter on his way.

The meal was wonderful, certainly the best food he had tasted in over a week. Not that the cooking at the Brooder home had been disagreeable the previous night. It had, in fact, been great, but the food on his plate now was on another level, and he was thankful for that.

"Alright," Ben said with a smile. "You've interrogated me long enough; it's my turn to ask you some questions."

Ellen nodded in agreement. "That's more than fair," she replied. "Do your worst. I can take it."

The meal left Ben feeling very full, but the conversation was perfect. He insisted on paying the bill, despite Ellen's protest. After James had returned his credit card, he signed the slip and added in the tip before he slipped a copy of the receipt into his pocket.

The night air outside the restaurant was cool and crisp, the kind of weather that hinted strongly at the approach of autumn. Ben was certain that a few more nights like this would nudge the foliage into a collection of yellows and reds.

"Did you walk from the library?" he asked her as they stepped out onto the sidewalk.

"Yeah, my car is in the lot," she replied. "It's not far, though. I don't mind the walk."

"Well, I'm going to insist that you let me walk you there," he said. "Considering what I stumbled upon this morning, I don't think you'll argue."

Ellen shook her head. "Not on your life," she said. "I was hoping you'd ask."

"Good," Ben said.

He fell in beside her and they began their walk back toward the library. The town around them was quiet, as if even the buildings had gone to sleep. Ben wasn't sure when he had last walked through a town that was so inactive after the sun set.

"Thanks again for dinner," Ellen said, interrupting his thoughts. "The food was great, and the conversation was even better. I'm not sure you're ever going to let me forget that story about my college roommate and the vacuum cleaner, though."

They both laughed and the sounds echoed across the dark street. "No," Ben replied, "that's not a story anyone could forget. It certainly beats my tale of—"

A scream, shrill and piercing, broke through the silence of the night, cutting Ben off in mid-sentence. They both stopped and looked at each other. The sound repeated itself almost immediately, though it was weaker the second time, almost half-hearted in comparison.

"What was that?" Ellen asked, glancing back down the street, past the restaurant.

"I have no idea," Ben replied, "but it didn't sound good." He began to walk back the way they had come, and then turned to Ellen. "I don't think we can ignore that. Someone needs to go see what it was. You don't have to come with me, though."

Ellen looked down the street in the direction they had been walking. The library was just beginning to come into view at the edge of a pool of light thrown off by one of the town's street lamps. It seemed safe enough to walk there, but that was only if one ignored the scream, and the gruesome discoveries that Ellen and Ben were full aware of.

"No," she said. "There's no way I'm walking the rest of the way alone in the dark. If you're going that way, so am I."

"Alright then," Ben replied. "But I think we better hurry. Someone could be in trouble."

Ellen kept up despite shoes that were definitely not designed for running, and within two minutes the pair had arrived at the front of a recognizable Kettering institution: Angela's. The lights were on inside and the lot was full of cars. A handful of young people were milling around near the door, smoking and laughing together, but they didn't seem to be alarmed. Ben didn't know why, but he was sure that whoever had screamed hadn't done so from there.

"I think it came from farther down," he motioned into the darkness.

"The only thing down there is the cemetery," Ellen replied.

"Well, let's check it out," Ben said and then started off toward the last remaining street light on their side of the road. Ellen reluctantly followed.

They moved quickly past the patch of wooded land between Angela's and the graveyard and then stopped beneath the glow of the lamp. The low stone wall that separated the cemetery from the sidewalk looked ancient in the pale light, and beyond it Ben could see the white shapes of dozens of gravestones.

"Do you see anything?" Ellen asked him.

Ben stepped closer to the wall and he felt the hair on the back of his neck stand up. A twig snapped somewhere off in the trees to their right. A dark shape, like black on deep gray, moved somewhere beyond the reach of the light.

"No," he replied, scanning the visible tombstones. "I don't see—"

"What?" Ellen snapped. "

"I'm not sure," Ben replied. "I thought I just saw one of the stones get smaller. Like the top of it was cut off or covered."

He had seen more than that, though. There had been a shape. It wasn't clear, and the light was too poor for him to see any detail, but the shape did not seem natural. It was too large, too quick. And the shape had moved away from the now-shorter grave stone.

He glanced back at Ellen. "You're going to hate me for this, but I think I need to climb over the wall and go look."

Ellen shook her head vigorously. "Oh no," she declared. "You're not leaving me here alone, Ben. Where you go, I go. But let's make it quick."

He helped her over the wall, which was nothing more than a knee-high line of granite fieldstone, and then joined her. She had pulled out her cell phone and showed it to him.

"I've dialed in the number for the sheriff," she said softly. "As soon as you see what you wanted to see, I'm calling for help."

Ben nodded. "That's the best idea I've heard all night," he said. "Follow me."

The tombstone Ben had focused his eyes on was just a few paces away, but the darkness had made it difficult to make out any details. As they approached it, though, the dark patch began to take shape. He felt his stomach tighten as his mind connected the dots.

It was a body.

CHAPTER SIX

IT WASN'T A BODY.

Not in the sense that Ben had been expecting, at least. What he saw as he approached was the torso of a woman. She had been draped over the top of a tall, wide granite slab that had been scoured by years of exposure to the harsh New England weather. Her arms hung down, framing the pale stone. Dark streaks ran down the surface of the tombstone, originating from the woman's head.

Her eyes were staring vacantly in their direction. It was clear she was dead already, and when Ben stepped around to the other side of the grave stone he understood why. Her left leg was completely missing, torn free from the body at the hip. White bone jutted out of the wound and ended in a jagged fracture.

Much of her midsection had been torn open, allowing her entrails to spill out and down to the ground. It was as if something enormous had taken a bite across the woman's middle, and then dropped her onto the stone. He was pretty sure her spine had been broken or severed, judging by the way her body was folded backwards over the grave marker.

It's not all there, Ben thought. *Half of her is gone. Just like the man from this morning. What was his name again? Alfonso. That was it. Just like Alfonso.*

"Oh God oh God oh God," Ellen moaned from behind him. Ben watched her sway on her feet for a moment before her knees gave out and she stumbled forward. Leaning forward on her hands, she wretched and vomited her dinner with a wet gagging sound.

"Ellen…" he said as he walked back over to her, but the words escaped him. He glanced one more time at the woman's body, and then stooped to help Ellen regain her feet.

"I really don't think we should stay here," he told her as he slipped an arm around her waist. "It's not safe. Whatever did this might be close."

Ellen nodded. Her eyes were wet with tears and a few pieces of regurgitated food still clung to her lips. "We need to call the police," she muttered.

"We will," Ben said reassuringly. He didn't let himself look back, but he could still feel the dead woman's eyes staring at him. It felt as if he were being watched, and he walked them both quickly back to the wall.

Ellen managed to step over on her own, and Ben followed her. Taking her arm, he led her back toward the busy parking lot outside Angela's. There, Ben took her phone and checked to see if the number she had entered was still on the screen, and when Ellen confirmed it was, he pressed the *Call* button.

The rest of the night was a blur. Sheriff Roberts arrived within a matter of minutes, and he brought help with him including an ambulance and a pair of off-duty deputies. This led to a few awkward moments where Roberts was beyond words that Ben had somehow managed to stumble upon yet another victim.

"This is going to take a lot more explaining," the Sheriff had said. They were standing on the sidewalk outside the cemetery, and Roberts kept pointing into the graveyard toward the body. "Once is a coincidence, but twice—"

"Twice is just as coincidental," Ben interjected. "It's a small town, and the odds are pretty high that someone out walking around is going to stumble on something like this. That is, of course, when there's a mysterious wild animal killing people."

Sheriff Roberts glared at him with cold blue eyes. "I don't trust you," he said. "But I trust Ellen's word. She vouches for your whereabouts. You're lucky for that, Mr. Simmons."

"Screw you," Ben replied. "Are we done?"

Roberts glanced one more time into the cemetery, where a large work light had been set up, illuminating the tombstone where the body had been found. The county medical examiner was working alongside one of the deputy sheriffs to collect any evidence they could find.

"You're free to go," the officer replied. "But I'm going to be watching you."

"I think you're focusing on the wrong puzzle," Ben said. "Something is killing the people in this town—*your* town. Rather than harassing me, maybe you should be pouring your energy into finding the animal that's doing this."

"Thankfully, I can do both at the same time," Roberts replied.

Ben shook his head before he turned and walked away. Ellen was sitting on the bumper of the ambulance with a blanket around her shoulders and a small plastic cup in her hand. She smiled weakly as he approached.

"Has Gil been giving you a hard time?" she asked him.

"That man is a blind fool," Ben replied. "And he has the personality of a wet rag."

Ellen chuckled. "I actually went to high school with him," she said. "That's not an excuse, mind you; I just thought it was worth mentioning that I'm more than familiar with his foolishness and rough personality. He's been like that for as long as I've known him."

"Feeling any better?" Ben asked her.

"A little," she replied. "That was horrible. I can't get the image out of my head. That woman…"

Ben nodded slowly. "I know what you mean. I'm not sure how well I'm going to sleep tonight, considering what we've seen today. But unless we both get home, we're never going to have a chance to try. Mind if I try walking you to your car again?"

Ellen nodded. She set the blanket on the back of the ambulance as they walked off in the direction of the library. They didn't talk much on the way to her car. Ben understood that she had been through a lot, as had he, and he was sure another deep conversation was the last thing she needed.

When Ellen found out that Ben planned to walk back to the Brooder farm in the dark, she protested and told him to get in the car. She claimed that it wasn't out of her way, but he didn't believe her. As much as Ben hated imposing on others, walking over half a mile through the dark outskirts of a town that seemed to have a problem with wild animals was the last thing he wanted to do.

He had hoped for a more cheerful ending to their evening, but that was not meant to be. Ellen drove up the gravel path and stopped beside Jack's old truck.

"Thanks again for dinner," she said as he unbuckled his seatbelt. "The night might not have ended ideally, but I had a lovely time at the restaurant. Really, I did." She gave him another weak smile.

"I agree completely," Ben replied. "You're tired. I'm tired. So how about you head home and get some rest, and I'll do the same. And if you're willing, perhaps you'd like to get a cup of coffee tomorrow, or a bite to eat."

"I'd like that very much," she replied. "Jack knows my number—it's a small town, so don't jump to conclusions. Just ask him in the morning and give me a call. I'm happy to drive over and pick you up if you need me to."

Ben thanked her and then climbed out of the car. "Goodnight, Ellen," he said with a wave.

"Goodnight, Ben."

⸻

Jack was still awake when Ben walked in through the kitchen door. The clock over the stove said it was half-past nine, but he thought it felt a lot later. Stress had a way of hacking your brain and playing with the settings, and Ben was feeling very tampered with.

"Evening," Jack said with a nod as Ben took a seat across from him at the table.

A small tin ashtray sat near his elbow and the remains of a cigarette still gave off a thin wisp of smoke. Jack was working at a rusty lock with a wire brush, but looked up at his guest.

"You look tired, Ben," he said. "Everything go alright tonight? Ellen's a great gal. I hope you treated her well."

"Dinner couldn't have gone better," he replied. "She's smart and fun, and that makes for a great evening out. But things kind of fell part when we left the Old Dog. There was some trouble."

Jack set the lock down and looked up at him. There was a glimmer in his eyes, a fearful expectancy, that didn't sit well with Ben. He had a feeling that Jack knew what he was about to tell him.

"Trouble, you say?" Jack asked. He picked up a rag and cleaned his hands absentmindedly. "I've heard that word tossed around a lot lately. It's become a word burdened with ill feelings over the last week, I'll tell you that."

"I bet it has," Ben replied. "And tonight's only added to it, I think."

"Tell me about it, then," Jack said. The man leaned forward onto his elbows, picked up the still-smoldering stub of his cigarette, and took a long pull. "I get the feeling that you need to tell it. It'll be good for you, and it's better than me making assumptions."

So Ben told him everything. He began with the incident this morning involving the body of Alfonso, but Jack had already heard about that. The smaller the town, the lower the friction between the message and the crowd.

It was exactly as Jack had assumed, he told him. Well, not exactly, but close enough. Jack had no way of guessing who the victim was, or where the attack had taken place—he'd have to be clairvoyant to know those details ahead of time.

But Jack still knew. He said he felt it in his gut, deep down in the core of his being. He knew that there would be another death. The confidence that Ben had sensed in the man just a day before now seemed diminished and somehow cornered.

"Lori is upstairs," Jack said, "and I made Tyler come home from his friend's house today. I want them under my roof, you know? I want them where I can see them, and where I can protect them. Not out there."

He pointed out into the darkness beyond the thin pane of glass in the window. Both of them gazed outside for a long moment, neither one willing to speak.

Ben understood what Jack meant. Something was out there, something vicious and savage, something that no person should have to encounter. Jack was thinking proactively and doing what any rational family man would do in his shoes: circle the wagons and bring the settlers inside.

"Jack, can I ask you something?" Ben said. "I don't know you very well, but all things considered, I'm not sure I'm in the mood to be diplomatic."

"Shoot," the man replied. "I'm an open book."

"I get the feeling that you know something," Ben said. He kept his tone casual, doing his best to avoid sounding accusatory or paranoid. He was a guest in this man's home, after all. "I'm not sure what it is. Maybe a look in your eyes, or something in your body language. I can't pin it down, but there's an air of familiarity with these attacks that you seem to be giving off. What am I not seeing?"

Jack inhaled deeply on the remains of his cigarette and then slowly mashed it into the ashtray, twisting and grinding the paper stub deliberately until the smoke ceased. For a few seconds, Ben wasn't sure if the man was going to answer him. Finally, though, he spoke.

"No, I don't know anything for certain." His voice shook slightly, proceeding without confidence. "I've got ideas, but hell, I think everyone has ideas. Until I've thought them through completely and am sure I'm not going to make a fool of myself for mentioning them, I think I'll keep my ideas to myself."

Ben didn't know how to respond. The man was clearly afraid of something, but not enough to push him over the edge. The fact that Jack was essentially a stranger—give or take thirty hours of casual conversation—didn't give Ben the right to push the man. Not too hard, at least.

"And if you end up being right?" he asked. "What if your ideas pan out, but more people die in the interim? Is that something you can live with?"

"It'll have to be," Jack replied. Slowly, like an exhausted man, he pushed away from the table and stood. "It's late, and I have a lot on my plate tomorrow. Which reminds me: I need help on a repair project in the afternoon. Would you be interested in helping me out, assuming you'll still be here?"

Ben nodded. "Absolutely," he said. "You've gone out of your way to give me a place to stay and the least I can do is lend a hand. Besides, Buster was clear that he wouldn't have the part he needs for my car until

Monday at the earliest. Maybe I better start paying rent."

Jack smiled. "An extra pair of hands tomorrow will be rent enough, Ben. Thanks for being so accommodating."

"I'm glad to contribute," he replied.

"Anything else you need?" Jack asked. "Are you comfortable in the room? Got enough space and all?"

"I'm good," he replied. "Unless you plan on installing internet before I leave on Monday, that is." He grinned half-heartedly.

"You'd be better off petitioning Lori on that one," Jack replied. "She's of the mind that we need to wire this place up and get with modern times. Me...well, I'm an old fashioned guy. I've got a feeling our boy is going to benefit from growing up without constant connection to the internet, if you know what I mean."

Ben did. Sure, he had grown up in a time without cell phones and the internet, but he had watched them enter society in his late teens. The internet didn't just attach itself onto culture; it burrowed inside like a parasitic organism, slowly taking over as the primary driver.

Of course, Ben saw the benefits that came along with the always-connected culture. In the last few years of his mother's life, email and instant messaging was a blessing beyond words. He had been able to communicate with her almost daily. The internet made it possible for them to maintain their small familial community while many miles apart.

But Ben remembered enough of the world before that to know that the changes weren't all good. During his time at Boston University he became hyper-aware of the isolated nature of the students around him. The deeper they allowed themselves to step into the digital world, the more disconnected they had become from the human beings around them.

Skills that had been hallmarks of humanity for thousands of years were withering away all around him. Body language was lost to the advent of the emoticon. Rather than being present and fully alive in each moment, people were choosing to have their noses pointed at small electronic screens.

Why live through something amazing when you could just take a picture, apply a muted filter to it, and then share it with thousands of strangers you refer to as friends? Why spend time talking with friends, sharing laughter and stories and experiences and wisdom, when it's so much easier to blog from a soap box and block out any voice that you disagree with?

No, the internet wasn't helping parents like Jack and Lori raise thoughtful, well-formed human beings. It wasn't equipping the next generation to improve society and community. It had become focused on the individual, and with the advent of that change, something deeply important had been lost.

"I sure do," was all Ben said in reply. "Thanks for everything, Jack. I really appreciate it."

Jack nodded politely at him. "I'm happy to help."

Ben stayed at the table a while longer after Jack left the room. He used the welcome alone time to collect his thoughts. What exactly had Jack been withholding from him?

Ben had no idea, but he wanted to find out. Maybe the time spent tomorrow helping Jack would give him another opportunity to press the issue further. One thing Ben *was* certain about, though, was that everyone in town that he had bumped into seemed to have an odd mix of fear and recognition. It was as if they understood and accepted what was happening, even if only on a subconscious level.

He couldn't help but think of his childhood on the playgrounds at the countless schools he cycled through as his mother moved them around. He was the perpetual new kid, never part of the established cliques and gangs, always a target of the class bully.

He remembered getting knocked down beside the monkey bars during recess. It might have been third grade, but possibly fourth. Hell, it was probably both. The image in his mind was still clear: a boy with the body of a middle schooler and the brain of a toddler was standing over him. He could feel the hot, sharp gravel pressing into his elbows and buttocks, and his stomach ached from being punched.

The pain in his gut didn't bother him as much as the laughter did. A dozen other kids had gathered around to watch them. Bullies usually only did it for the attention, and when the show started, it was hard to keep the audience away. They gathered around like pigeons at a park bench, waiting for the crumbs to fall.

What Ben saw in the eyes of those kids—and what he noticed now in the faces of the people in Kettering —was always that same mixture of fear and recognition. They were all frightened beyond words, but cradled that fear within resignation. *This is the way it has to be*, their vacant glances seemed to say.

Not everyone was like this, of course. Ellen struck him as different. Maybe his nascent feelings for her were somehow clouding that impression, but he didn't think so. She seemed different, more defiant and unbending to the tide of fear. He couldn't help but wonder, however, what the events of the evening might have done to her resolve.

Then there was Sheriff Roberts. He couldn't tell for sure, but he suspected that Ellen knew him better than she was letting on. Although the man was clearly stubborn and quick to judge, he didn't give off that same terrified acceptance that Ben had noticed in others.

Sure, he represented the local law enforcement. He also didn't have the luxury of wearing his fear on his sleeve while the town around him was being terrorized by some wild animal. He had somehow managed to remain above it all. Despite his aggressive personality, the man clearly wanted to help.

Ben wasn't happy about their interactions so far. It would be fair to say that they had gotten off on the wrong foot. Ben was pretty sure that the man disliked him, although he wasn't sure if that was because Ben was an outsider, or because he had managed to appear at two of the most recent crime scenes. Did it even matter what the reason was?

Of course it matters, he thought. *If I know why he doesn't like me, I can make efforts to repair that.*

That gave Ben an idea. He planned to meet Ellen for lunch, and Jack needed his help after that, but perhaps he should use his morning to find Sheriff Roberts and speak with him and request some kind of a social do-over. And maybe, just maybe, he could find a way to reason with the man and talk with him about what's really going on.

Ben stood up. Though his body was exhausted, his mind continued to race. Sleep would be good for him, but he wondered how long it would take for that to happen. Whenever his mind took hold of a problem that it couldn't resolve, he had a tendency to work it over and over until he cracked it. That was never good for sleep.

He climbed the stairs and quietly slipped into his room. Once he had kicked off his shoes and slipped out of his clothes, he pulled on an old t-shirt and a pair of running shorts before climbing into bed.

The sheets were cool and the pillow was soft, and despite his concerns that sleep would be elusive, it didn't take long before his eyes drifted shut. If some rabid animal, wild and vicious, lurked outside his window that night, he was completely unaware of it.

CHAPTER SEVEN

JACK AND LORI WERE in the kitchen when Ben came downstairs the next morning. He was surprised to find their son Tyler sitting at the table with them. In the two days he had spend with them so far, the young teen had somehow managed to elude him.

It hadn't been intentional, of course. Tyler, like a lot of thirteen-year olds, had a busy social life. Sleep-overs, homework, and early bedtimes all conspired to turn him into a mythical creature, like a white stag or the jackalope. Ben used this rare opportunity to introduce himself.

"I didn't actually think I'd ever get to meet you," he said with a grin and an extended hand. Tyler, a thin boy no taller than five feet, glanced up at him from under a mop of tangled brown hair. He didn't look awake yet, that was clear.

"Hi," he muttered and then went back to his bowl of cereal.

"Don't mind him," Lori apologized. "His brain is still upstairs. Once it wakes up, he'll put it in and transform into a lovely boy. Right now, though…"

"Mom," Tyler said. "Stop."

Jack had been reading a paper—the Boston Globe, from the looks of it—and he lowered the page to glance up at Ben. "Welcome to family life," he said. "It's a wonderful time in the Brooder household."

Ben appreciated the light mood, especially after the tension of the night before.

Tyler didn't say another word the entire meal, but Ben and Lori had a long conversation about the evening before. It was clear from the pained look in her eyes that Jack had told her about the new attack, but she kept her focus on his time with Ellen. Discussing a horrific murder at the table with a child was never a good idea.

"She's a wonderful woman," Lori said. "I've only gotten to know her through the library, having not grown up in town like Jack did, but she's always been warm and welcoming to me and Tyler. We spend a lot of time in that building, between home work and personal reading."

"Last night was a lot like that," Ben agreed. "If I can dare to call it a date, I'd have to say that it was a memorable one. Which reminds me: I offered to buy her a cup of coffee today. She said you and Jack would have her number."

Lori stood up and walked toward the refrigerator. "Absolutely," she said, lifting an old, worn magnet shaped like a panda bear and removing a long paper. "You'll find Ellen Hornsby listed about halfway down," she said as she handed it to him.

"Thanks," he replied sheepishly, suddenly aware that he was blushing. He felt the need to explain himself. "It's nothing, really. I just wanted to see if she was alright after what happened last night."

Lori looked away, glancing out the window rather than at him. "No need to explain it to me," she said with forced humor. "I'm not your mother, and you're both adults. You can get coffee as much as you like."

It's not the date that bothers her, he thought. *It's the attack. She's afraid for herself, and for her family.*

"Thanks," he said again. "I'm going to step outside and give her a call. Thanks for breakfast, by the way. You've gone out of your way to make me feel like I'm part of the family, and I really appreciate that."

"You're very welcome, Ben," Lori replied, turning back around. Her smile was genuine. "We're happy to help."

<hr />

Ben's walk into town was refreshing. The late morning sun had warmed the chill from the cold night before, leaving behind dew on the grass. Not wanting to get his shoes wet he walked along the very edge of the road, being careful to stay out of the lane of traffic. Thankfully, the road was empty and quiet. Sundays in New England were like that.

He rounded the corner marked by Kettering's lone traffic light sometime around 11:00 AM. He chose to stay on the right side of the street as he walked toward downtown, not wanting to repeat what had happened the day before. He had no desire to walk along that stretch of sidewalk, but he did give the cemetery and parking lot a wary sideways glance.

Yellow police tape marked off the area in the cemetery that contained the tombstone where he had discovered the woman's body the night before. The stone itself stood in the center of the cordoned area, and he couldn't help but notice the obvious patch of darkness that seemed to have been painted down its middle.

He shivered. He could still see the dead woman's eyes staring at him even now in the bright light of day. Her eyes had been full of pain and fear, wide and white amidst the darkness around her. He didn't know how long he would be haunted by those eyes, but he feared it might be years.

Past the small strip of woodland that separated the cemetery from the rest of town was Angela's. The parking lot was empty except for the first batch of fallen leaves and a few random bottles. Ben glanced toward the back end of the lot and was surprised to see a small pile of cut flowers. They had been arranged like those along a highway that mark the scene of a tragic accident.

The town understands, he thought. *They know their loss and fear. But do they have the strength to end it?*

Music could be heard pouring out of the garage as he passed Buster's. Ben admired the man for working hard even on the weekends to help repair vehicles for the people in town. He felt a pang of jealously that someone's car might be back on the road today when his was sitting off to the side awaiting some obscure replacement part. He wanted to go home.

That desire to escape to his home was still strong, but it had waned slightly over the last twenty-four hours. Ben knew the reason for that, and she could usually be found sitting behind the desk in the library down the street. She had certainly bewitched him, that much was certain.

When he had asked Jack where he could find the County Sheriff's office, he was told to walk a couple of blocks past Buster's place and to take a right turn onto Hall Street. Moving in that direction took him toward the library. He saw the Old Dog across the street, and the abandoned movie theater as well.

A good number of the shops and businesses that lined the street were closed because it was Sunday. Hopefully the Sheriff's office would still be open and accessible. Ben hadn't even thought to call ahead and find out.

He would know for sure in a few minutes whether that assumption had made an ass out of him—as the old saying goes—or a very lucky man. Luck shouldn't have anything to do with it, though. He didn't see how it would be possible for a town's law enforcement office to be closed, Sunday or not, with a string of mysterious deaths weighing on the public mind.

The only phone call he had made that morning was to Ellen. She had sounded tired, but glad he had called. He told her that he planned to visit Sheriff Roberts that morning, so it would be better to meet for lunch. She recommended a café that was, coincidentally, right next door to the Old Dog, and they agreed to meet there at noon.

He couldn't tell from her voice on the phone whether Ellen was looking forward to meeting again, but Ben knew that *he* certainly was. Perhaps it was the past week he had spent in the woods and historic sites surrounding the Great Swamp, or maybe it was the decade-long drought his dating life had experienced. Either way, the notion of seeing the same female friend two days in a row had a very comforting ring to it.

And he liked her, too. That was the kicker. He had expected to just get his car repaired and drive home as fast as possible. Not in his wildest dreams did he expect to meet someone as enthralling as Ellen Hornsby. Was he smitten? That remained to be seen, but he was willing to see it out. In the meantime, he planned to enjoy the journey.

His walk had finally brought him to the corner of Main and Hall, and he took the right turn that Jack had told him about. There on the right side of the street, just a dozen yards or so from the corner, sat the County Court House. It was an unimpressive cement structure that lived up to its heritage as an example of Brutalist architecture. It was wildly uninviting.

Ben approached the front and read the sign staked into the flowerbed to the left of the sidewalk, which gave directions to the various departments housed in the building. The County Sheriff's office was apparently located on the left side, accessible from its own entrance. Following the sign, Ben headed in that direction.

───❈───

Once inside, the cold nature of the architecture really began to shine. Low-hung drop ceilings, buzzing fluorescent lights, and a chest-high counter that ran the entire width of the visitor's area were all about as welcoming as a North Korean border guard.

The office was quiet, and that didn't surprise Ben. Most of the staff would be off on a Sunday in a small county like this. But the lights were on and the occasional crackle of a radio could be heard off in another room. He stepped toward the counter and was about to knock on the faux wood surface when a familiar face peeked around the corner.

"Simmons," said Sheriff Roberts. "I didn't expect to see you here. Still stuck in town?"

"Buster's doing everything he can to get me out of your hair, Sheriff Roberts, believe me."

"Gil," he replied. "Call me Gil." The man approached the counter from the other side and extended a hand. Ben shook it.

"Look," Ben began, but the man cut him off.

"I know," the Sheriff said. "We got off on the wrong foot. I'm sorry for that. My guess is that, by now, you've managed to wrap your mind around the mess I've got on my plate. I let the stress push me too far. I apologize for that."

Ben was stunned. He had honestly expected to spend the majority of his conversation with this man battling accusations and defending his honesty. Here he was actually apologizing to him. It made him feel uncomfortable and victorious all at the same time. He wasn't sure how he felt about that.

"I, um…" he stammered. "Thanks. That's kind of you."

"Probably wasn't the best way to welcome you to town. That's not good for tourism, for sure."

Roberts grinned at him from across the counter. It was the polished, practiced smile of a politician, but it also felt genuine. Maybe that was all part of the show, but Ben wanted to give him the benefit of the doubt. If Roberts said he was sorry, he meant it.

"So what brings you in today?" Gil asked.

"I wanted to talk more about last night," Ben replied. "It was late and we were both pretty rattled by what we saw. I'm wondering if it might be helpful to talk about *everything* this time. All of it, not just the stuff I managed to remember through the adrenaline and fright."

Gil looked at his watch. "I've got about twenty minutes, and then I need to meet with the county medical examiner. If you can be quick, go for it. I'll listen."

Ben set his arms on the counter and leaned against it. "Clearly, you saw what I saw last night. The body, I mean. I'm not sure we need to rehash all of that. To be honest, I'm doing my best to forget it, but there was something else I saw."

"Changing your story, Simmons?" Gil asked with a smirk, but given their limited experience with each other, it took Ben a moment to catch the humor in the man's question.

"No," he replied. "Nothing's changed. There are just some additional details—things I think I saw—that might be important to your investigation."

"Go on," the man replied.

"Well, before we found the body, we heard a scream," he said. "You already know that. We left the restaurant, heard the scream, and then ran to see if someone needed help. Before we set foot in the cemetery, though, I glanced inside. It's not hard; that wall is low and more of a decorative barrier than a privacy shield. Anyway, I looked in, and even though it was pretty dark in there, I saw something moving. A shape, near the tombstone where the body was found."

"Well, logic would dictate that if Mrs. Sorenson was attacked by something, then you stood a good chance of seeing that something."

"Right," Ben replied. "But I have a feeling you're expecting the…thing…that's doing this to be an animal."

"It's certainly not human," Gil replied. "I'd hate to think that a person could descend to that level of savagery, but even if someone *was* insane and amoral enough to do so, I don't see how a human being could physically accomplish the level of mutilation we've found. It simply has to be an animal."

"Then you're going to be disappointed," Ben said. "The shape I saw in the darkness was big. Very big, in fact. Thinking back on what I saw, and knowing how big that tombstone is, I think the shape was at least eight feet tall. Maybe ten."

Sheriff Roberts forced a smile and shook his head. "Mr. Simmons, I honestly do appreciate your interest in the case. But I can assure you that there are no wild animals in the woods around Kettering that can stand ten feet tall on their hind legs. Black bears are rare out here, and they only get to about seven feet, tops. I have a feeling the darkness and trauma of the night might have muddled your memories of what you saw."

Ben didn't know what to say. Yes, it was possible that the distress of the previous night's events played with his mind, but he didn't think it was likely. And the best way to find out if that were true would be to talk with Ellen. She was sure to have seen the same thing.

"That's easy for you to suggest," he told the Sheriff. "Why are you so quick to discount the report of what I saw?"

"Because you couldn't have seen anything like that," Gil replied. "Come on, Mr. Simmons. It almost sound like you're suggesting something...I don't know... supernatural. I don't believe in ghosts, sorry."

"And neither do I," Ben replied. "I'm not taking my ideas in any direction in particular. Call it supernatural, call it unexplained. I couldn't care less. My agenda isn't there. What I need you to understand is that I saw something last night that scared the shit out of me, and my brain can't seem to put it in a box and label it."

Roberts sighed. "Alright, Mr. Simmons. What do you propose I do about this, then?"

That's when Ben froze. He hadn't thought that far. Honestly, he had expected the local law enforcement to be able to take this information and run with it. It hadn't occurred to him that, just maybe, his alleged observations were a bit too odd for someone to follow up on. What exactly *did* he expect a small town Sheriff like Roberts to do about it? Hunt down the thing he saw? Ben wasn't even close to understanding what that thing *was*.

"Exactly," Roberts said in reply to Ben's silence. "I can't do a thing, Simmons, because I've got nothing to go on. No evidence. Just the day-after memories of a startled man who found a body."

"Hey, now," Ben said. "That's not entirely fair—"

"Listen," said the Sheriff, cutting him off. "Your time is up. I've got a meeting to get to that might actually give me some helpful information for this case. If I have to choose between listening to stories of ten-foot tall shadow men and meeting with my medical examiner, I think you know which way I'm leaning, right?"

Gil stepped back from the counter. Ben saw his chance slipping away. He thought it was clear that something had to be done. There was a chance that he was right about whatever was killing these people. If it wasn't an animal, then the entire investigation was pointed in the wrong direction.

"Look, Gil," he said. "Just give it some thought, alright? I saw what I saw. I'm not making things up to get attention, and just like you, I'd be much happier with a more logical explanation. I'm not trying to make this complicated, but I know what my eyes saw."

"I need to go, Mr. Simmons," the Sheriff replied. "If it helps, consider your account of the events recorded and submitted to public record. Even the shadow-man. Fair enough?"

Ben sighed. It was as if there was a barrier between he and Roberts, much like the physical counter they were both standing at, that was preventing them from agreeing. He didn't know what that obstacle was, but if he could, he was going to help Sheriff Roberts overcome it. Maybe not today, but soon.

"Alright," he finally said. "But I'm not giving up. You'll hear from me again."

"Fine by me," Roberts said. "You have a good day, Mr. Simmons."

Without waiting for Ben to reply, the Sheriff stepped back around the corner and disappeared. Ben waited for a moment, wrestling with his conviction that something deeper, something darker was going on. Without an outlet, though—without a Sheriff who was willing to listen and honestly consider his ideas—he was impotent.

He glanced at the clock on his cell phone. He had just ten minutes until he was set to meet Ellen at the café downtown. This battle would have to wait.

***

They had finished their food nearly half an hour before, but there seemed to be no end to the conversation. Over a plate of ham and swiss sandwiches, kettle chips, and a pair of delicious pickle spears, they had managed to sort out how they were digesting the previous night's events. Ellen might very well have been more successful than Ben, it seemed.

She admitted that getting to sleep had been difficult, something Ben couldn't sympathize with. Ellen, though, had the common sense to locate the cough syrup in her medicine cabinet, and had drifted off to sleep quickly. Ben made a mental note to remember that trick.

He filled her in on his visit to see Sheriff Roberts, and how the man refused to accept the full story of what Ben saw. Bringing it up again caused him to stop and ask her if she had seen the same thing he had.

"You mean the dark shape that moved away from the stone before we went in there? Of course I saw it. I'd have to be blind to miss something like that."

"Really? he asked. "You saw it too?"

Ellen nodded and took another drink. "It was massive, Ben. At first I just assumed it was a trick of light, so to speak, but I've never seen a shadow move like that. There was something in the cemetery last night."

"Hey, no need to sell me on it; I agree with you completely," he replied. "Unfortunately, Roberts isn't on board with that theory. He thinks I'm imagining things. I think he and the rest of his team are still convinced they're looking for a wild animal that's sick or desperate."

"Considering what we saw last night, I'm not sure how that's possible," she said. "I know occasional attacks happen in the area, but I'm having a hard time believing there's some animal out there that's capable of doing that kind of damage."

"Well, not everyone is as level-headed as you. Most people I see in town seem to be rolling over and just accepting that this is somehow normal. Others, like Roberts, are just being obstinate."

"I have a confession to make," Ellen told him after taking another sip of her iced tea.

"This is where you tell me you're actually married, right?" Ben replied with a grin.

Ellen shook her head. "I dated Gil in high school," she said. "Senior year. We were voted 'Cutest Couple', according to the yearbook."

"Wow," Ben said. "That's not something I expected to hear. I'm not sure I could see the two of you together. How long did that last?"

"Less than two years," she replied. "We graduated and then after a great summer together, he headed up to the Lowell campus of UMass while I went to Simmons in Boston."

"Let me guess: long distance didn't work for him?" Ben asked.

"No," she replied, "it didn't work for *me*. He could have waited it out, but once I was miles away from him, I needed to move on."

"I'm impressed," he said. "A bit ironic that in the end you both ended up coming back to your home town, isn't it? What stopped you and him from starting things up again?"

"I wasn't really interested at that point," she said. "But it didn't help that he moved back with a wedding ring and a pregnant wife."

"Ah, I can see how that might shut some doors."

"But," she added, holding up a finger, "I think he'll listen to me. Maybe I should visit him today as well. Tell him my side of the story, you know?"

"I can't see how it could hurt," Ben said. "Go for it."

The door to the café opened, and Ben glanced up to see a young man, possibly a college student, walk through. He was dressed in baggy pants and a shirt that was a bit too large for his slim body. The clothing was nice and well-kept, but he wore it like a homeless man. Ben nodded toward the man.

"Do you get a lot of students in town?" he asked Ellen, nodding toward the newcomer.

She glanced over her shoulder. "Occasionally," she said. "Most dress better than that, though."

Ben smiled and glanced back to the young man. He had paid for whatever it was he had ordered and had wandered over to the counter where the café kept their napkins and condiments. Ben couldn't stop looking at his unique appearance.

The young man seemed to have grown a short beard, but shaved the areas that most men used for a goatee. He had a metal stud in his nose, but it was the three rings in his lower lip that really caught Ben's attention.

He's a modern hippie, Ben thought. *Everything comes back around, doesn't it?*

"And you're helping Jack with something this afternoon, you said?" Ellen's voice brought his head back around.

"Yes," he replied. "He said there's a section of the wall that's collapsed, and thought I would take some pleasure in learning how to repair it. Long story."

"I bet," she grinned. "How about I give you a call at the house after I've chatted with Gil. I'll let you know if I've made any headway with him."

Ben stood up and grabbed their plates. "Sounds good to me," he said. "Let me drop these off and I'll walk you out."

"Such a gentleman," she said.

Ben walked over to the condiment counter. The café had set up a bin on top of the trash can where customers could drop off their used utensils and dishes. When he got there, the bin had been freshly emptied, so he dumped their scraps and napkins into the trash and reached up to set the dishes in. That's when he saw the note.

Ben carefully picked up the small scrap of paper and looked around. No one else was in the café except for Ellen and the teenage girl behind the counter. The young hippie had vanished.

He looked down at the note and read the three words that had been penned with the skill of a drunken draftsman: 'Ellen's friend: manitou'.

Manitou? What the hell does that mean?

He decided to keep it and tucked the paper into his pocket. It had clearly been written for him, and by someone who knew that he was a friend of Ellen's. But what it meant was beyond him.

He set the dishes in the basket and walked over to where Ellen was waiting for him. He smiled and held the door for her, but when they were finally outside he pulled the note out and handed it to her.

"I found this by the trash, waiting for me," he told her.

Ellen scanned the words for a moment. "It's for you," she said. "But why? And what does that word mean?"

"I have no idea," he said. "I've never heard of it before."

Ellen handed the paper back to him. "Well, you're welcome to come by the library tomorrow and do some research if you want. We've got thousands of books and something called *The Internet*. Have you heard of it?"

Ben laughed. "No," he said, feigning ignorance. "Are you offering to teach me about it?"

"Happily," she smiled back. "Listen, I'm going to go chat with Gil. I'll give you a call later and let you know how it went, alright?"

"Sounds good to me," he replied. "Thanks for lunch. I had a great time."

She began to walk away, heading back down Main Street toward Hall Street. She turned around and took the next few steps backwards, waving to him. "Me too, Ben. Me too."

She smiled one last time and then spun around. Ben watched her for a moment and then headed in the opposite direction. He had a long walk ahead of him. Thankfully, though, he had plenty to think about.

CHAPTER EIGHT

BEN NEVER THOUGHT HE would find himself squatting at the edge of a stranger's property while digging at the stoney earth with his fingers, but here he was. More surprising was the fact that he was enjoying himself. His fingertips throbbed and his back ached, but he felt alive.

They had walked out toward the west edge of Jack's property as soon as Ben had returned from lunch. He changed into some of the clothes that he had worn during his hikes through the Great Swamp the week prior. He could still smell the potpourri of the wildlife sanctuary on them, earthy and fragrant. Then, with one of Jack's shovels resting on his shoulder, they had both headed off toward the tree line.

The walk back to the Brooder homestead had given him a lot of time to think, and Ben had used it well. In fact, he had managed to convince himself, after wrestling with his doubts for most of the day, that there was a perfectly good explanation for everything he had seen since arriving in Kettering. The moment he had settled on the answer, he could feel a great weight slip off his shoulders.

Most of what he had witnessed had simply been the scenes of the two attacks. While the bodies had certainly been badly mangled—perhaps dismembered was a better adjective in this case—he was clearly unqualified to make the assumption that no human being could have been responsible. How many dead bodies had he seen through the course of his life, really? Not counting his mother's after her passing in a cold hospital room three years ago, none.

Ben's best guess was that there was indeed a very disturbed person in the town of Kettering, someone twisted enough to commit the level of violence that he had seen firsthand. These kinds of people were rare, but history reminded him that they existed. Jack the Ripper came to mind immediately. So did Jeffrey Dahmer and Edmund Kemper, both of whom had been capable of not only killing people, but dismembering and consuming their corpses.

That left only the shadowy shape to explain. The dark shape that had flashed across the cemetery had been indistinct, but both he and Ellen remembered seeing it. It could only have belonged to something real, and now that Ben was sure that the suspect was a deranged killer—and most likely a man—he knew the shadow must have belonged to him.

He could only guess as to why the shadow had seemed so large. Perhaps it was a trick of the light as a result of the street lamp being so far from where they were standing. Maybe it had to do with the dark sky and the darker trees behind the gravestone. He couldn't be sure, of course, but he was comfortable chalking this mystery up to confusion and the graveyard's version of smoke and mirrors.

When they reached the edge of the property, it was clear why Jack needed his help. A long portion of the old stone wall, perhaps six feet in length, had collapsed inward. The large field stones that had constituted the barrier for so many decades now lay in a heap that spilled into the grass.

"How'd this happen?" he asked. "I swear I haven't had my car out this way at all."

Jack smiled. "Who knows," he replied. "It happens every now and then. My best guess is that really cold nights can sometimes cause the wet ground to heave a bit. Most of these walls are sturdy and can't be shaken, but the weak spots are prone to crumble. I fix them as it happens, with the hope that I'm making the wall stronger one section at a time."

"So how do we put this back together?" Ben asked.

"Carefully," the man said with a smile. "And one stone at a time."

"You're beginning to sound too much like a grandfather," Ben replied. "You're much too young for that."

"Well, I was raised by my grandfather," Jack said. "That could explain it."

Jack spent a few minutes walking Ben through the process of repairing the wall, and then both men set to work. It wasn't rocket science, but it wasn't a walk in the park either. It involved finding the stones that had clearly been at the bottom of the wall—most of which were now at the bottom of the *pile*—and move them back to the property line. Then, it was a bit like putting a puzzle together.

Ben would hold each stone up and turn it over and over in his hands until the shape made sense for the opening. Jack was the final word on all the difficult stones, but they quickly managed to fall into a productive groove.

"Your grandfather raised you, eh?" Ben asked. "Can I ask what happened to your parents?"

"Died when I was young," Jack replied without looking up. He heaved another large stone onto the intricate stack. "Car accident up in Providence when I was seven."

"Wow," Ben replied. "That's rough. I'm sorry to hear it."

"Don't be," Jack replied. "Looking back, it brought a lot of positive change into my life."

"How so?"

"Oh, my father was an alcoholic and my mother wasn't much better. She preferred pills, though. Unlike most generations of the Brooder clan, rather than staying on the homestead here, they chose to chase after the pleasures that only big city life could offer."

"And by pleasures," Ben said, "you mean alcohol and drugs?"

"You got it," he replied. "The police told my grandfather that the accident wasn't their fault, that some college kids had blown through a red light and plowed into the side of their old AMC Gremlin, but I'm sure they were loaded. They were almost always loaded. I'm just glad I wasn't with them. At least they had the forethought to get a babysitter before they got shit-faced."

"That's when you came here to live with your grandfather?"

"Yep."

"No grandmother, though?" Ben asked as he pushed another rock into place.

"That's a longer story," Jack said thoughtfully. "I think it's enough to say that she died young, just after my father was born. But I didn't want for lack. Grumps took good care of me."

"Grumps?" Ben straightened up and grinned at Jack. "Is that what you called him?"

Jack nodded. "That's what I called him when I was little. It stuck, I guess. Got to the point that even people around town were calling him that. It was all in fun, and the fact that he was one of the most positive, cheerful people you'd ever meet helped it feel more like a joke than anything. To me, he was always Grumps."

"Hard to argue with that," Ben said. "And he raised you by himself? That was pretty noble of him."

"Yeah, but he did it because it was just the right thing to do. He wasn't looking for a badge of honor. I can't imagine what my life would have been like if my parents had been the ones to raise me. I wouldn't be here, that's for sure. Grumps did a good job and kept me out of trouble. Lori and I try to do the same with Tyler."

"Lori mentioned that you spent time in the military," Ben said as he placed another stone on the wall. "What branch were you in?"

"United States Army," Jack said with a voice that still had a bit of pride left in it. "I was in the 6th Special Forces Group. We handled…ah…*unique* missions." Jack gave Ben a knowing grin.

"Exciting," Ben replied. "Didn't see yourself as a career military man, though?"

Jack shook his head. "No, not after everything I saw and did." He studied one of the stones a bit longer than usual, gathering his thoughts. "Soldiers in that line of work have a tendency to be more like road flares than scented candles; we burn hot and fast and bright, but it's over way too quickly."

The conversation fell off for a few moments while the two men thought through the placement of a few difficult stones. While Ben was lowering one of them into place, Jack stood tall and watched him. He took off his hat and wiped his brow with the sleeve of his shirt, and then pulled it back on.

"I've been thinking more about our conversation last night," he said. "About my ideas and about your concern, I mean. And I think I might be ready to talk about it."

Ben stopped what he was doing. "I appreciate that, Jack," he replied. "And you're welcome to talk me through your thoughts. But I'm pretty sure I've managed to talk myself down from a very unreasonable ledge."

"How so?" Jack asked.

"It's just that I was pretty convinced last night that I saw something in the cemetery. Something too unnatural to be human. The kind of stuff nightmares are stitched from, if you know what I mean.

"But I think I was seeing it through the lens of the victims, and that might have colored my opinion. I probably had too much faith in humanity to think that a person could hurt people like that, but of course I'd be wrong to think that way. We don't need fairy tales or horror movies to show us what evil is; humans have that ability within themselves. I think that's what we're seeing here in town."

Jack picked up another stone and turned it over in his hand. "Hold that thought," he said. "Let me tell you what I know, and then maybe we can find a place to meet in the middle. I'll tell you this now, though: I wish you were right, but I'm not so sure you are just yet."

"Well, I'll try to keep an open mind," Ben replied. "History is full of people whose stubbornness prevented them from seeing the truth. I aim to be more flexible."

Jack sat down on a section of the wall that was still intact and took off his hat again. "When I was nine or so, the kids at school were whispering about something they were hearing from their parents. Someone had died, they said. Maybe more than one person, too. And no one knew how or why, and that the grown-ups were pretty frightened.

"The kids, though, they were all buzzing with excitement. You know how kids can get. A mystery is a mystery, regardless of the danger or risk. That's why kids sometimes make stupid choices; they don't see the consequences or the price, only the thrill and excitement. It's natural, I think. It helps kids enjoy their childhood and really live life to the fullest. But it's an incomplete view of the world. Parents know this.

"So when I was nine, there were rumors and whispers at school. Some people had died and no one had an answer. The sheriff had called in the State Police —their barracks are just to the East in North Kingstown—and there was some kind of a manhunt going on. They were looking for a serial killer."

Ben took in a sharp breath. *What are the chances*, he wondered. *What if we're looking for a copycat. Or maybe the killer from thirty years ago has just come out of retirement?*

"I don't remember all of the details," Jack continued. "Most people around here won't talk about it, either. But I know that the murders were brutal. So brutal, in fact, that the people who *should* have been

141

able to talk about them never *could*. It was fear, Ben. They were afraid to even talk about it. Afraid it might somehow happen to them."

"That sounds like folks in town today," Ben said. "I don't know everyone as well as you do—obviously—but that's my impression. They're gripped by a fear that's absolutely paralyzing them."

"Yep," Jack agreed. "And that's why I've been thinking about those times. Because—and you should know this better than most, I'd think—history has a way of repeating itself."

"Yeah, but crimes like this don't," Ben said. "Unless we're talking about a serial killer who's been snow-birding in Florida for three decades and has finally decided to get back into the swing of things."

"No," Jack said, shaking his head. "See, you wouldn't think that if you knew the rest of the story."

"Then tell me," Ben said.

"I only know pieces of it, myself," Jack replied. "Hearsay, really. What I do remember is that Grumps had a friend—Dorothy—who would sometimes come over and cook for us and do some cleaning. She was a sweet woman, and she knew how hard Grumps worked on the farm and how our house lacked the feminine touch. I think she had been a friend of my grandmother's and she sometimes helped us out, maybe out of obligation to that friendship.

"When all of this was going on back then, Grumps did his best to not talk about it when I was around. It's probably a lot like how Lori and I keep the internet out of our house in hopes that Tyler will be a better person. Maybe Grumps filtered what he could as his own way of helping me grow up on solid ground.

"Whatever the reason, I don't remember Grumps ever sitting me down to talk about the murders. Everything I learned, for the most part, was through friends at school. And eavesdropping on grown-ups."

"Something kids love to do," Ben said.

"You bet," Jack replied. "When there was a chance you might overhear a discussion about Christmas presents or a secret party, you got mighty good at pretending to be asleep or engrossed in a good book. And that's how I overheard Grumps and Dorothy talking one day.

"They were in the kitchen," Jack said, glancing toward the house. "I'd come down from my room all quiet-like, and was standing in the hall just around the corner from where they were. Even though they thought I was upstairs, they were talking in whispers, as if saying anything out loud might somehow conjure up the killer himself right there in front of them.

"They sometimes got loud enough for me to hear them, though, but not regularly. What I heard was a collection of broken phrases and ideas. Things that made my stomach tighten up with nervousness, like I had to go to the bathroom in an urgent way."

"I know that feeling," Ben said. "I used to sneak into the movies as a teen. I loved the horror flicks, but they scared the crap out of me, sometimes literally. I would spend an hour under the stress of that building tension and then have to slip out to use the bathroom before it got too bad."

Jack smiled, but it was vacant and thin. "That's the feeling," he replied. "The things they said scared me like that, Ben. Sometimes I'm glad I didn't catch all of it. But what I *do* remember is that Dorothy kept asking Grumps if he thought it was the same thing that had happened in 1954."

Ben's heart skipped a beat. "Wait," he said, trying to wrap his head around what Jack had just said. "You mean, you think whatever was happening thirty years ago reminded your grandfather and his friend of something that had happened before that?"

"I think," Jack said, "that the killings that happened when I was a kid weren't the first. And it's pretty clear now that they aren't the last, either."

Ben shook his head. "No, you're moving into crazy territory now. At least sixty years of killings, Jack. That's what you're suggesting, isn't it? Sixty-fucking-years!"

"I know, Ben. I know it sounds insane. Hell, I feel a bit crazy for even bringing it up. But I've never told anyone about overhearing that conversation, and I have a feeling—deep down in my gut where hunches and inspiration come from, you know?—that there's a connection somehow."

"Did they say anything else?" Ben asked.

"Nothing much that made sense to me at the time," he replied. "There was a bit of talk about how gruesome the killings were. How savage—that's how Dorothy said it. *Savage.*"

"I can see how that might stick with you after all these years," Ben said.

Jack nodded in agreement. "Something else was discussed that night, but they were so quiet that I could barely make sense of it all. They talked about 1954 a bit, but they also talked about something that made my grandfather really angry, and sad too. I don't know what it was, only that he didn't want to talk about it. He was clear about that."

Ben was quiet, waiting for Jack to go on, but he never did. The man was still looking off across the field toward the house, his eyes vacant and pained. Finally, though, Ben had to say what was on his mind.

"Jack," he said. "I think you're nuts. But I also think you're telling the truth. And that scares me."

"Why?" Jack asked.

"Because you're talking about a killer who's been active for sixty years, if not longer. You're claiming this is a threat that's visited your town not once before but twice. I'm not sure what to do with information like that. It doesn't fit neatly into a category in my mind."

"Maybe that's to be expected," Jack replied, still gazing off across the field. "Something is evil, by definition, when it doesn't play by the rules society has established. There's a moral code and when someone crosses that line, bad things happen. The world isn't perfect, Ben. Evil happens far too often, and in a whole range of forms. Who says evil has to conform to *our* interpretation of what is natural?"

"I guess we'll never know for sure," Ben replied. "Your grandfather is gone, though it sounds like he wouldn't have talked to us about it even if he were still alive. Whatever happened must have hurt him deeply."

Jack's face snapped back around to face Ben, as if something profound had just occurred to him. He held up his hand while he struggled to find the right words. And then he spoke.

"Ben, *Dorothy* is still alive." There was a sense of wonder in his voice, as it he had spoken a truth too powerful to have ever been forgotten. "She's alive, Ben. Why did I never think to talk to her about this?"

"Sometimes we stay kids," Ben replied. "With some people, the people we interacted with most as children, we have a really hard time graduating to adulthood. We spend the rest of our lives thinking of ourselves as children whenever we are around them.

"They might see us as adults now, all grown up and doing well, but our perspective is skewed. Maybe you've never thought of yourself as an adult in relation to her, and that's prevented you from assuming you could talk to her about it."

Jack thought for a moment. "That's probably true," he said, "but it needs to change. I have a feeling Dorothy knows something we don't. Something we should probably listen to. Would you be willing to do that with me? Go and visit Dorothy and ask her to relive those nightmares and tell me what she knows?"

"Are you kidding?" Ben asked. "I'd love to. We need answers, and I have a feeling she's got them."

CHAPTER NINE

ELLEN WALKED ACROSS THE lobby of the County Sheriff's office and stopped at the desk. The place was empty as far as she could tell, but there was a sound off in the distance. She tilted her head toward the noise.

It was a radio. She couldn't make out the artist, or even the genre, but the unmistakable beats and trills of a song were drifting across the office toward her. Someone was home, at least.

The counter was far from bare. There were three wire baskets along its twelve-foot length, each one holding forms for various reports. There were four acrylic brochure holders that held trifold pieces extolling the benefits of not texting while driving, or how driving sober is safer.

Beside the basket in the center of the counter was a bell. It was the old-fashioned kind that you would expect to find at the desk in a library, and she knew instantly what it would sound like. She remembered a bell just like it sitting on the counter at the library when she first returned home from graduate school to assist the previous Head Librarian, Henry Epscomb.

Personally, Ellen hated bells like this one. When Henry retired five years ago, opening a door for Ellen to succeed him, it was one of the first changes that she had made. Bells were better at distracting the people in the library than they were at getting the attention of staff. Instead, Ellen tried to be near the desk as often as possible, and that meant that the bell would be redundant.

She hovered her hand over it for a moment. It wasn't hatred that held her back, or even a weak dislike for the sound. It was just a part of her past that she had left behind so many years ago, and it was difficult to allow it back into her mind.

Like Gil, she thought.

She and Gil had been inseparable in high school. They had known each other for most of their lives, attending grade school together and even participating in some of the same after-school programs. When Gil was on the football team, Ellen even became a cheerleader. Had it been stereotypical? Perhaps. Did they enjoy every minute of it, though? Absolutely.

Their breakup after the start of their first semester of college was harder on her than she had let Ben believe. She had poured a lot of hope and energy into Gil, both before they dated and during their time together. Walking away from that investment had been one of the hardest things she had ever made herself do. But it had been for the best. She was good at telling herself that, at least.

Other than a few casual dates throughout her time in college, Ellen pretty much avoided another relationship. College was a tricky place to meet a guy. Not just because Simmons College was an all-female undergrad school, but because the men that she *was* able to meet from other nearby schools were almost always from a town or state too far from her own. She knew how it would end; once graduation came around, so would that difficult decision: break up, or follow him home?

Ellen knew Kettering was an old town without a lot of room for growth, but she loved it and couldn't see herself moving away. Rather than helping her become more comfortable outside the nest, her time in college seemed to replenish her deep love of this small New England town. She wanted to return home more than anything, and so she remained single.

That didn't mean she didn't have hopes. They just weren't the kind of hopes that she shared with anyone. One of those hopes, though, was that Gil Roberts would return from college single, bump into her some afternoon at McMullen's Market, and their six year break would end. That wasn't how it ended up working, however.

Ellen rang the bell. The sound was sharp and piercing, with that hollow metallic vibration that seemed to carry for miles. The sound continued to reverberate for a moment longer, weakening with each second until it finally stopped. In the distance, Ellen heard a chair move on the tile floor and then footsteps. She gripped the counter tighter.

Gil Roberts walked briskly around the corner. His face was unwelcoming and tired, but when his eyes spotted her and recognition set in, those features softened.

"Ellen," he said with surprise. "I didn't expect to see you here. Everything alright?"

"Hi, Gil. Yes," she said. Her tongue felt like it was caught on something and the words were coming out clumsily. "How are you?"

Gil sighed. "Honestly?" he asked. "I'm exhausted. These murders are like a bag of cement mix on my shoulders, and I haven't slept more than a couple hours a night all week. I'm spent, and I'm ready for a vacation."

"I can't imagine the stress," she said. "That's a lot of responsibility for an elected official. I'm not sure they could pay me enough to do what you're doing."

"Well," he said, resting his hands on the counter. "It's not like I didn't ask for this. It comes with the job, I suppose."

Ellen glanced down. The gold ring on his left hand glinted slightly and she looked away. "Any progress? I talked with Ben earlier today. He said you were going to meet with the medical examiner."

Gil frowned slightly. "Officially, it's none of his business. Or yours, really." He paused and his face softened again. "Unofficially, I think I'm out of my depth and I don't like it. And I'm beginning to think you and Ben might have been right."

"How so?" she asked. Gil was a very confident man. He always had been. Some saw it as arrogance, but Gil would be quick to tell you that he didn't mean to come across that way. He was just very sure of his abilities, and knew his limits well.

He glanced at the counter for a moment and then spoke. "Ellen, the wounds...they're not natural. Dr. Kaur said he might need more time with this last victim, but he's almost positive that the injuries found on the body weren't from a man-made weapon."

"Meaning what?" Ellen wasn't sure she understood yet. "That it was an animal after all?"

Gil shook his head. "Not that he can tell. Dr. Kaur is the same county medical examiner who handled the Robertson autopsy a few years back. Do you remember that?"

Ellen did. She had taken over the role of Head Librarian just a month before when the news broke. A hiker traveling southeast of town along the Queen River was found dead near the Glen Rock Reservoir. The state police had suspected foul play at first, but the autopsy showed conclusive evidence that it had been a bear attack. It had come as a surprise to most people, but the occasional black bear did wander into the area. That bear was later found and removed by wildlife experts.

"I do," she replied. "He's an expert in animal attacks, from what I remember. The State Police call him in on big cases, don't they?"

Gil nodded. "The Robertson case really increased his profile. I'm glad he's stayed around our little county; he could probably go work anywhere with the kind of credibility and reputation he has. So, obviously, when he examines three bodies in one week and then comes back to me with his professional opinion, I listen."

"So what did he say?"

"That the wounds do *look* like they were inflicted by a wild animal," he replied. "But if they were, he has no idea what kind of animal that might be. He says the lacerations are too deep to be from a bear, and too far apart." Gil held up a hand and spread his fingers wide. "It doesn't fit any profile Dr. Kaur has ever encountered. This, from a man who has encountered everything."

"Are you still looking for a serial killer, then?" she asked. "You don't have to answer that. I realize I'm not really supposed to be privy to that information."

"Until about an hour ago," he replied, "that's exactly what we thought we had. Some wacko hunting the locals. Violent, but still human. Now…"

Ellen nodded soberly. "Nothing is simple, is it?" she asked.

Nothing had ever been simple for them, as far as she could remember. Returning from college and hoping to find Gil single and available had turned out to be far from simple. His reaction to seeing her, their awkward conversation; it had far too many layers of complexity.

"No," he said, but his eyes said more. "It never is."

"So what's your plan now?"

"I've made a call to the State Police barracks," he said. "They're trying to put together a team of seasoned troopers that we can take out into the woods and do a search. We know where most of the attacks have occurred, and can focus our attention there. Hopefully, if there *is* some kind of animal doing this, we can flush it out and capture it. Or better yet, kill it."

"That's something to hope for, at least," she said. "But what if that *doesn't* work?"

Gil looked at her from across the counter. She no longer saw any of the confidence that he normally exuded. Instead, his eyes were full of honest-to-God fear. She found it to be more than disconcerting; it was absolutely unnerving.

"If it doesn't work?" he replied, "If that's the case, then we've got a major problem on our hands."

Allenby Village was at the northwestern edge of Kettering, on the north side of Main Street. It was a sprawling old manor house that had been converted in the early 1970s into an assisted living facility. Many of the acres of land that once surrounded it had been sold off to developers, but a generous portion remained, lending the building a stately appearance.

Jack eased the old pickup into one of the parking spots along the side of the building, and he and Ben made their way to the front entrance. The sidewalk along the front of the facility was apparently a favorite place for some of the residents to take their afternoon walks, as evidenced by the handful of elderly folk who were scooting along behind aluminum walkers. Ben smiled to each he passed.

Inside, the foyer area opened up to reveal the grand staircase that had been a centerpiece of the manor home in its day. Set just ahead of the stairs was a large reception area, much like the front desk of a hotel. A woman who appeared to be in her late fifties sat behind the desk. She had her phone held up to one ear, and was jotting down notes on a pad of paper.

"Will do," she said to the person on the other end of the line. "Thanks again, Bill. I'll let Margaret's family know."

She set the phone down gently and looked up. Recognition washed over her face.

"Well, if it isn't Jack Brooder," she said with a warm smile. "I haven't seen you in ages. How are you, dear?"

She stood and came around the desk in a flash, catching Jack in a tight hug that almost seemed comical. Ben took a quiet step backwards.

"I'm doing well, Sally," he said. "You staying out of trouble?"

Sally giggled in a way that seemed out of character for a woman her age and then let go of Jack. "I never behave, Jack. That's my secret to a happy life."

"I'll be sure to make a note of that," he replied with a smile.

Sally turned her attention to Ben, who fought the urge to back up another step. "And who's your friend?"

"Ben Simmons," he said, extending a hand to her. "I'm visiting from out of town. Jack is playing host to me."

"Ben is a writer, Sally," Jack added.

Her face lit up, and she took his hand in her firm grip, nearly shaking his arm off at the shoulder. "Romance novels, by chance?"

"Ah, no ma'am," Ben replied. "I'm more of a history man. Not that there's anything wrong with romance," he added.

"Oh well," she said with a grin. "I've always wanted to snag me a romance writer. I imagine they'd be perfect for a lonely old spinster like me."

Then, turning back to Jack, she asked, "So what can I do for you today, Jack. Here to see someone?"

Jack nodded. "As a matter of fact, I am. You don't know if Dorothy Abington is up and about, do you?"

"Dorothy?," she said as she walked back around her desk. "Let me make a quick call and find out."

Sally picked up her phone and punched in three digits with the grace of a fifth-grader playing Whack-a-Mole. There was a pause, and then someone answered.

"Hellen, it's Sally. Listen, Dorothy has a couple of visitors. Is she up to it today? Let her know one of them is Jack Brooder."

Another pause.

"Sounds great," she said cheerfully. "I'll send them right over."

Sally set the phone back in the cradle. "You're in luck, gentlemen," she said, setting a clipboard on the desk in front of them. "Dorothy is taking in some television while she waits for dinner. You can find her down the hallway to the left in the main common room. Can't miss it. I just need you to sign in before you go."

"Many thanks, Sally," Jack said.

He grabbed the clipboard and quickly wrote down his name and the current time. He handed it to Ben who did the same and then gave it back to Sally.

"Good to see you, Jackie," she grinned. "Don't be a stranger, alright?"

"I'd never think of it," Jack replied as they walked away. A moment later they were entering the Allenby Village common room.

The room was situated toward the back of the facility, separated from the hallway by a low wall. The opposite side of the room was lined with large windows that looked out on the old gardens and courtyard that once held gatherings of the elite from Newport and Providence. The fading afternoon sunlight spilled in through the open windows, casting a weak yellow glow on everything near them.

A large flat-panel television was set up on the western wall, and a collection of old, comfortable furniture had been arranged within viewing distance. Perhaps a dozen residents were seated near the screen, which was filled with a rowdy talk show audience.

Jack found Dorothy almost immediately. She was in a recliner close to the hallway, a tattered paperback book in her gnarled hands. Her hair was snow white, and her skin had that near-translucent quality that was so common among octogenarians and those older.

Dorothy was certainly older. Jack had informed him on the way over that she had turned ninety-three over the summer. She was weak and lost her balance every now and then, but her mind was still as sharp as it had ever been.

"Jackie," she said when she saw him enter the room. Her voice had an elderly warble to it, but it was clear. "So good to see you."

Jack smiled, and Ben thought it was the first time he had really seen the man relax. They both took a seat on a couch arranged near her chair, with Jack closer to her.

"Good to see you as well, Dorothy," Jack replied, taking one of her hands in his. "How are you doing?"

"I'm ninety-three, Jack," she replied. "If I can get out of bed when I wake up, I'm ready to call it a good day. Who's your friend?"

Jack made the introduction and explained to her how Ben had come to be staying with his family for the weekend. Dorothy was delighted to hear that Ben was from Hollesley.

"My sister married a man from there," she said. "Of course, they passed away many years ago, but I remember visiting them there. Lovely town."

"I've enjoyed my time there for sure," Ben said. "When were you last up that way to visit?"

Dorothy thought for a moment. "Oh, it must have been twenty years ago if it was a day," she replied. "I don't remember what year it was, but I'm pretty sure it was right after that young boy died in the accident in the old mill building. The newspapers spent a lot of ink talking on and on about it. A tragedy, for sure."

"That was a bit before my time," Ben replied. "I think I've heard rumors about it, though. I moved there about three years ago."

"Well, welcome to Kettering," she said. "Another lovely small town, most of the time."

"That's why we're here, Dorothy," Jack said. "I have some questions for you about Kettering and the past. I was wondering if you would be willing to try and answer them."

Dorothy's eyes flashed across both of them for a moment, and Ben thought he saw anger in them. Or perhaps fear. But she nodded her head.

"I still read the papers, Jackie," she said. "I know why you're here. But go on, ask your questions. Maybe it's about time you heard the whole story. No one else in town seems to want to talk about it, if they even remember it at all, so maybe it's my job to tell it. But I warn you, Jackie: you aren't going to like what I have to say. No one will."

CHAPTER TEN

"YOU WERE A YOUNG boy back in 1984," she said, the hint of a smile at the corners of her mouth. "You were, what, eight?"

"Nine," Jack replied.

"Yes," she agreed. "And it was a horrible early autumn. It had been a cold summer. I remember thinking, as the leaves changed color, that we'd been cheated. We had waited for summer all through that long, dark New England winter and spring, and what we got at the end of it just wasn't worth it.

"I think most people were feeling depressed about that. Depressed, and maybe a little resentful. I don't blame them, but I did my best to keep the mood light whenever I could. Then, in October of that year, things got dark."

"Dark?" Ben asked. "In what sense?"

"Dreadful, Mr. Simmons," she replied. "Everything —every*one*—turned dreadful. And it all started with Billy Gaines."

"Who was he, Dorothy?" Jack asked. Though she wasn't his grandmother, Jack sat before her with the respect and devotion reserved for one.

"Billy was the janitor at the middle school," she replied. "He'd been there many years. You know how sometimes the young ones can take a shine to someone because of a quirk or trick but the parents get a bad feeling about them? Not Billy; everyone loved him, the kids *and* the parents. A genuinely good man.

"I don't remember when it was exactly, but I do know it was early October when they found him. Some boys were playing out behind the buildings north of Main Street, just along the edge of the woods, and they found him there. Of course, I never saw the body myself, but the police said it had been messy. I think if it had been any other person, they probably wouldn't have been able to recognize him.

"But these kids knew Billy well. They'd spent years in school around him. I remember one of the boys telling me that he had come to school sick and vomited in the classroom, and it was Billy Gaines who brought in the mop bucket and cleaned up the mess. The boy—I think it was Gene Nolan—said Billy gave him a piece of gum. He was a real sweet man."

"Did the police think there was anything to worry about when they found him?" Jack asked. "At that point, I mean?"

Dorothy slowly shook her head, but kept her eyes on Jack's. "Did they think it was horrible? Of course they did. But they didn't jump out of their skin from fright and raise the alarm. Billy was a well-loved man in town, and I think perhaps they tried to keep his death out of the papers. I can understand, but it sure left a lot of people unaware of the danger that seemed to have crept into their lives."

"Like Edith Powell last week, you mean?" Jack asked. "People took her death as an accident and nothing to be concerned about personally, and just went about their lives. Is that what you mean?"

"Exactly that," she replied. "The whole town was unaware, for the most part. I have a feeling that the sheriff at the time, Don Blackwell, maybe expected another murder, but he never said so. He was just a lot less surprised than the rest of Kettering when the second body was found a few days later."

Ben interrupted again. "Is he still in town, Mrs. Abington?"

"Don?" she asked. "Oh no. He retired in the late Eighties, I think. Passed away a few years ago. No, I doubt there is anyone left who might have been directly involved in the investigation back in 1984."

"But you think Sheriff Blackwell knew more than he was letting on?" Jack said.

"No," she shook her head. "I just think his instincts told him that Billy Gaines wouldn't be the last. Maybe it was the nature of the crime, or the place the body was found. I don't know. I wish I could remember more about that. I just recall thinking that Don seemed less shocked than the rest of us when they found Patti Fuller's body.

"I can't remember where they found her, but it was just like Billy Gaines—the mess and horror of it all, I mean. Patti was less known around town. She was a college girl and her family had only just moved to Kettering a few years before. I think she might have been a cheerleader during her time at Kettering High, but I can't say for sure.

"She was pretty, though. My goodness, she was gorgeous. And that might have been what helped the people in town to take an interest. When a well-loved, blue-collar man dies, it's sad for those who know him. When a beautiful young woman is killed, though, people identify. Maybe they mourn the loss of that beauty, or the potential she represented. I think they also feel closer to the pain and fear she must have felt at the end.

"All those feelings caused people to invest in her death. They cared more, I think. And they started to fear for themselves. So when news broke about her murder and how similar it was to that of Billy Gaines, people took it real hard."

"They finally felt the gravity of the situation," Ben mused out loud.

Dorothy nodded once toward him. "That's exactly it," she said. "Whatever was happening finally settled on the town with a heavy weight."

Jack tilted his head to the side, as if an idea had moved it. "It seems that history is repeating itself today, then. Edith Powell, Alfonso Quezada...they aren't random murders, are they, Dorothy?"

The elderly woman grew quiet for a moment. She turned and looked out the window into the fading light. It was a beautiful afternoon outside, and the sky was clear and blue. Then, as if waking from a dream, she returned to them.

"They found something on the Fuller girl's body," she said, as if Jack hadn't asked her a question. "Did you know that? They found a claw."

"A *claw*?" Ben asked. "You mean, like an animal claw?" He was hopeful, but that hope felt weak and flimsy.

She shook her head. "Not from any animal we might know," she replied. "At least, that's what I heard through the grapevine. You know how people can talk. Rumors spread like gangrene, sometimes.

"I bumped into Don Blackwell once after he retired, and I couldn't help but ask him if it were true. I said, 'Donny, they say you found a claw buried in that poor Fuller girl's body. They say it wasn't natural, that claw. Is that a fact?' And I'll tell you, Don thought long and hard before he answered me."

"What did he say?" Jack asked, leaning forward.

"He told me couldn't talk about it. 'Retired or not, those are things I had to leave behind when I left office,' he had said. Maybe he didn't think it was his place to answer my question, but I tend to think that was enough of an answer for me."

Ben had produced a small notebook from one of his pockets, and he scribbled quickly on the page. Jack spent a moment in thought, and then decided to press on.

"Did it stop with Patti Fuller, then?" he asked her.

"No," she said weakly, almost with a sigh. "No, I wish it had, but it didn't stop. Not then. Just like 1954, in fact."

"Wait," Ben said. "I thought we were talking about 1984."

"Yes," she replied. "But you can't talk about 1984 without mentioning 1954. You'll find many people in town who still remember those dark days in October thirty years ago, but very few can say the same about '54. There aren't many of us left," she said, looking around the room at the other residents. "Not many who can remember, at least."

"Do you need to take a break, Dorothy?" Jack asked. He reached out and placed a hand on hers.

She forced a smile and patted his hand appreciatively. "No," she said. "It will be better to have it all out on the table. You need to know these things."

"So, about 1954—" Ben started, but the elderly woman cut him off with a wave of her hand.

"I'm not ready to talk about that yet," she replied. "The final murder in 1984 came just a couple of days after the Fuller girl. Jimmy Brubeck was an alcoholic who had drunk himself out of his job, his marriage, and eventually his home. He lived off the charity of many people in town, myself included, but I can't say anyone was relieved when his body was found out by

Hog House Pond. Drunk or not, he didn't deserve to die. Especially not that way.

"A group of men from Exeter found his body while they were out fishing on the pond. I think the police tried to get them to stay quiet about it, but it's hard to keep stories from spreading. One of the men—I don't remember his name but he was from here in town—said they could see the body from the middle of the pond, hanging from a low branch near the water's edge.

"They thought a hunter had bagged a buck and then discovered he couldn't get it out of the woods and just left it. When they rowed closer to shore, though, it looked less and less like a deer carcass. The man was insistent, though, that the body looked as if someone had tried to dress it, cutting it open all over. Just not in the neat and clean way you'd expect."

"And then it ended?" Ben asked. Dorothy nodded, closing her eyes for a moment.

"What stopped it, do you know?" Jack asked.

"I don't," she replied. "The whole town got more and more tense, like someone was winding us up. We could feel the springs getting tighter every day that October. You could take a walk through town in the middle of the day and feel it in the air, like an emotional humidity. Everyone was waiting for another murder. We were helpless and afraid. And then nothing happened."

"But no one knows why it stopped?" Ben repeated. "Something had to have frightened off the killer."

"Killer?" Dorothy almost spat the words out. "You say that as if you were talking about a man, Mr. Simmons. I don't think a man could have had anything to do with those crimes. Not with those same murders happening again thirty years later, and knowing that Billy and Patti and Jimmy weren't the first. No, there's no man behind the veil, hiding and waiting. I won't believe that for a moment."

"You mentioned 1954 earlier," Ben said. "You said most people in town have forgotten it happened. What can you tell us about that year?"

Dorothy's face grew pale. Her eyes took on a glassy, shimmering quality. It was as if Jack's words were an incantation, exhuming some ancient pain. She raised a hand to her face and Ben saw it tremble slightly.

"It was much the same as 1984," she said. Her voice was choked with emotion. "There were four murders in 1954, but I don't remember all of them. I was young and busy. My husband and I had just brought our fourth child home from the hospital and our life was beyond chaotic. I just remember the newspaper at the time making a big deal over what they thought were some accidental deaths."

"They didn't suspect murder?" Ben asked.

"Well, like Don Blackwell, I'm sure the sheriff's office back then assumed something sinister was going on, but I think people were a lot more trusting back then. It was easy to believe that people in Kettering just didn't get murdered. It must not have been until the third victim was found that they really started to take it seriously."

Jack leaned forward again. "Dorothy, you seemed pretty broken up when Ben brought up '54 again. You said you didn't know most of the murder victims, but I have a feeling you knew one of them. Personally, even."

She sighed again, and for the first time in the conversation Dorothy seemed unbelievably old. It was clear that she was reaching deep inside for these memories, and the process of bringing them to the surface was hurting her. Jack seemed aware of this, but he gently nudged her again.

"Who was the victim that you knew, Dorothy?" he asked quietly.

"She was my best friend," she finally said. She spoke the answer quickly and with much pain, like a bandage being torn off.

Ben was scribbling again in his notebook. Jack kept his hand on Dorothy's.

"I had known her my entire life. We grew up on the same street, played together, went to school together, and even double-dated in high school. She was the first person to be killed that year, the first of four. They found her in a tangle of trees and fallen leaves along the side of Exeter Road, just beyond Maple Hill Cemetery."

She stopped, unable to continue, and brought both of her gaunt hands up to her eyes. Her cheekbones, fine and high, were wet with tears.

"That must have been horrifying," Jack said. "I can't imagine that loss. She sounds like she was very special to you."

Dorothy nodded, but looked at Jack with a pained expression. Ben could almost read her thoughts, so clearly were they broadcast on her face. *She's holding something back*, he thought. *Why would she be doing that?*

"Dorothy," he said softly, carefully, as if he were approaching a frightened animal. "Who was your best friend? What was her name?" He readied his pen and notebook.

She never stopped looking at Jack. That moment of time between Ben's question and her answer might have been brief, but it felt eternal. Her eyes studied Jack's face and then, after taking a deep, calming breath, she spoke to him.

"You have her smile," she said, and her voice was full of recollection and emotion. "Every time you smile, I see her in there, smiling back at me."

Jack's face knotted in confusion. "I don't understand..." he trailed off, waiting for her to finish.

"Your grandmother, Jackie," she said, reaching out one of her frail hands to find his. "She was your grandmother."

The conversation came to an end with the approach of one of the nursing assistants. The woman, with her short, stocky build and severe expression, made it clear that it was time for the evening meal and Dorothy was needed in the dining area. Ben and Jack had no choice but to leave.

Dorothy gave Jack a final embrace. Her tears were mostly gone by then, as if telling her story had somehow extracted much of the pain she had felt. After a rushed farewell, he and Ben found their way out of the common area and back to the building's lobby, while Dorothy was slowly guided, arm in arm with her nurse, down the hall toward the clatter of plates and the smell of cafeteria food.

Jack was silent as they made their way to the lobby, and Ben didn't dare intrude on the man's thoughts. He knew that the last two days had accelerated whatever process helped two people become friends, but the last thing he wanted to do was overstep his boundaries.

There are always walls to watch out for, aren't there? he thought. Walls to mend, walls to protect, and walls to tear down. He wondered if Jack might be wishing for higher, stronger walls right about now.

They turned the corner into the lobby. Ben wasn't excited about passing by Sally. He felt like a crab walking the beach at low tide, nervously watching the seagulls on the rocks deeper inland. This image brought a smile to his face, and he nearly laughed. The thought dissipated instantly when he looked up and saw who was standing at the front desk signing the visitor clipboard.

It was the young hippie from the café.

CHAPTER ELEVEN

THEY WERE SITTING ON one of the stone benches that lined the strip of lawn between the building and the circular driveway. A large white van was lowering a hydraulic lift while an elderly man in a wheelchair waited patiently inside. Most of the residents, though, had gone inside for the evening meal.

The young hippie had introduced himself as Chase when they approached him at the front desk. Ben most likely came across as more than a little confrontational, but it was easy to feel paranoid after the weekend that he had experienced. He felt as if he were being stalked, and that pissed him off. He needed to know who this man was, and why he was seeing him for the second time that day.

It had been Jack's idea to step outside. Ben's tone of voice had verged on the edge of anger when he approached the young man, drawing a curious glance from Sally. When she looked up from her paperwork and raised an eyebrow at them, that was their signal to leave. Jack led them out the front door despite the young man's protests, and directed them to one of the benches a few yards from the entrance area.

"Let's back up a bit," Jack said with a tone that reminded Ben of a guidance counselor. Jack's eyes studied Ben's face. "How do you two know each other?"

"I saw him today while Ellen and I were eating in the café downtown," Ben replied. "We didn't speak, but I think he left something for me on the counter. A note."

The young man resembled a trapped animal, but he didn't seem ready to bolt yet. He was close, though, and Ben could tell he was uncomfortable with the conversation.

Jack turned to him. "Is that true?" he asked, gesturing toward Ben. "Are you following my friend here? And why don't I know you? Kettering is a pretty small community. I think I know nearly everyone in town."

The young man named Chase seemed to collapse inward. His shoulders slumped and he dropped his head. "Yes, I was in the café," he replied. "I'm Chase, I told you that inside. Chase Abington."

Jack's head cocked slightly. "Abington? Wait, are you related to Dorothy?"

Chase nodded. "She's my great-grandmother."

"Then why don't I know you?" Jack asked. "I've known Dorothy since I was a little kid."

"I grew up in Providence," the young man said. "My parents divorced when I was in grade school, and my dad—her grandson—stopped visiting here. Mom would bring us as often as she could, but, well, it was awkward sometimes. So I don't get down here much anymore."

Jack was quiet and thoughtful. Ben was doing the math in his head and decided that the young man—boy?—was telling the truth. He couldn't be much older than college age, so it was possible. But it still didn't explain everything.

"You left a note for me today," Ben said to Chase. "It was cryptic and unclear, but I have a feeling you knew who we were, and that we were looking for answers to something. What I don't understand is how. Are you following me?"

Chase shook his head so hard that one of his lip rings rattled faintly, like the sound of two coins colliding off in the distance. "No," he insisted. "It's not like that at all. I don't really know who you are, but I know what you've seen."

Jack interrupted. "How would you know what Ben has seen if you weren't stalking him around town?"

"Because I was at Angela's last night," Chase replied. "I was smoking outside and saw you and a woman running past. And I saw the police show up later. All I had to do was read the paper this morning and put the pieces together. You guys saw something, and it was connected to the other deaths, I'm sure of that."

"But what about the note?" Ben asked. "It just had one word on it: *manitou*. What the hell does that mean? How is it supposed to help me?"

Chase stood up. "Listen, I want to answer your questions. Really, I do. But Nana—Dorothy, I mean—is waiting for me. She'll be worried, and I don't get to see her too often. Maybe we can meet later tonight?"

Ben looked at Jack. "Do you believe him?"

"I do," Jack said, not taking his eyes off of the young man. "We'll meet at my place tonight. Seven o-clock, alright?"

Chase nodded.

"Here, give me a piece of paper from your notebook." Jack reached out to Ben, who tore out a sheet and handed it to him, along with his pen.

Jack wrote his address and phone number on the page and gave it to Chase. "Call me if you have any trouble finding the place."

"I will," he said. Turning to Ben, "In the meantime, you should look into that note. I think you'll be surprised how obvious it really is."

Chase nodded at both of them and then walked back toward the facility entrance. When he was out of sight, Ben turned to Jack, who stood and motioned for them to head back toward the truck.

"You believe him?" Ben asked.

"Yeah," Jack nodded, pulling his keys out. "I don't think he has any reason to lie, to be honest with you. What would he gain from pretending to be related to Dorothy?"

"Nothing, as far as I can tell," Ben replied. "I'd sure like to know what he thinks he knows about these murders, though. And what that note is supposed to mean."

They approached the truck. In the fading light of the early evening the horizontal chromed grill bars had lost much of their luster, but the white paint almost seemed to glow. Ben opened his door, hearing that heavy creak of the old hinges, and then slid onto the bench seat.

He pulled out his cell phone. "Listen, I'm going to skip dinner with you and Lori. Do you think you could drop me off at the library on your way by?"

"You bet," Jack replied. "What do you plan to do?"

"I'm going to give Ellen a call," Ben replied. "I think I have some digging around to do before our little meeting tonight."

—◦∞◦—

Jack had dropped Ben off at the library after a short drive. He had quickly explained to Ellen what he and Jack had learned during their visit with Dorothy. News of a similar series of attacks in 1984 did not seem to shock her as much as he had expected, but the 1954 murders did. He filled her in on their meeting with Chase for later in the evening, and she quickly added herself to the list of attendees.

After a moment of conversation, he had asked her to meet him at the library. She told him it would take a few minutes to get there, but she was happy to help. Ben hoped it was more than just these murders and their amateur investigation that had earned her company.

While the building was open on Sundays until 7:00 PM, Ellen had the day off, having left the desk in the hands of one of the semi-capable teens who helped her out. Rather than go inside without her, Ben had chosen to sit on the front steps and enjoy the cool evening air. It gave him time to think, and there was a lot of thinking that needed to be done. He was beginning to feel overwhelmed by the details and events of the last few days, and needed a chance to pause and examine it all from a new perspective.

He knew that there was a serial killer in Kettering, though he didn't know if that killer was human or some rabid animal wandering the wooded area north of town. He knew that the townsfolk were afraid beyond words, almost paralyzed by it. And he knew that this series of murders wasn't unique, that in the recent—as well as distant, he reminded himself—past, similar events had taken place.

That's the part that didn't sit well with him. Two sets of murders separated by three decades seemed odd and unlikely, but not impossible. Three strings of violence across sixty years, though? That just couldn't happen.

But, of course, it *had* happened, at least according to Dorothy Abington. Even more shocking, one of those 1954 victims had been none other than Jack's grandmother. Not to mention the others who had been killed over the course of that long, unlikely timeline. Nearly ten, as far as he could tell from his notes. It was more than compelling; it was frightening.

There was also the question of why no one else in town seemed to remember the 1954 murders. Surely there were still many in Kettering who were alive back then. Had they simply chosen to keep their dark memories to themselves? Depending on how close to the vest the local authorities played their investigation back then, there was a chance many people just didn't know how bad it was. Tragic accidents and nothing more, possibly. Even in a small town, people tend to mind their own business and miss details.

The problem wormed into the back of his head like a parasite. He could feel his mind working it over, turning the facts around in circles to find an answer. His years as a research assistant, as well as his own research-heavy attempts at writing, had helped him develop a strong sense of logic, and yet the pieces did not yield to him.

It was maddening.

He was about to talk it through—he had learned years ago that he was a verbal processor, and that speaking things out loud had a way of lubricating difficult challenges—when a small car pulled into a parking spot along the street and Ellen's tall, elegant figure climbed out.

"Aren't you cold?" she asked with a grin as he stood to greet her.

She had a light jacket on, and for the first time that evening Ben became aware of how cool the air had become. He couldn't see her breath in the air yet, but he knew that day was just around the corner.

Ellen climbed the stairs and gave Ben a warm hug, and there was a moment where she lingered close to his face ever so slightly before backing away. Ben felt the urge to pull her back.

"I'm alright," he replied. "Thanks for giving up your night off to come back here. I think I need the help of the Head Librarian tonight."

Ellen straightened up and leaned her head back in an air of mock professionalism. "Happy to be of assistance, sir." They both laughed and then mounted the rest of the stairs together.

Inside, the air was warmer and an overwhelming feeling of silence greeted them. The teenage girl at the desk looked up briefly and then did a double-take when she recognized Ellen. She straightened up and forced a smile.

"At ease, Rebecca," Ellen said softly as they approached the counter. "I'm here unofficially. My friend Ben needs help with some research, and he thinks that I'm somehow qualified to help him out."

Rebecca glanced nervously at Ben and then back to Ellen. The humor of what she had said somehow missed the target, sailing instead over the girl's head.

"Oh," she whispered, still serious. "Okay. Do you you need anything from me?"

"No," Ellen reassured her. "Act as if I'm not even here."

Rebecca nodded nervously, clearly put off by having her supervisor in the building during her shift at the desk. Ben nodded politely at her and then walked with Ellen toward the microfiche machine in the corner of the reading room.

"What are we looking for?" she asked him, taking off her jacket and hanging it over the back of a chair. "Is this about that note you found today?"

Ben nodded. "Long story," he said when she looked at him inquisitively. "I'll tell you about that later. For now, we need to see if we can figure out what that word means."

"Got it," she said. "So why are we at the microfiche machine?"

"Ah, that's our second goal," Ben replied. "While you're working on the mystery word, I have some old newspapers to read. Any chance you can help me find some old films?"

"Sure," Ellen replied, walking toward the cabinet that housed the archive of decades of Kettering news. "What period of time?"

"October of 1924."

Ellen stopped momentarily, enough for Ben to notice. "1924?" she repeated with her brow furrowed. "Don't you mean 1954?"

Ben grinned. "Just a hunch," he replied. "I have a theory to test. Though, I'll be honest, I don't want it to be right."

"Well then, let's hope you aren't." She pulled a small box from the shelf and handed it to him. "September through November of 1924. I'll be in the reference section if you need me."

She patted him on the back as she passed him, and Ben felt a tingle run down his spine. Her touch was a new sensation, and he found himself wanting to experience it more often.

Ben opened the small square box and pulled a roll of film out. It resembled a miniature version of footage one might find in a movie theater, only this film was different. Each frame was a detailed photograph of a single page from the Kettering *Times Press*. All along the strip, dark boxes filled with pale typography were lined up in meticulous, rhythmic order.

He fed the front edge of the film through the base of the machine, across the viewing plate, and out the other side. After affixing the film to a second spool, he flipped the switch and the monitor flickered to life. A motor somewhere inside the metal housing purred quietly, telling him that it was ready.

It took a moment for Ben to find his groove. He had used machines similar to this during his time at Boston University, and again during the early research phase of his first novel, but he was out of practice. Like a video game, it took a few minutes of practice to wrap his mind around the controls and the movements they created on the screen. As his comfort level increased, so did his speed.

The motor whirred as Ben sped through the early portion of the film. The murders that had taken place in 1954 and 1984 had all occurred in October, and so he felt safe skipping over September for now. He was willing to be proven wrong, but he needed to at least start where it made the most sense.

He paused the film and checked the date in the header of one of the pages. He had reached the last week of September. Advancing more slowly now, he counted the front pages that slid by on the screen. Large black and white photos moved silently from right to left, marking off the start of each new issue of the paper.

Finally, he stopped and began to move through the papers one by one. He wasn't entirely sure what he was looking for, but he scanned each and every headline on each and every page. Local events from the Roaring Twenties scrolled by, and Ben couldn't help but smile at the innocence and optimism of these ancient small-town journalists.

Then he saw it. The photo was large and centered on the front page of the October 10 edition. While the reproduction of the image wasn't of the best quality, the headline more than made up for it. Ben scanned the article for a moment longer, and then felt around on the sides of the microfiche machine for a print button.

He couldn't find it. The machine was fairly new—a modern Canon Carrier, at least—so he assumed he would have the ability to print any screen he wanted. As frustrating as that was, he was sure Ellen could help him once she returned. In the meantime, he pulled out his notebook and began to write down the details that he needed.

It's a shame I can't take that image with me, though, he thought. *They don't print pictures like that these days.*

He moved on to the next edition of the Times Press and then the one after that. He found what he was looking for nearly a week deeper into the roll of film. No photograph this time, but the headline was still splashed across the paper's front page.

Taking notes, Ben moved through the rest of October, and when he was sure he had found what he was looking for, he rewound the film and snapped off the machine. As if summoned by the sound, Ellen appeared from around the corner with a large leather-bound book in her hand.

"Success?" she asked him with a nod toward the now-silent machine. "It sounded like you were flying through that thing."

"Better than I had expected," he replied, "but it's not good news. What about you?"

Ellen set the book down on the table beside the microfiche machine. "I think I have an answer, though I'm not entirely sure how it helps. But you first." She motioned toward his open notebook.

"Oh no," he said. "I'm saving this for tonight. Tell me what you know about *manitou*."

Ellen studied him intently for a moment, as if it might cause him to give in and reveal what he had learned. Ben, though, set his notebook aside and leaned toward the book. He flashed an expectant glance at her.

"Well," she said, giving up, "there are a few options. The first is pretty much useless. As it turns out, there's a summer camp called Manitou Camp for Boys. But that's all the way up near Derry, Maine, so I think we can rule that out."

"That's a good assumption," Ben replied. "Unless you think middle school boys have been traveling down from the woods of Maine every thirty years with the goal of killing locals here in town."

"The second reference," Ellen said, ignoring Ben's sarcasm, "is a stop on the Hudson Line of the New York rail system about forty-five miles north of New York City. Again, that's not a match."

Ben decided to just nod in agreement this time, foregoing the witty comments that he actually wanted to make. "Is there an option that *does* make sense, though?"

"There is," Ellen replied, and then opened the large book she had brought over. She pulled out the small slip of paper that marked the page she wanted to show him, and then pushed the book toward him.

He leaned over and scanned the page. "What am I looking for?" he said. "This is an encyclopedia entry for Algonquian Spiritualism."

"Yes it is," she nodded, "Read it, Ben."

Ben did as he was told. After a few moments he leaned back and gave her a long, thoughtful look.

"Do you understand what this is saying?" she said without really meaning to ask. "The Algonquian peoples, one of the largest collections of Native American tribes on the continent, used the word *manitou* to collectively represent everything in the spiritual, supernatural world. The life force that flows through everything, as well as good and evil spirits. Primarily, though, the term refers to evil creatures."

"A dark spirit," Ben wondered out loud. "But the word could just as likely mean something positive, right? Could we possibly be reading into this, given the circumstances?"

Ellen shook her head. "I don't think so. You and I both know that what is happening in this town is far beyond the realms of the natural and sane. Something darker is going on. And the one word we've had suggested to us points to a similar answer. I think we have to assume a negative connotation to this term."

"Yeah, but this Chase kid isn't an expert," Ben replied. "Hell, he's barely out of college. Why should we put any stock into his theories? He's guessing, just like we are, right?"

"We are, yes," she said, "but we haven't heard him out yet. I have a feeling he's going to tell us why he wrote that word down when we see him tonight. If it's just a hunch, a guess out of nowhere, then I agree that we might be able to discount what he thinks. But what if he knows something that we don't, Ben? What if he's right?"

Ben didn't answer. He glanced back at his notebook, and at the list he had made while going through the old newspapers. He didn't want to think that Chase was right, but he also didn't feel like he had the luxury of pretending things were alright when they weren't. People were being killed, and turning a blind eye would only lead to more blood.

The names and dates that he had written in his notebook, along with other details, told him he had little to hope for. He wanted a logical explanation, for the real killer to be laid bare and found to be nothing more than a misunderstanding dressed in shadows and violence, but every sign—every single one—pointed to an answer that his mind struggled to grasp.

Fear, much like the mysterious thing that was killing the people of Kettering in the dark of night, began to grip Ben's heart. He might find answers tonight when he met with the others, but he didn't want to. What he wanted to do was cowardly and weak. It would leave the mess in someone else's hand and let him avoid it all.

Ben wanted to flee.

CHAPTER TWELVE

THEY HAD BEGUN TO wonder if Chase Abington would actually show up. Jack and Ben had parked themselves on the sofa in the Brooders' living room where they had a clear view of the driveway. Every few moments, like an obsessive-compulsive child repeatedly washing her hands, Ben would glance out through the glass at the darkness, hoping to see headlights approaching from the road.

Ellen had settled in the kitchen with Lori, where they were discussing books. Ben could hear Ellen's laughter, genuine but tight with nervousness, as the two of them recommended book titles to each other. He had just heard Ellen mention *The Lovely Mrs. Walker* by William J. McCarthy when the phone rang.

Jack made as if to get up and answer it, but Lori beat him. All conversation ceased for a few heartbeats while the person on the other end spoke to Lori. When she replied, everyone relaxed.

"No, thank you," she said. "We're happy with the news we get through our local paper. No need to add the Wall Street Journal to our lives. Have a good night."

The click of the phone being hung up was audible even in the living room. Ben smiled apprehensively at Jack, who was peeking out the window.

"False alarm," he said. "Though, I'd think if he was going to cancel on us, he wouldn't even—"

"He's here," Jack said, cutting Ben off. "I'll go let him in."

Jack rose and walked over to the front door. Ben had only ever seen the family use the kitchen door the entire time he had stayed with them, so seeing the large antique front door unlatched and pulled open felt odd. When Chase, no more than a stranger to all of them, stepped through the doorway, it felt even more peculiar.

Chase had changed clothes sometime since their chance encounter this afternoon. A thick peacoat was now buttoned up over his dark jeans and leather boots. Something about the outfit felt much less hippie this time, and Ben wondered if he had perhaps judged the college boy too quickly.

"We're glad you made it," he said as he stood and offered his hand to Chase.

The young man shook it, but his eyes glanced around the room, taking everything in. "Thanks. I almost didn't come," he said. "Something in the back of my mind told me I should, though. That, and Nana insisted on it."

Jack raised an eyebrow. "You told her about our meeting?"

"Not exactly," Chase replied. "You guys kept me talking long enough for her to wonder why I was late. One of the nurses apparently looked outside and saw me talking with you and mentioned it to Nana. I guess she put the rest of the pieces together."

"Speaking of," Ellen's voice came from the other side of the room. She and Lori were moving toward seats by the sofa. "We have some pieces of our own to put together tonight, don't we? Let's get started."

"Good idea," Jack said, and then motioned toward an arm chair near the fireplace. It was one of the old Colonial-styles, filling up much of the wall between the room and the kitchen on the other side. Chase unbuttoned his coat, hung it over the back of the chair, and sat down.

"Let's get introductions out of the way," Jack said. "Obviously, I'm Jack Brooder. That's my wife, Lori." He pointed toward her, where she sat beside Ellen. "Next to her is Ellen Hornsby, head librarian at the town library. And you've already met Ben Simmons. He's not from around here, but he's stuck with us at least until tomorrow."

Chase waved to the middle of the room. "Chase Abington," he said in response. "I'm not from around here, either. That's to say, my family is, but I grew up in Providence. I go to school at the University of Rhode Island where I'm in the graduate program studying cultural anthropology."

Ben cast a glance at Ellen, who raised an eyebrow at him. *That's one checkmark in the column of qualifications*, he thought. *The kid might really know something after all.*

"Can you explain why you've taken an interest in Ben and Ellen, and why you thought it would be helpful to leave them a cryptic note instead of helping them directly?"

Chase didn't respond for a moment. He turned his gaze toward the fireplace, which was dark and unused. The old brick lining was well-kept, and the right side of the space still had the bread over and wood storage areas that were a staple in Colonial homes.

"I only noticed Ben and Ellen because they happened to run past the restaurant last night," he finally said. "I told you that already."

"Yes, but why try to make contact?" Ben asked. "Why not ignore us and go back to school?"

Chase sighed. "Because I've been in town since Thursday, and I've heard a lot of whispering. Mostly from the people I met at Angela's last night, but you hear it all around you if you get out and walk through town.

"The thing is, almost everyone talking about it is scared out of their minds. Like, really scared, not just concerned or worried. I've heard multiple people say they've bought new locks for their homes, and lots of people have decided to stay inside once the sun goes down. I don't know the last time I've seen an entire town shift its behavior in response to something like this."

"Why did you think we were the ones to approach, then?" Ellen asked.

"Because you guys clearly saw something last night," he replied. "I could hear it in your voices. I stuck around outside and watched the police show up and everything. That county sheriff you guys have here was quite the jerk to you from what I could tell.

"Anyway, you two saw something," he continued. "I'm not sure anyone else in town is making that claim. I bet the only other people to have seen something are the ones who are dead. So when I had a chance to think about it—to really think it through and try to connect the dots—I didn't have many options for people I could share it with."

"What dots?" Jack asked. "You mean the murders?"

Chase nodded. "Yeah, those, and some of the clues around them that people seem to be ignoring."

"Such as?" Ben asked.

"Well," he replied, "each of these murders happened on the north side of town. And all of them happened in or near the woods. And at night, but I think that part is obvious. Anyway, part of me thinks those people who refuse to go outside at night are missing the point. They can leave their homes all they want; they just need to avoid the woods. I know *I* plan to."

"So how does *manitou* come into all of this?" Ellen asked.

"Did you look it up?" Chase asked. Ellen nodded in reply. "Well, then I think it's clear."

"Even still," Jack said, "enlighten us. Pretend we're not all anthropology majors."

Chase's mouth twisted into a frown. "You can call me superstitious or a nut-job, but I think what's happening isn't natural. People don't rip open other people, man. It's just not natural. That might make me assume there's a wild animal out there, sick or hungry or territorial or something, but then again, I also heard you talking to the sheriff. I'm not sure that the things you've seen can be explained away as easily as that."

"So you jumped over the fence from the natural to the supernatural," Jack replied. "What are you thinking it *could* be, then?"

"The things I don't know far outnumber the things I do," Chase replied. "Remember that. I'm just guessing. But I also happen to know a lot about this area, and the cultures that make up its history."

"The Algonquian peoples, right?" Ellen asked.

Chase's face lit up. "So you *did* figure it out." His voice was far too cheerful to be appropriate, considering the gravity of the events of the last week. "Yes, *manitou* is a reference to the Algonquian legends about spirit creatures. Beings that exist outside of what we would consider to be the natural world. But according to the Native Americans who trace their roots to this area, those legends aren't just stories; they believe these forces actually walk among us."

Ben leaned forward, resting his elbows on his knees. "So you think these murders are the result of some evil spirit in the woods, is that it?"

Chase nodded. "You got it, man. It's Occam's Razor, right? On a list of explanations for why something is happening, the best choice—the most logical and most likely to be correct—is the one that has the fewest assumptions required to be true."

"Yeah," Lori replied, jumping into the conversation, "but you're making a huge assumption here. Evil spirits?"

"I'm making *one* assumption," Chase corrected her. "Let's say it's a person, an actual human being, who has been committing these murders. We'd have to assume that there's someone capable of that. We would also have to assume that this person would be strong enough to do what people are saying the killer is doing. And, lastly, we'd have to assume that person—crazy and strong—is living among us without being noticed.

"That's one hell of a laundry list of assumptions, Ma'am. And I have a feeling Ben here has learned some other things that might make that list even longer, if we were to keep chasing the notion that a human being is doing this. Am I right, Ben?"

Ben swallowed. He didn't like how correct Chase was. The logic was sound and the facts did indeed point toward the supernatural hypothesis being true. What Ben had learned this afternoon didn't provide any arguments against it, either. In fact, he was pretty sure that it only confirmed Chase's assumption.

He nodded and looked around the room. "I did some digging today, after talking with Chase's great-grandmother, Dorothy. And my guess is that he's already learned a lot of what I know from her, isn't that right, Chase?"

The young man nodded. "She told me about 1984, and 1954 before that, yes." His eyes shifted toward Jack for a single heartbeat, and then back to Ben. "Between that and my college studies on the cultures rooted in this area, I've managed to connect some of the dots."

Ben nodded. "Well, I spent some time at the library after seeing you at Allenby Village today. It pays to know the head librarian, I suppose, and she helped me do some digging into old newspapers. I wanted to see for myself if the things Dorothy remembered were rooted in a pattern."

"So you looked up the 1954 murders?" Jack asked.

"No," he replied. "I just assumed Dorothy was telling the truth and then dug deeper. Each of the three waves of murder that we know about happened thirty years apart. Long enough for Dorothy to remember a couple of them, but far enough apart for elected law enforcement to miss the pattern."

"I don't follow," Lori said.

"Think about it this way: if Gil Roberts' predecessor had remained in his position for decades, he would surely remember any unsolved cases if they appeared to be happening again. But he never did. A

County Sheriff is elected into the job, and they rarely stay on for more than a decade. My guess is that after Don Blackwell retired in in the late Eighties, there must have been half a dozen other sheriffs in that chair downtown."

Jack nodded slowly. "Not that many, but I'd say at least three others between Blackwell and Roberts."

"See?" Ben asked excitedly. "Who's left to see the pattern? The people of Kettering? They're blinded by fear. And by the time they've seen enough to notice a pattern—as Dorothy has—they're too old to do anything about it. If they even live that long, that is."

"Wait," Ellen said with a hand held up. "You're saying that these murders happen on a schedule, but the spacing is so wide that no one ever notices it?"

"I wouldn't say 'no one' sees it," Ben replied, "but *most* people don't. So that's why I had you pull the microfiche for the newspapers dating back to the Fall of 1924. I wanted to go back another notch in the pattern, thirty years before the earliest murders Dorothy could remember."

"Shit," muttered Chase. "I never thought to ask her about that. What if she's heard stories about it, from her parents or something?"

"I don't know," Jack said. "She seemed pretty broken up about 1954, but she also never hinted at anything older. I don't even think *she* thought it could go back that far."

"But it doesn't really, does it Ben?" Lori asked her question without hope. It was the kind of question that came with its answer already embedded within, as if she knew that asking it was pointless.

Ben nodded, a grim expression on his face. "I'm afraid it does. There were five deaths in 1924." He pulled the notebook out from his back pocket and opened it. "The first victim was a young mother named Ivy Horton. She died in the first week of October of that year. The four other deaths proceeded hers over a three week period."

"God help us," whispered Ellen. "What animal could possibly live that long? Certainly no human could. I think I see what Chase meant. If we assume a person is doing this, not only would they have to be crazy beyond understanding and viciously strong, but they'd have to be at least a century old. Too many assumptions, I think."

"Now do you guys see what I mean?" Chase asked. "There's something out there that isn't human, or animal, and it's been killing people for decades. Who knows, it's probably been doing it longer."

Ben paused and thought through all the pieces of the puzzle as they understood them. Something about it didn't seem right. Not the facts; no, the facts were solid. It was the pattern.

Every thirty years, he thought. *It's too rhythmic, too perfect. It's almost intentional. As if there's a purpose to it, or a...*

"It's not killing people," he declared to the others. "Killers don't follow patterns like that. Murder is an impulse behavior, not something planned to a schedule. Whatever this thing is, it's *feeding.*"

"Intentionally, you mean?" Jack asked. "That would assume a level of intelligence that's far beyond an animal. I think you're right, don't get me wrong, but I sure don't like it. You're suggesting that there's a sentient being out there, most likely of supernatural origin, that's methodically feeding on the people of Kettering in small, thirty-year gulps, and has been doing it for at least a century."

Ben could do nothing but nod in response. The fear was paralyzing, and he wanted nothing more than to get in his car and drive north.

What about Ellen, though? She'd be left here without me. Left to be taken by the creature. Left to become the next meal, one more name on a list that will be forgotten in thirty years.

He glanced over at her, but she was looking at the floor. No one else seemed to be ready to speak. Jack sat rigid on the sofa, one hand clenched into a tight fist.

Lori had put her face in her hands, and Chase was playing nervously with one of his lip rings while staring into the dark fireplace.

It suddenly occurred to Ben that this thing, whatever it was, had the entire town captive. On the surface it was just killing people, devouring their flesh and their lives. But by doing so, it had also cast a spell of fear, and even the living had been consumed by it. Unless something changed, thousands of people would remain prisoner to this evil force.

"We have to do something," Ben said, breaking the silence.

"What? How?" Ellen asked.

"No idea," Ben replied. "But what if we're the first group of people in this town to catch on to what's really happening? Don't we owe it to everyone, including ourselves, to find a way to end it?"

"Yeah, but Ben, that's not as easy as it sounds." Lori was speaking from inside her hands, like a child too frightened to look.

Jack stood up suddenly. "Ben's right," he said. "But we need to know more if we're going to be able to do anything. I say we get some more answers, and then act. The quicker, the better."

"What do we need to know?" Ellen asked.

Ben saw strength in her face, and bravery. If he needed another reason to admire her, this was it. Here, in the face of danger, she was resisting. Perhaps she, too, was tired of the fear.

Ben, however, felt ashamed. All he wanted to do was run and abandon these people to whatever might—or might not—happen. Despite his deep desire to not be an imposition to the people around him, he felt a strong pull toward home. Ellen, though, did not seem to be feeling that same urge to run away.

Chase spoke up next. His voice was strained and weak.

"We'll need to see if we can identify what it is," he said, as if it were the easiest task in the world. "Maybe we can get the local police involved?"

"Our County Sheriff isn't the kind of man who buys into the supernatural," Jack replied. "I'm not sure we'll get much help from him."

"Actually," Ellen said, "you might be wrong about that."

"How so?" Jack replied.

"I spoke with him earlier today," she said. "He's at the end of his rope dealing with this case, and I got the feeling that he might be open to exploring ideas that sit outside the accepted realm of possibility."

Jack was visibly impressed. "I'll take it," he said. "How about Ben and I go visit him in the morning. And do you and Chase think you can put your heads together and figure out what we're up against?"

"Jack," Lori said with a trembling voice. "Why do you have to get involved? We need to be careful. What if something happened to you? Think about Tyler, for God's sake."

Jack shook his head in protest. "Lori, I *am* thinking about Tyler. And the kids he goes to school with. I'm thinking about his friends, and their families, and the people around town who try to crank out a living in this withering, backwater town. I'm thinking about my grandmother, who died at the hands of this...this thing. And dammit, I want it to stop."

"Then it's settled," Ben declared. "We find a solution tomorrow and put a stop to this. No more lives should be lost."

Jack motioned to Ellen. "Are you going to be alright going home tonight? And what about you, Chase?"

"I'm fine," Ellen replied. "My place isn't near the woods. I'll be scared out of my mind, but I don't think I'll be taking a risk to run from my driveway to my house."

"Same for me," Chase said. "I'm staying with a cousin near downtown, but south of Main Street. I think I'll be okay. I have no plans to die tonight."

"Nobody does," Jack said. "Let's hope things go according to plan."

Everyone except Lori stood and gathered near the door. Chase, who seemed more than eager to leave, pulled the door open and let in the cold night air. Jack stopped him, shaking his hand and giving him a forced smile. They spoke quietly for a moment, and Ben thought he saw Jack writing something down on a slip of paper.

Ellen tugged on her jacket and dug through her purse for her keys. She flashed Ben a nervous smile and then stepped closer to him. Without thinking, he reached up and placed a hand on the small of her back.

Instead of flinching or moving away, Ellen leaned closer. Ben was becoming convinced she had feelings for him. He imagined those feelings were nothing more than pity and friendship, but at least they were something.

Chase slipped out the door after mumbling his farewells. Ellen made to follow, and then paused, glancing back at Ben. There was courage in her eyes, and a look that he couldn't quite interpret.

Pity? he wondered. *Or just sympathy. There's a big difference.*

He opened his mouth to say something humorous and light-hearted, but before he could do so, she leaned toward him and pressed her lips on his. The moment was over before it even registered, but the softness of her mouth and the sweet scent of her breath lingered.

"Good night, everyone," she said while keeping her bright eyes locked on his, and then she was gone, slipping into the night like a specter vanishing into misty woods.

CHAPTER THIRTEEN

DOROTHY ABINGTON HAD LIVED at Allenby Village for nearly seven years, but the assisted living facility had never truly become her home. That was understandable considering that she had spent the vast majority of her long life raising a family and managing a home with her husband Robert. Independence was hard to give up.

Robert was gone, though, and so was the house. The former was lost to a stroke and subsequent heart attack eleven years ago, and the latter to an estate sale that was necessary to fund her incarceration here. That's how she saw it, of course; her family had grown tired of babysitting her, and they made the executive decision to let someone else do it.

Allenby Village wasn't actually that bad, and on her good days she had a much better attitude about it. Her room might be small, but she had managed to keep a good number of her favorite pieces of furniture and she took great pleasure in dusting them. Their edges were as familiar to her as the curves of her own aged body, defects and all.

The number of housekeepers who had come and gone over the last seven years was remarkable. The facility's rate of employee turnover was similar to that of a lightbulb, and it seemed that every few months she was being introduced to one more fresh face tasked with mopping her floors and vacuuming the rugs. Always young, usually unmarried, and—as if stereotypes needed to be reenforced—typically Hispanic.

Some were lovely and offered pleasant conversation, even friendship, if you allowed yourself to call it that, but others were as bitter and prickly as a patch of nettles. Each one, though, required one piece of training when they entered her apartment for the first time: the furniture is off-limits. They could clean anything else they wanted, but the furniture was her responsibility.

The buffet that barely fit along the wall between her eat-in kitchen and the living room always reminded her of her late husband Robert. He had been a truck driver, making the run between Providence and California, where he was originally from. In fact, they most likely never would have met had a coworker not taken sick and needed a substitute back in the Spring of 1947. She thanked God for that stomach flu or whatever it had been. There's nothing like intestinal discomfort to bring a couple together.

Of course, Robert had been with the Merchant Marines before that, making a tour of the Pacific that ended shortly after his time in the Battle for the Philippines. Moving goods was what he did well, so after his discharge he settled into the world of long-distance trucking. He found the open road to be a wonderful place and performed that service for the rest of his life.

Robert had discovered the buffet on one of his trips through Pennsylvania in 1967. He had found a truck stop on the I-76 turnpike that served the best coffee for miles, and after stopping there on one of his regular trips through, he noticed a large antique shop just down the road. The buffet caught his eye immediately, and because he was headed toward home with only a half-load, he figured he could pick it up and bring it back with him.

He had probably been swindled by the shop owner —they insisted the piece was over a century old and priced it as such—but she and Robert loved it regardless. Dorothy could still remember him unloading the thing from the back of his trailer with the help of Richard Brooder, Jack's grandfather. She and Elizabeth had watched them from the kitchen table, wondering aloud at the long, dark shape of the object the men were extracting from that trailer.

She stood beside that buffet now and ran her fingers over its smooth, worn surface. It was nearly ten feet long and stained a deep color that reminded her of coffee grounds. She knew its lines and firmness as one might know a lover's body. She cherished it now, but that had not always been the case.

She initially hadn't wanted to keep it. It was too big for their dining room, and they didn't even have enough dinnerware to warrant the additional storage. But it had been the wide grin on her husband's face that won her over. He loved it, and was certain that they would get many useful years out of it. He'd been right, of course, and forty-seven years later, here it was. She couldn't say the same about Robert. Or Elizabeth.

Elizabeth had been on her mind the entire evening, ever since Jack's visit and their conversation about the past. She missed her old friend, even more deeply now than in the decades past. Perhaps it was the busyness of life that had helped her forget that loss for a long while. Four children had been enough to keep any woman on the verge of insanity, never mind the weddings and grandkids.

But life has a way of slowing down at the end. Dorothy had found the last eleven years without Robert to be quiet and lonely, and times like that gave the mind freedom to wander. She drifted into the past more and more, unearthing memories like an archaeologist kneeling in the middle of an arid dig site. A lot of what she uncovered was pleasant. Those memories put smiles on her face and warmth in her bones. They kept her company in much the same way as a sleeping dog in the corner might.

Some memories were harder to lift from the dirt and hold up to the light, though. The loss of Robert was recent enough to still cause her throat to tighten and turn on the tears. She missed him terribly, his voice and touch and silent companionship in the middle of the chaos of life. He had been her rock, and in those dark moments when she remembered that loss, she felt untethered and adrift.

The loss of Elizabeth was deeper, though. Elizabeth, the girl she had known since her earliest memories. Elizabeth, who taught her to read a watch and tie her shoes. She sat beside Dorothy on the back seat of her father's 1929 Model A Tudor as he drove them to their Junior Promenade. She was beside her again twelve years later, when Dorothy married Robert.

Elizabeth had always been there, until she wasn't.

What she had told Jack was true. They had indeed found her body thrown carelessly under the low-hanging branches of a dying pine tree along the side of Exeter Road. Dorothy knew this because she was there. She had, in fact, been the one to find Elizabeth, long before the County Sheriff arrived and the flashing lights lit up the edge of the forest with a sickly red glow.

They had simply gone for a walk. How many of the others had done the same? Had Billy Gaines been out for an evening stroll along the edge of the woods, perhaps admiring the changing leaves that hung from the branches in bright orange patches? Even last week, poor Edith Powell—Dorothy had known her mother for many years and thought very highly of her—seemed to have just been out for a walk. That's all it was, just a walk.

They had spent the day with their two young families. There was a farm in Exeter that opened their orchard for apple picking each autumn, and they had worn the kids out walking all over those lovely acres of land. After a big dinner and some raucous singing—Robert could find his way around a piano, and Richard knew how to clap out a rhythm—they put the kids to bed.

The men wanted to sit around the fireplace and sip on some bourbon Robert had brought back on a recent drive. Elizabeth, though, wanted fresh air, and a walk sounded like just the thing to fill that need. They had grabbed their shawls and headed out into the night, tired but happy to have some peace after such an exhausting day.

She remembered the air being crisp and cool, but very still. Had there been much of a wind, they most likely would have turned around and headed back, but the clear night sky and stillness was seductive, drawing them out.

Dorothy and Robert's house had been just down the road from the Brooder farm, but they chose to walk north that night for some reason. She had reflected on that decision over the years, and whenever she did, her mind filled with regret and doubt. What if they had chosen to walk toward Elizabeth's home instead? What would their lives have been like had they not walked north?

So much loss, she thought. *So much pain.*

The walk north left them with another decision as well. One more choice for Dorothy to spend decades second-guessing. Should they cross Main Street and keep going north, or head east into town? It was Elizabeth who settled that choice for them when she pulled out a crumpled pack of cigarettes and grinned at her.

They were like school girls again, getting into trouble and hoping the adults wouldn't find out. Elizabeth suggested that instead of walking down Main Street, they should stroll through Maple Hill Cemetery. It was dark and set off from the rest of the town, but that was what she wanted. Dark, and quiet.

It wouldn't be quiet for long.

They had walked and laughed and chatted about their lives before kids and husbands. Dorothy remembered debating which one of them had kissed Hal Weaver first—even though they had both only been about eight at the time—but they couldn't get their stories to line up.

When they were sure that they had travelled far enough away from Main Street, the women had stopped in front of an ancient fieldstone and mortar hut that sat at the edge of the graveyard. It was the small sort of building that could be found in many New England cemeteries, typically used to store tools and funeral supplies.

Elizabeth lit a cigarette with a thin paper match, and when she tipped the package toward Dorothy, she gave her friend a hell-why-not grin and pulled one out. It hadn't been her first time smoking, but it wasn't something she did all the time. Not like Elizabeth, who snuck a smoke when her husband was out in the field or inside reading after a long day.

The rest of the night was a bit of a blur. Fear and loss has a way of muddling the memory sometimes, like one of those faux-finish painting techniques that was all the rage in the Eighties. What she did remember was that they walked deeper into the graveyard, and then Elizabeth suddenly had to go to the bathroom.

They had a brief conversation about walking into town. Back then the building that now played host to Angela's was a night club called The Back Room, and they had a restroom near the entrance. Elizabeth said it was pretty urgent, though, and she finally declared that she was just going to step into the bushes and do it right there.

Dorothy had giggled at her friend. Their nighttime walk without kids and spouses had already led to smoking. Relieving herself in the bushes somehow seemed fitting and comical all at the same time.

Her friend had stepped on the crisp, dry leaves that littered the grass at the edge of the cemetery and then lifted her skirt and squatted with her back to the trees. Dorothy remembered feeling a slight twinge of embarrassment, and then looking away. A car horn honked back in the direction of Main Street—someone leaving The Back Room, most likely—and she watched for its headlights to pass by.

Then there was the sound of wind. It was a dry, raspy noise, like the exhale of a breath, but more subtle. She had initially thought it was the wind, but when she didn't feel a breeze on her face she shrugged it off as shifting leaves.

That's when Elizabeth screamed.

Dorothy had spun around as quickly as she could, but the cry was muffled almost immediately. When she cast her gaze over the spot in the bushes where her friend had been just a moment before, all she managed to see was a dark shadow slowly dissolving backward into the trees. A shadow that was much too large to be human.

She called out for her friend, but there was no answer. When she stepped closer, she felt something crunch beneath her shoe and bent down to find the package of cigarettes. There was no other sign of Elizabeth, though, and that did more than worry her. It made her feel very alone, and completely vulnerable.

She ran up and down the edge of the trees for what seemed like an eternity. First she had whispered Elizabeth's name, but that soon gave way to desperate crying. Her friend was gone, and she didn't know what to do. There were sounds in the trees, and though she did her best to follow after them, she couldn't get herself to leave the grass of the cemetery.

Finally, after what must have been a quarter of an hour of frantic searching, she had clambered over the low stone wall on the western side of the graveyard and walked along Exeter Road, scanning the tree line by the dim starlight. She hadn't gone far when something pale and irregular caught her eye. It had been Elizabeth, of course, but in many ways it hadn't been.

Dorothy ran her hand over the buffet again. Then, without thinking, she pulled open one of the wide drawers and took out an ancient, crumpled pack of cigarettes. Elizabeth's cigarettes. Suddenly, she wanted nothing more than to taste one, to inhale their warm, acidic smoke and remember that night more clearly.

She found her robe and wrapped it around herself before tucking the cigarettes into one of the pockets. In the kitchen she found a half-used book of matches and added them, and then took her keys and slipped quietly out the door.

The hallway was silent and deserted, as it usually was at this time of the night. Dorothy didn't always sleep the best, so she would often take slow walks up and down the hallway to tire herself out. Tonight was different. Tonight she felt energized, and let her feet take her toward the common room.

The large room was dark, but enough moonlight filtered in through the windows to allow her to pick her way through the maze of oversized sofas and square folding tables. Many of the residents in the facility had an enthusiastic relationship with card games, but the only evidence that could be seen now were a handful of boxed decks on each of the tables.

The room was quiet, which Dorothy found refreshing. Daily life in Allenby Village could be noisy, especially when one of the patients with geriatric dementia had an episode in the hallway and four nurses had to find a way to restrain them. She continued to be amazed at how strong a woman her age could be when under the influence of a dementia-induced rage.

Dorothy had none of those troubles, however, and she was thankful for that. She had watched friends decline around her for decades. Some of them had crumbled physically while maintaining a tight grip on their sanity. Others took the opposite approach to old age. None of them had any choice in the matter, of course, but that was the way of things. She seemed to have skipped both paths and slipped into her golden years intact. Weak, but intact.

She reached out to test the knob on the door to the courtyard, expecting it to be locked. If it was, she would simply shuffle back to her room, stow the cigarettes away, and attempt to let sleep drive these painful memories from her mind. It wasn't, though, and the door swung silently open.

Cold air washed over her. October had begun to turn on them, it seemed. A few more nights like this would finish off all of the leaves and usher in that period of the year that felt desolate and barren. She could smell the decay of the foliage that had already fallen, and it stirred more memories. Pulling her robe tighter against the cold night, she slipped outside.

Allenby Village was the palatial home of a wealthy Nineteenth-century industrialist. He had the home constructed on the north edge of town, facing south, and pattered the rear of the property after the formal gardens of England, where his parents had been born. Beyond the gardens, fountains, and ornamental hedges was the front edge of trees that acted more as a barrier than a feature. Beyond them, a tangle of darkness and branches.

The industrialist's family continued to own the sprawling residence up until the 1970's, when it was sold and converted into a home for the elderly. Acreage around the manor home was sold off to developers who filled the land with homes for the growing number of commuters who preferred raising their children away from the stress and chaos of the big city.

The courtyard was all that remained of those beautiful English gardens now. Dorothy remembered how it looked before the family sold the estate, though. She had been friends with one of the staff employed by the owners and had been given a private tour once. She knew, perhaps better than most, that the courtyard as it existed today was but a shadow of what it had been.

Dorothy walked slowly down the gravel path toward the back of the property. She was fairly certain that none of the nursing staff would think to look out the windows into the yard behind the building, but if they did, she wanted to make sure none of them saw the glow of her cigarette or the smoke it would produce. Even on a night with so little wind, she didn't want to take that chance.

There was a stone bench along the back edge of the yard, overlooking the trees and the nature trail that passed by. Someone once told her that the path, installed just two years before, went all the way to Exeter, but she couldn't fathom why anyone would want to walk that far. That didn't stop them, though, and most afternoons—if she managed to find the bench empty—she could watch as dozens of young folk ran up and down along the edge of the woods.

The stone seat was cold beneath her body, and she tugged her robe tighter around her shoulders. She felt for the package of cigarettes and pulled it out, along with the book of matches. They felt light, as if the package might be empty, but she knew better.

They weren't fresh, of course. They were dry and stale and a lesser version of what they once were, much like herself. She wasn't even sure how she still had them. They must have been in the buffet when her family moved it into her apartment years before, the last remaining piece of evidence of what had happened to

—

No, thinking about that night in the cemetery was not wise, but how could she stop now? The memories were there, like an animal crouched in the bushes, waiting to attack. She had paced frantically along the tree line at the back of the graveyard, crying out her friend's name in hoarse whispers that grew louder as the minutes passed, her heart pounding wildly in her throat.

All the while, poor Elizabeth had been somewhere nearby having her body torn apart.

She pulled one of the cigarettes out of the cellophane and paper packet and pushed it between her dry lips. With practiced hands she struck a match and held it up, catching the tip on fire before shacking it out and dropping it on the gravel beside her feet. Then she breathed deep.

The air was still, but the wind seemed to call out regardless. It was a dusty sound, like the exhale of someone off in the distance. The smoke from her cigarette floated straight up, yet she could still hear the wind.

Rasssp...

The sound was familiar to her. It caused her skin to tighten into gooseflesh, and she felt the hair on the back of her neck stand on end. Something about that sound tugged at the strings of her mind, and she didn't like the memories it evoked.

It was the sound she had heard while Elizabeth squatted in the bushes. The sound of whatever had taken her.

She was imagining that, of course. How could she not, after dragging up all of those old feelings and memories? It was nothing more than her mind playing tricks on her.

With the taste and smell of the cigarette around her, it was so easy to drift into the past. The scent of the dead leaves, the pungent odor of damp earth of the woodland just beyond the path, and even the dark night sky—all of it was conspiring to recreate those moments in her mind.

Rasssp...

And yet…and yet, there was the sound again. Before, she would have sworn she had only imagined it, that it had come from within her, from her memories of that night. This time, though, she was certain she heard it nearby. Close by her, not *within* her.

Dorothy sighed and felt the weight of decades slip off her shoulders. Maybe she knew this moment would come. Perhaps it had been set in motion the instant she heard her dear friend cry out, and turned to see the shadow that took her away. She wondered if her life—everyone's life, really—was nothing more than a wind-up clock that ticked toward a predetermined time, determined by some invisible clockmaker.

In that moment she knew her time had come. She wasn't afraid, though. Not now, not with such familiar sensations surrounding her. The scent of tobacco mingled with damp earth, the chill night air and the bright stars above. All of it took her back.

Rasssp…

Now it was here, ready to take her back, whatever it was. But she was ready. Robert was already gone, and so was Elizabeth. She had told Jack her story as best she could. The torch had been passed and her race was done. She had reached her bitter, haunted finish line.

She stood up slowly, her ancient knees struggling against the pull of gravity, and then faced the the woods. The sound came with more frequency now, and it was louder. Whatever it was, it was now much closer.

Dorothy took another long pull on her cigarette and felt the warm smoke fill her lungs. Then, with a weak flick of her wrist, she tossed it to the gravel. She stepped forward, extinguishing it beneath her foot, and then stepped farther. Step by step she crossed from the path to the tall grass beyond it, and then onto the walking trail.

Rasssp...

Between the trunks of the tree, shadows congealed and thickened and formed a darker patch within the blackness. The sound had grown yet louder, bringing movement with it. She wasn't afraid, though. Not tonight.

Elizabeth had gone this way. Elizabeth, the friend who sat with her during the horrible labor at the end of her first pregnancy. Elizabeth, who had passed notes to her during their countless classes together. She had left this world through a door that Dorothy had never been able to follow.

Until now, that is. Now she could do one last thing —*the* last thing—just like her oldest friend.

Rasssp...

Now the sound called out to her. It filled her ears and mind and heart. Where before it was nothing more than the sound of a dry, scratching wind, it had become something more. It was a voice calling out to her. It beckoned.

Come...

Her slippers left the path and she felt the tall grass scratch at her ankles. The first branches of the woods were within reach now. The shape in the shadows seemed to quiver with anticipation, pulsing darker and lighter. The air had grown icy cold, and even though she had stamped out the cigarette, her breath rose in white tendrils through the chill air.

I'm ready, she thought. She reached into her pocket one last time, withdrew the crumpled cigarette package, and dropped it in the grass. Then, as if an invisible cord were tugging her forward, she took the last two steps.

Shadow enveloped her, followed closely by pain, and then finally death.

CHAPTER FOURTEEN

THE LIGHT THAT FILTERED through Ben's window hinted at a cold, gray morning. He reached over and checked the time on his old mobile flip phone which lay charging on the night stand. It was early, but that was good.

He opened the door to his room and listened. The house was silent, and he hoped that meant everyone was still asleep. Gathering his toiletries and a change of clothes, he slipped into the bathroom and did his best to get ready for the day.

He found that much of his best thinking occurred in the shower, a sentiment that many people had echoed over the years. Some had suggested it was because of the sound of water, while others thought perhaps it was the act of stripping naked that somehow encouraged the mind to empty itself and reboot.

Ben preferred to believe it was because the bathroom was a place where distraction was absent. Most people showered alone, and it was hard for anyone to hold an electronic device while they bathed. Stepping through the door to a bathroom was almost like passing through airport security in the post-9/11 era.

Untethered from social obligations and digital distractions, Ben felt free to process ideas and work through problems. He didn't always have the privilege of deciding which problem his brain was going to tackle, though. It was a grab-bag, and he always had to take what he was given.

Today it was the story he was trying to tell in his new novel. He had been stuck on a few key pieces of information that had been uncovered during his research phase, making him unsure of where to end the story. He felt that sophomoric pressure to make the best decision he could, because a wrong choice might damn his chances for publication.

The Great Swamp Fight, the name given to a decisive battle fought between the militia from a handful of New England colonies and the native Narragansett tribe, ended the same way many battles did: messily. For some, the battle signaled the end of an era of cooperation between people groups. For others, such as the Native American-turned traitor Indian Peter, it signaled judgment. And for a small handful of Narragansett warriors, death and starvation in the harsh winter conditions.

Ben wanted to be sure to paint both sides of the battle with as much realism as possible. There were heroes on both sides of the fortress walls, and both forces paid dearly. He simply wanted to paint an accurate picture, and tell a compelling story at the same time.

Easier said than done.

His time in the shower delivered on its promise, though, and he stepped out into the quiet hallway with enough inspiration to sit down in his room and flesh out the outline he had been building. It felt good to organize his thoughts and get them onto the page— even if that page was digital.

The smell of bacon drifted into his room around 8:00 AM, providing enough distraction to end his writing session. He had made great progress and that temporarily lightened his mood, which continually felt dark and fearful no matter how he tried to keep his mind off of it.

Breakfast was brief, and Lori left to take Tyler to school shortly after Ben sat down at the table. He and Jack drank their coffee and made the kind of small talk that two people use to dance around a topic that no one wants to address. At some point, though, you couldn't dance anymore.

"Any idea how we're going to learn more about a creature no one has seen or tracked?" Ben asked as Jack folded his paper and tossed it aside. "I have this horrible feeling we're all just going to have to wander off into the woods and hope we bump into it."

Jack grimaced. "Man, I sure hope not," he replied. "You're wrong, though; a few people *have* seen this thing. They just didn't live to tell the rest of us about it. If there's a way for us to learn more about it without joining that elite group, I'll vote for that option."

"I'm with you, trust me," Ben said, nodding. "I have high hopes that Ellen and Chase might turn something up at the library today that will help us out."

"I don't know," Jack said with a sigh. "I don't think it really matters what this creature is. We know everything we need: it's hunting people, feeding on them at night and disposing of the bodies where others will find them. And I believe that it's literally mocking us by purposefully creating more fear and tension with each passing day."

"It's as if the thing is feeding on fear as much or more than it's feeding on the people it kills," Ben added.

Jack was quiet for a moment. "You know, that's an interesting observation. Have we heard anything about the conditions of the bodies, aside from the fact that they were mutilated and torn to pieces?"

"Not that I have ever heard," Ben replied. "But Sheriff Roberts would certainly know more. He told me that he had called in the County Medical Examiner to look at the most recent victim. Maybe we should ask him?"

Jack nodded. "We need to do *something*," he said. "But you're going to need a coat."

———⦿⦿⦿———

Their drive to the Courthouse took longer than expected. For the first time since he had arrived in Kettering, Ben got to witness the traffic light in use. A small line of cars had been waiting at the light, and as Jack steered his old truck up to the intersection, they all headed west toward I-95.

Downtown felt more active than it ever had, as well. Ben pointed out how many cars were parked along Main Street, and Jack nodded in acknowledgment.

"Ayup," he replied. "Commuters. They live here, and work in the city. I know a couple of folks who get to drive to North Kingstown, but the majority have to get in line and join the march toward the interstate."

Ben shook his head. "I've never had to commute," he said. "For the last couple of years I've even had the privilege of working from my own home. Nothing beats that commute: it's three steps from my kitchen table to my writing desk. Compared to this, it's bliss, pure and simple."

"That's why I love farming after spending all those years commuting to military bases. Some of them were in lovely areas, but most were horrible. It was better when I lived on base, but once we got married, Lori and I really wanted a real house. Something we could put some equity into, you know? And that meant driving in each day."

They passed the library, and Ben felt something in his chest unhitch. He wondered if Ellen was already hard at work digging for information, or if she was waiting for Chase to arrive at some unknown time. He was hopeful that he would find time to visit her, and realized that seeing her face was something he had grown very fond of very quickly.

It was a bitter-sweet emotion. Ben had been assuming since Friday that he would receive a phone call from Buster Moynahan today. His car would be back in action and ready to be picked up. After than, some time on the highway would take him home, away from this unfortunate detour. Suddenly, though, Ben was much less excited about going home, and he had a strong suspicion that Ellen had something to do with that.

Jack turned onto Hall Street and parked in one of the available spots along the sidewalk, directly behind one of the three police cruisers the county owned. Ben stepped out and zipped up the heavy coat Jack had loaned him. It looked to be army-issued, complete with an olive drab cotton shell. It was the quilted lining that Ben was thankful for, though, considering how cold it had turned overnight.

Sure, the day before had been brisk, but that was typical of autumn in New England. Today, however, it felt as if they were on the threshold of winter. Ben could see his breath and his fingers felt numb. He tucked his hands into the pockets of the coat and shrugged his shoulders up against the chill.

"I hope Roberts is in," Jack said as they headed up the short sidewalk toward the building. "I'm pretty sure that *he'll* answer our questions, but I doubt any of his deputies will."

Ben was about to reply when the door ahead of them burst open. Gil Roberts was moving fast, pulling on his own coat while attempting to trot. When he noticed the others, though, he stopped.

"Brooder," he said. There was tension and adrenaline in his voice. "Shit, you've got some great timing. I think you're going to want to follow me." He glanced at Ben, and then added, "Both of you, as a matter of fact."

"What's going on?" Jack asked. "Anything you're allowed to share?"

"Screw protocol," Roberts replied. "Keeping all of this crap private isn't helping anyone except the very suspect we're trying to find. I'm done hiding behind this badge and rules. If you want to help, follow me."

"Alright, then. Where are we going?" Ben asked as they all turned and headed back toward the street.

"Allenby Village," Roberts replied. "Dorothy Abington was killed last night."

Ben expected Jack to weep. He had known Dorothy his entire life, and having just seen her the day before, the news of her death—her *murder*, rather—seemed all the more bitter.

Jack wasn't weeping, though. Jack was ablaze with anger. His hands were gripping the steering wheel of the truck so hard that his knuckles seemed to be painted white. Ben didn't want to be the first person to speak, either. He was afraid of what Jack might do or say.

They were moving quickly, following close behind Sheriff Roberts' cruiser. His lights were on, splashing red and blue across their windshield and drawing the attention of those who were out and about along Main Street. Each and every one of them looked both frightened and undisturbed, as if they had been expecting yet another horrible event.

It was barely 9:00 AM, according to the clock on his phone, but Ben already felt exhausted. He had a feeling that today was going to be a long day. News of another attack only served to increase the urgency he felt regarding the creature. He felt more helpless than ever.

Jack followed Roberts into Allenby Village's parking lot. Both men exited their vehicles with amazing speed, and Ben struggled to keep up with them as they ran toward the facility's entrance. Thankfully there were no residents milling about on the front sideway this morning.

They were greeted inside by Sally, who was pacing back and forth in front of her long counter. Roberts passed right by her, and Ben guessed that the Sheriff knew where he had to go. Jack paused, though, and allowed Sally to speak with them.

"Oh, Jack," she said fearfully. "I'm sorry. I don't know what to say."

Jack took her hands in his. His anger seemed to have been left in the truck, and Ben observed how gentle his touch was. Sally was sobbing, and Jack put an arm around her.

"It's alright," he reassured her. "What can you tell me?"

Sally heaved a moment longer with waves of sadness, and then nodded. "One of the residents found her this morning, after breakfast," she said. "The nurses thought it was odd that she wasn't at breakfast, but she's skipped before. They just assumed she needed a bit of extra sleep."

"So no one noticed she was missing?" Ben asked from beside Jack.

"No," Sally said, shaking her head. "At least, not until right after breakfast. Nurse Hesser went to check on her but found her apartment empty. That's when they started searching."

She reached over the counter and pulled a tissue out from some hidden box. Before she continued, she dabbed at her watery eyes and then wiped at her nose.

"It was Mr. Mollenaur that found her," she said. "Well, he saw her, that is. He didn't go near her."

"Where, Sally?" Jack asked.

She pointed down the hall in the direction the Sheriff had run. "Outside. At the back of the courtyard."

Jack nodded. "Thanks, Sally," he said. "We'll be outside if you need me for anything."

Sally nodded, and then the two men ran on. They paused at the door that led outside from the common room, and Jack pulled out a piece of paper.

"Chase's number," he said, extending it to Ben. "I got it from him last night. He's going to want to know about this. Call him and tell him to get his ass over here."

Ben took the paper and pulled out his phone. "You've got it. I'll join you in a moment."

Jack nodded and stepped outside, making his way toward the back of the property. Ben watched him go, and then dialed the number into his cell. There was a pause while the line connected, and then three long rings on the other end. He was about to hang up, assuming the young man wasn't planning to answer, when there was a *CLICK* followed by a familiar voice.

"Hello?" Chase answered.

"Chase, it's Ben Simmons. There's been another murder."

The line was quiet for a moment, then, "Who was it this time?"

"I'm really sorry, Chase," Ben replied. "This is tough news to pass on. It was—"

"It was Nana, wasn't it?" the younger man interrupted.

"Yes," Ben answered. "Jack and I are already here at Allenby Village. Sheriff Roberts asked us to follow him here, but he doesn't know about you. I think you should join us. Can you come?"

"Already on my way," Chase said. "I'll be there in a couple of minutes."

"Sounds good," Ben replied. "We're out back in the courtyard. Come right out when you get here."

Chase didn't reply. The line simply went dead and Ben knew he understood. The young man was going to have a tough morning. Ben hoped he was ready for it.

He closed his phone and headed out the door. The chill air felt like a slap in the face after the warmth of the common room, and he pushed his hands back into the pockets.

God, it's cold, he thought.

He found Jack standing with Roberts on the narrow gravel path at the back of the courtyard. The Sheriff was speaking with an elderly man, and all three of them were looking out toward the trees behind the facility.

"...didn't expect to see something like that after breakfast, I'll tell you that," the elderly gentleman was saying. "Hard to miss her, though, all pale and crumpled off at the edge of the trees."

The man pointed toward the wooded area, where a large white sheet had been spread over what Ben assumed were the mangled remains of Dorothy Abington. As if on cue, Ben heard sirens in the distance, and he guessed that the county ambulance had finally arrived.

"Thank you, Mr. Mollenaur," Roberts said. "If I have any other questions, is it alright if I stop by and talk with you again?"

"You bet, young man," he replied. "Anything you need, just ask."

The elderly man shuffled his way back down the path toward Ben, who smiled politely and nodded as they made eye contact. The man seemed both sad and alive. Ben guessed that the events of the morning qualified as the most excitement Mr. Mollenaur had experienced in years.

"Is Chase on his way?" Jack asked as Ben approached.

Ben nodded, and the Sheriff gave them a curious glance.

"You two aren't abusing my transparency, are you?" he asked.

"Not at all," Jack replied. "Mrs. Abington's great-grandson has been in town all week. He visits her from time to time. We thought he would like to know about her death as soon as possible.

"What a mess," Roberts said. "I'm helpless, guys. I'm out of my depth and I've got nothing to hold onto."

"No," Jack replied. "You have us. Chase Abington as well. And Ellen."

Gil Robert's expression changed at the sound of her name, but he gave no other sign than that. "Don't go dragging her into this," he warned. "I like Ellen. I'd hate for her to get hurt, too."

"Good luck telling her that," Ben replied. "She doesn't strike me as a woman who enjoys taking orders from others, badge or no."

"That's the truth," Roberts said with a grim smile. "So, what help can you guys offer me?"

"Well," Jack replied. "For starters, I'm going to guess that you'd be alright with a former Army Ranger assisting in the hunt, correct?"

"Crap, I forgot that about you," Roberts replied. "You better believe it. Still got a gun?"

Jack nodded. "A few. Back at the house. I'm happy to strap one on if you need me to."

The expression on the Sheriff's face was more than enough to answer that question. "The more the merrier, at this point," he said.

"Mind if I check out the area around the body?" Ben asked, motioning toward the white sheet a few yards away. "As you've so nicely pointed out before, I've managed to find myself at two other crime scenes since arriving in town. Maybe something will jump out at me."

The Sheriff considered the idea for a moment, but relented easily. "Take Brooder with you," he said. "But don't touch anything. The ambulance just got here, and I want to make sure the medical examiner has a clean scene to process."

"Understood," Ben replied, and then he and Jack stepped off the gravel and headed toward the edge of the trees.

The grass was crisp from the morning frost, and it crunched beneath their feet. Ben stopped when they reached the walking trail and glanced down the path, first to their left and then to the right. The trail followed the contour of the tree line in each direction as far as he could see.

"Where does this trail go?" he asked, pointing toward the west, the direction that led to downtown.

"That way?" Jack replied. "It heads northward after crossing Exeter Road. Follows the edge of the woods for about ten miles, and then bends westward again. Used to be an old railroad, but they converted it over the year Lori and I moved back to town."

Ben nodded and then crossed the path. There was a strip of grassland between the gravel running surface of the trail and the edge of the woods, like a buffer zone. It was on the far side of that small field that the body of Dorothy Abington lay beneath a white sheet.

Ben skirted the body, keeping a healthy amount of space between himself and the sheet. The Sheriff didn't want the scene disturbed, and he wasn't about to disobey those orders. Jack, however, walked more closely to where she lay, enough to make Ben nervous.

The white sheet was stained with blood in the dozen or more places where it touched her torn body. He could smell the acrid, coppery scent of blood. Jack broke the silence.

"She was the closest thing I had to a grandmother," he said quietly. "She filled a hole that mine left vacant. And now..."

Ben understood. Dorothy had done more than follow in the footsteps of Jack's grandmother. In the end, both women fell victim to the very same creature, reunited across a gulf of sixty years. It was tragically symmetrical.

Ben was looking at the ground, trying not to let his eyes fall on the bloody silhouette of the elderly woman, when he saw a flash of white. He bent and pushed aside some of the grass to reveal something red and white and glossy.

A pack of cigarettes.

"What did you find?" Jack asked from a few feet away.

"Just some old trash," Ben replied, tossing it back to the ground without a second thought. "I doubt there will be any clues we could find. This *thing*, whatever it might be, doesn't strike me as the kind of killer that leaves evidence behind."

That wasn't right, though. Something in the back of Ben's mind jumped and shouted for attention, but he couldn't catch it. He almost said as much to Jack, but the other man walked away before he could find the words.

Jack moved toward the edge of the trees and stopped, the low branches of the underbrush pressing against his legs. He was peering into the dimly-lit woods with the trained eyes of a soldier.

"Do you see something?" Ben asked in a hushed voice, the kind of voice one might use if they were worried about frightening off a doe.

Jack gave a dismissive shrug. "I don't know," he replied. "Hang on."

He stepped into the bushes, and Ben's heart jumped.

"What are you—" he tried to say, but Jack waved him off.

It was in that moment that Ben believed Jack's claim about serving with an elite group of Army soldiers. His body seemed set like a coiled spring, and he moved with smooth, silent steps. Jack didn't push the leaves and low branches out of his way so much as they dissolved around him. Before Ben could question him again, the man was gone.

The quiet of the morning seemed suddenly oppressive. He was alone, standing mere feet from the body of a murdered woman, and the only person he knew well enough to trust, the man who had provided shelter and friendship during his unexpected stay in Kettering, had vanished into the woods.

The *woods*.

Somewhere inside that cathedral of autumn leaves and bent boughs was a creature that shouldn't exist. How could it? No animal known to science lived and hunted for nearly a century. But this one had.

Probably longer, thought Ben. *Much longer, in fact.*

He wasn't sure how he knew that, but he did. Whatever it was that had been hiding in the darkness and shadows of these woods had been doing so for a very, very long time. And it was still hungry.

"Ben!" came a voice behind him.

It was faint enough to sound like a loud whisper, and for a moment he thought it was Dorothy, crying out to him from beneath her blood-stained cover.

"Hey!" the voice called again, louder this time. Mingled with the voice was the distinctive crunch of gravel, followed by the rustle of grass. Ben turned to see Chase running toward him. Even though he knew the dead did not actually cry out to the living—or did they?—he sighed with relief.

Chase's sprint ended abruptly when he caught sight of the covered body of his great-grandmother. He stopped a few paces away from where she lay, and then slowly, painfully crept closer.

Ben saw tears in the corners of the young man's eyes. His face was twisted in a hybrid of pain and sorrow and anger, and when he dropped to his knees, he let go of a deep, wretched sob.

"Oh, God," he muttered, his voice hoarse with emotion. "Oh, no…"

"Chase, I'm so sorry," Ben said softly.

The younger man nodded, eyes closed, and took deep, hitching breaths. "We have to stop this thing, Ben," he replied. "I wanted to leave town and just put this all behind me, you know? But now...this is just too much. No more people can die. It has to end."

"I agree," Ben said. "I agree more than you could know. We'll stop it, alright? There's enough of us. Maybe it's time this thing found out what it's like to be hunted."

A rustle in the bushes behind them caught their attention, and Ben whirled around to face whatever might be waiting for them there. What emerged from the tangle of branches and undergrowth wasn't a monster, though. It was Jack.

"Where the hell did you go?" Ben spat as the man stepped out into the tall grass.

"I went tracking," Jack replied, as if it was the obvious answer. "I wanted to see if I could find signs of a struggle, or even something tangible. Evidence of some kind. Anything that might help us track the thing, or identify it."

"And?" Chase said, approaching the others. "Did you?"

Jack noticed the young man and stopped. "Chase, I'm sorry for your loss. *Our* loss, really. She meant a lot to me, too."

Chase nodded. "You found something, didn't you," he said, pointing to Jack's closed right hand.

"I did," Jack replied. He held up his hand and opened it, palm upward. "Any idea what this is?"

Resting in the center of Jack's hand was a curved object that looked remarkably like the tip of a claw. Only this piece was nearly three inches long. Blood covered most of its bone-like length, and no one felt the need to point out where that blood might have come from.

"A claw," Ben said with sudden realization. The memory he had been trying to retrieve suddenly floated to the surface, and he pulled out his notebook, riffling through the pages. When he found what he had been looking for, he looked up.

"They found a claw in 1984 as well. On the body of a young woman named Patti Fuller."

"That's right," Jack said. "Dorothy told us that yesterday, didn't she?"

Ben nodded. "She said it was just rumor, but here it is." He pointed to Jack's hand. "Proof that something real—tangible and physical—is out there."

"Better yet," Jack added. "It's proof that this thing can be injured."

CHAPTER FIFTEEN

THE LIBRARY WAS QUIET when the three men walked in. Their footsteps were soft, echoing like thunder through the open space of the foyer. Ellen was sitting at the desk, and when she saw them enter the building she smiled. Ben and the others didn't smile back, though; they were grim and serious, and they approached Ellen with determination.

"What's wrong, you guys?" she whispered to them, sensing the tension among them. "Has something happened?"

"Dorothy Abington," Ben replied. "They found her dead this morning."

"It was that fucking monster," Chase added, his voice a bit too loud for the quiet atmosphere of the library.

Ellen brought a hand up to cover her mouth. "Oh, dear God," she moaned. "Ben, we have to stop this. So many lives…" She trailed off. The rest didn't need to be said.

"Sheriff Roberts is open to our help," Jack said. "He's willing to work with us to take care of this. I think he's finally coming around."

"Or is finally desperate enough," Ben suggested.

"Well, either way, it's a step forward," Jack continued. "I'll give him a call later today and get a plan put in place. I think he's going to be busy this morning with Dorothy's crime scene, but maybe that'll provide some urgency as well. We need to act on this. *Today*."

Ellen nodded. "I've been thinking about that," she said to Jack. "It might be a good idea to have Lori and Tyler leave town for a few days. Just in case things get bad. There's no sense getting them caught up in all of this. Is there some place they can go?"

Jack thought for a moment. Finally, "She has a friend down in Narragansett. I'm sure she'd be willing to do that, especially if it meant keeping Tyler safe. I'll have her pick him up early from school."

"Maybe you should go with her," Ben said to Ellen. "I get the feeling Roberts would prefer if you're out of harm's way too."

She shook her head vigorously. "No way. Nope, not going to happen." Her voice rose above a whisper. "I'm in this to the end, whatever happens."

Ben held up his hands in mock surrender. "I won't argue," he said. "Hell hath no fury, they say."

"*They* knew what they were talking about," she replied with a grin. "But *you* better catch on."

"Any progress on learning more about what we might be up against?" Chase asked quietly. "Sorry I haven't been able to help you here."

"Don't worry about it," she replied. "As a matter of fact, I *have* found out some new pieces of information, but I need a bit more time to dig deeper."

"Mind if I stick around and help?" Chase asked, taking off his coat. "I have a few ideas I want to look into as well."

"More minds working on this puzzle can't be a bad thing, as far as I'm concerned," she replied. Then, to Ben, "When should we meet again, then?"

"Why don't you come over to the house after your part-time help takes over," Ben said. He turned to Jack, "Sorry, I shouldn't be inviting people over to your house without asking."

Jack just shrugged. "It makes sense. The sooner we know, the better. Can you make it by dinner?" he asked her.

"Yes," she replied. "Let's say 5:00 PM. That will give me time to run home and change."

"Alright," Jack said. "We'll let you work. See you tonight."

As the other men walked back toward the main doors, Ben set his hand on Ellen's. "I don't want you to get hurt," he said. "Are you sure you won't leave town with Lori?"

She smiled warmly at him. "I'm not leaving you to do this alone, Ben."

"I won't be alone," he replied. "I have Jack. And Chase, and the Sheriff now."

"I know," she said. "But I want to be there, too. I have a part to play in this. I don't know why I think that, but I'm sure of it now. Let me play my part."

"Hey," Ben said, "who am I to stop you? I'll see you later. Go get some work done."

He patted her hand one more time and then followed after the others.

Over the last few days, Jack's presence had begun to provide Ben with confidence and a sense of safety, something he sorely needed. Ellen, though, was giving him something more: hope and courage. Being near her helped him find purpose, a true desire to protect someone else other than himself.

Ben didn't know what the rest of the day had in store for him, but he knew that he would need everything his friends could offer if he was to survive it.

———— ❦ ————

"I'm *not* going to argue with you about it any more, Lori," Jack said with a stern tone. "Things are building to a head, and I want you and Tyler out of town until it's done. End of story."

Ben was in his guest room at the Brooder residence with his door closed. That didn't stop him from hearing every word of the discussion between his hosts, who were battling it out in the room across the hall. He suddenly wished he had brought his headphones with him.

"End of story?" she spat back. "And what about you? I want to know that *you* are going to be safe, too."

"You stayed at home for years while I went off on dozens of dangerous missions," Jack's voice replied. "You never acted like this back then. Why now?"

"Because this seems a hell of a lot more dangerous than escorting a diplomat or securing an embassy. Dammit Jack, you're going to fight a *monster*."

"That's right," he said. "And you're going to drive to Susan's. Pack what you need. I've already taken care of Tyler's things and put them in the car. You're going to finish up here and then go pick him up from school and drive. I'm done arguing with you about it."

Someone opened their bedroom door, and then slammed it shut. Ben waited a few moments for the thumping of angry footsteps to descend the stairs, and then followed after. He found Jack fuming in the kitchen, pulling a can of beer from the refrigerator.

"It's 5:00 PM somewhere," he said when Ben gave him a sideways glance. Pointing up at the clock on the wall, "Hell, restaurants downtown started serving beer an hour ago for lunch. I think this is perfectly socially acceptable."

"Hey, I'm not judging," Ben said. "I was just wondering if you had another for me?."

Jack grinned. "You bet."

He stood, grabbed another can, and then tossed it to Ben.

"We've got a wall to finish," he said. "We can talk more while we work."

"And Lori?" Ben asked.

Jack shrugged. "She's pissed at me, of course, but she knows I'm right. They're both safer away from town, and I don't want to be worried about them while we're out trying to stop this thing from killing again."

Ben just nodded. The last thing he wanted was to spin his wheels on a mundane task when he should be working toward a solution. The truth was, though, they weren't going to be able to do anything until Ellen and Chase arrived.

He followed Jack out the door and into the field. His mind was filled with puzzle pieces that seemed as large as stones, and wondered how long it would take him to put them all together.

—⚬⚬⚬—

It was already growing dark outside when Ellen pulled into the driveway. The men hadn't been idle in her absence, though; Ben and Jack had spent most of the afternoon finishing the repairs on the wall, and when Chase arrived they had gone over their ideas for the search they hoped to launch first thing in the morning. They all agreed that it would be unwise to begin tonight, no matter how urgent they felt the matter had become.

Ellen agreed with them, but she had also brought them information that would give them much to think about between now and then. When everyone was ready and settled around the kitchen table, she pulled out a notebook along with some photocopies that had been folded and tucked inside it.

"We already know that these killings have taken place every thirty years, going back to at least 1924. Ben was able to prove this pattern exists by going through old microfiche at the library and finding reports of violent, mysterious deaths, the ones usually attributed to animal attacks."

"There were five that year, as far as I could tell," Ben added. "But I'll admit, I never thought to look at years prior to that."

"No," Ellen said, "but I *did*."

"You found more deaths in 1893?" Jack asked.

"No, but I did in 1892," she replied. "Not in Kettering, though. These deaths were in Exeter."

"Hey," Ben spoke up, "wasn't that the same year Mercy Brown and her brother both died?

"Indeed it was," she replied with a raised eyebrow. "I also found more in 1861, that time in the town of Foster. Those deaths—there were four of them that year—appeared much more similar to the ones Kettering has experienced over the last century."

"Wait a minute," Jack interrupted. "You're not saying Mercy Brown was killed by the same creature, are you? From everything I've read, she died of tuberculosis, not something resembling an animal attack."

"No, but the deaths that happened around her in Exeter were much more suspicious, and they put the town on edge. That could certainly explain why all of those normal, sane townsfolk—people just a few miles from the social elite in Newport, mind you—would be willing to dig up her family and look for supernatural clues?"

"How far back did you go?" Chase asked.

"I looked for a pattern of thirty years," Ellen said, flipping through the pages of her notebook. "Some gaps were longer, some were shorter. On the whole, though, they average out to a three-decade respite, and then the killings would start again.

"Every beat in the pattern was like that, almost like clockwork, all the way back to 1675 near the town of Richmond, south of here. Before that date, there was nothing. I searched through local records for the ten years surrounding 1645 but found nothing. Granted, there aren't many extant records from that era, but I still think a series of grisly deaths would have been mentioned, even briefly. It's as if whatever triggered this creature's activity did so in 1675."

"That's odd," Chase said. "I'm not sure how helpful it is at this point, but it does tell us more about this creature. We thought it was old, but if these dates and records are to be believed, 'old' might not be the right term for it."

Jack nodded. "Any luck figuring out what we might be up against?"

"Not exactly," Ellen replied, tugging a piece of folded paper free from her notebook. "I have this small list of Native American myths that could be a match, but I haven't narrowed them down yet."

Ben reached for the list and began to scan the terms listed there. The first name, *Bigfoot*, was instantly recognizable. Others terms, though, were barely pronounceable.

"What is a *kewakwa*?" he asked.

It was Chase who answered. "A cannibalistic giant," he said. "But it belongs to the lore of tribes that are found too far north to be our creature."

Ben looked at the list again. "And a *jenu*?"

"Same thing," Chase said. "Similar monster, different region of the north. Mostly in Canada, if I remember correctly. My guess is that if this creature really has been active in this area for the last three-hundred years, then the local folklore is going to reference it. That means you'll want to stick to Algonquian mythology, especially that of the Narragansett tribe."

"Here", Ben said, handing over the list to the young man. "It might just be simpler for you to look this over and tell us what sounds right to you."

Chase took the list and studied it. He tugged nervously at one of the small metal rings in his lower lip while he scanned slowly down the page. Then, toward the bottom, his eyes opened wider.

"There," he said quickly. "Most of these are Inuit myths, so they're not an option. But the bottom choice is what I would bet my money on."

Ben took the paper back and looked at the bottom of the list. "Wendigo?" he asked.

Chase nodded. "It's similar to the myths of the *jenu* and *kewakwa*, and even the *wechuge* of British Columbia. All of them are described as icy-cold cannibalistic monsters that prey on humans. The difference between all the others and the wendigo is pretty simple: unlike the rest, there are stories of the wendigo in this region."

"It sounds familiar to me," Jack said. "Part of our survival training in the Army Rangers involved what-if situations. How would you adapt if this or that happened to you. We studied documented cases of people who were lost in the wilderness for days or weeks at a time, and pulled survival tips from their testimonies. One of them had to do with cannibalism."

"I don't follow," said Ellen.

"There's a diagnosis in modern psychology called Wendigo Psychosis, where the person has an unnatural craving for human flesh. Sometimes, this is a condition brought on by actually eating human flesh, and other times it's a chemical imbalance that seems to fixate on cannibalism."

"Yep," Chase said. "And that diagnosis gets its name from the Algonquian myth of the wendigo. Native Americans across the continent believed that if a person turned to cannibalism to survive, they would become open to an evil spirit, a *manitou*, that would posses them and transform them into a flesh-devouring monster."

"Wait a minute," Ben said, closing his eyes. He held up one hand as if to signal for their silence, and thought deep and hard. There was something in the back of his mind, tickling at his conscious thoughts, and he needed to wrestle it free. Suddenly the blockage melted away and he had it.

"The year 1675 is significant in Rhode Island because of the battle that took place at the Great Swamp. I've been reading a lot about it lately. Hell, I'm down here in Kettering because my car broke down on my way home from that area.

"Anyway, the battle was fought between Colonial soldiers and the Narragansett tribe. Hundreds died on both sides, but the only reason the Colonial militia was able to approach and attack the Narragansett fort was because it had been an unusually cold winter, and the swamp had frozen over."

"I don't see how it connects," Jack said. "Help us, Ben."

"You don't see it?" Ben asked, looking at the others. "When the battle ended, a handful of Native warriors escaped into the swamp. It was freezing cold, and many of them couldn't survive in the harsh climate. Some did, though—at least according to legend—and at least one of those survivors did so by eating the dead around him."

Ellen, who had been quiet for much of the conversation, spoke up.

"So you think a Native American warrior wandered off into the frozen swamp, ate some of his tribesmen, and then somehow turned into a wendigo? Seems pretty far-fetched, don't you think?"

"Far-fetched?" Ben asked. "We're trying to find the suspect behind a series of violent murders that spans more than three hundred years. I think we need to be open to answers that step outside the realm of logic, don't we?"

"You've got a good point there," she replied.

"So where does that leave us?" Jack asked. "What do we know about wendigo lore?"

"It's a possession," Chase replied. "Similar to the idea of demonic possession, according to most Native American folklore. It's a solitary creature that hibernates for long periods of time, and then feeds once it is awake. Some legends hint that the wendigo spirit might leave a host body as it wears out and jump to a new host. They are powerful creatures, perfect hunters, and possess superhuman strength and speed."

"That's it?" Jack replied sarcastically. "That doesn't sound so bad."

Ellen laughed nervously and Ben shifted in his seat. Chase was describing something that sat at an entirely new plane of existence. And here they were, a handful of weak humans, making plans with the assumption that they'll somehow be able to overpower it.

"This might be the most obvious question that hasn't been asked yet, but can a wendigo even be killed?" Ben asked.

"Fire," Chase said. "That's what almost all the stories say. Burn them and they die."

Jack stood up. "Well, I've got a box of strike-anywhere matches in the barn," he said. "I'll go get them. Maybe we can trap it and torch it."

Chase let out a nervous laugh. "We're not a bunch of explorers hunting for exotic animals along the Amazon, man. I'm a grad student, not an outdoorsman. Ben looks like he's spent about as much time in the woods as me—no offense—and Ellen is probably in the same boat."

"Hey," she replied. "I'm perfectly comfortable hiking through the woods. I hunted many times with my dad while I was in high school. I bet I'm the only one of us who knows how to field dress a deer."

"The only one of two," Jack said from the kitchen doorway. "But I have my survival training to thank for that." He slipped out into the dusk and closed the door behind him.

"Still," Chase continued. "I get the feeling Jack wants us to go looking for a monster, and I don't know the first thing about hunting. What are we supposed to do?"

"I have no idea," Ben said. "But if I had to trust one person to lead us into the woods, it's Jack. Sounds like Ellen can handle a rifle as well."

Ellen smirked at him. "It's been far too long, but I'll do what I have to."

Ben was about to speak when a flash of red and blue light caught his eye. He stood and looked out the window and watched as the Sheriff's cruiser sped down the driveway and stopped hard in the space between the house and the shed.

"What is it?" Ellen asked, standing to join him at the window.

"No idea," Ben replied. "Let's go find out."

They arrived at the cruiser at the same moment Jack did, just as Sheriff Roberts was climbing out.

"What's going on, Gil?" Jack asked as he skidded to a halt near the front of the car. "You came down my drive like a runaway train."

The Sheriff tipped his hat quickly at Jack. He did a double-take when he saw the others arrive. "You're *all* here, eh? Good. We've got a problem."

"What is it?" Ellen asked, stepping forward.

Something passed between Ellen and the Sheriff. It was fleeting, and barely noticeable, but Ben saw it in their eyes. Then it was gone, like a flame that had been blown out.

"I was out south of town a bit ago when I received a call from dispatch that there's been an attack out at Maple Hill Cemetery. One of my deputies managed to get there in time and stop it, and he's waiting for me there. I've got no more info than that, so don't ask. But if you want to come along, maybe this is as good a time as any to lend a hand."

Jack ran toward the kitchen door. "Let me get my guns," he shouted over his shoulder.

"I'll ride with you," Ellen said to the sheriff. "If that's alright, that is."

Roberts grimaced and then nodded, just once. "Back door's unlocked," he said. "I can take one more."

"I'll ride with Jack," Ben said. He glanced at Ellen, and was surprised to feel a rotting mass of jealousy low in his gut. Then, to Chase: "The truck seats two, so you better ride along with them."

Chase didn't need to be told twice. He walked over to the rear passenger door and opened it up, practically tossing himself on the back seat beside Ellen.

"Hurry after us," Roberts said. "I'm counting on Jack to help me level the playing field with this thing."

Ben nodded.

Roberts climbed back behind the wheel of his cruiser, and with the experience of a man twice his age he backed it into the grass beside the driveway and then sped back down toward the road. The two black ruts left by the car's tires in the lawn resembled wounds left by the talons of some great bird. The receding taillights cast a red glow over the yard.

Jack burst from the kitchen door, a semi-automatic carbine rifle over one shoulder, a pump-action shotgun in one hand, and a small black bag in the other.

"Ammo," Jack said when Ben glanced curiously at the bag. "I'm hoping we don't need to use it, but I'd hate to regret leaving it behind."

"I'm not going to argue," Ben replied. "You ready?"

"Almost. I have some flashlights in the shed, and I think we'll need them."

Jack found the lights and dropped those into the bag, and then they made a run for the truck. Ben slid onto the bench seat as Jack cranked the ignition. For a moment, it didn't seem that it was going to start—it made the sound one might expect from a hungry cat that's been stuck inside a closet. Then, with a cough, it turned over and rumbled to life.

Jack handed his rifle to Ben and dropped the bag of ammunition between them on the seat.

"Ready or not," he said as he guided the truck down the drive, "here we go."

CHAPTER SIXTEEN

THE OLD CHEVY'S HEADLIGHTS cut through the encroaching darkness of the cemetery as they turned the corner from Exeter to Main. The Sheriff's cruiser was parked across the entrance, nearly blocking the way. At first Ben wasn't sure why he had done that, but then he caught sight of a second cruiser parked a few yards inside the main gate and he understood. No one was supposed to get out.

Jack brought the truck to a stop along the far side of the road, turned it off, and nodded to Ben. They were as ready as they were going to get. Ben handed the rifle back to Jack, and they both exited the truck and crossed the road.

The first thing Ben noticed as they jogged across the road was that the cruiser's lights had been turned off. If someone didn't think to look out their window as they drove past, there was a good chance they wouldn't notice a thing. With no street light directly over the entrance to the cemetery, all of the action going on farther inside was far away from prying eyes.

"Do you see them yet?" Ben asked as they slipped between the cruiser and the stone wall.

"I think so," Jack replied. "I thought I saw a flashlight up ahead. Beside the car."

The air was cold. It seemed as though whatever warmth there might have been at sunset had vanished with the daylight. There was no wind though, something Ben was thankful for. Nothing was worse than wind on an already cold day.

"Up ahead," Jack said, pointing down the gravel path that ran up the middle of the graveyard. "I see them."

Ben did, too. The tall shape of Sheriff Roberts was silhouetted against the dark gray of the trees and tombstones. Chase stood a bit behind the Sheriff, and beside them, Ben could just make out the smaller shape of Ellen.

Good, he thought. *She's still safe.*

Beyond them, Ben could see three other shapes. As they approached it became clear what was going on. The on-duty deputy sheriff had arrived in time, and both the victim and the perpetrator were now in his care. He could see both of them now, by the light cast by Roberts' flashlight.

Ben recognized the deputy as Cranston, the same man who helped Roberts that morning at Angela's. He had broad shoulders and a face that appeared to be carved out of fine New England granite. Ben knew more than a few men who would happily sacrifice a goat on some dark altar for a jawline even half as chiseled as this man's. Cranston's attention was on the woman beside him.

Ben didn't recognize her face, but since he was a stranger to Kettering, that didn't surprise him. She was in tears, and the light of the flashlight caused the wet ribbons beneath her eyes to shimmer dully. The deputy was writing on a small pad of paper and nodding as the woman alternated between talking and sobbing.

In between scribbles on the notepad, the deputy was watching the dark figure of a man a couple of paces away. Sheriff Roberts stood closer to this man, and his sidearm was out and pointed at the ground near the man's feet. Ellen seemed to be watching it all, taking it in with the wonder of a child witnessing her first drunken brawl.

"What's going on?" Jack asked in a hushed tone as he approached the Sheriff. Roberts almost seemed to be caught off guard, and he spun quickly around to face them both.

"False alarm, it seems," he said. There was disappointment in his voice, but also a hint of relief. Ben couldn't blame him.

"Wait," Ben said. "I know that man. I've seen him before."

The man was Jasper Levett, the old caretakerr of the cemetery. His filthy overalls and unkept beard were almost like a costume, and Ben was sure that without them, he might not have recognized the man at all.

"Everyone knows Jasper," the Sheriff replied.

"No, that's not what I mean," Ben replied. He stepped closer to the old man. Jasper was hunched over and draped in shadows, but there was a glimmer of anger in the man's eyes.

"I saw him with all the others when I stumbled upon the second victim, behind Angela's. Alfonso, I think his name was."

The Sheriff nodded in reply.

"I also saw him walking toward the cemetery a short while before the third victim's body was found by Ellen and I."

"I saw him that night as well," Chase added. "I saw three people pass by Angela's that night, Ben and Ellen being the other two. Of course, they passed by *after* the scream."

"I work here," the old man spat, breaking his silence. "Damn kid, 'course I was walkin round here. But I ain't no killer."

"You've been suspiciously close to two of the recent murders, though," Ben replied. "And I have a feeling, if we started asking around over at Allenby Village, some of the residents there would probably admit to seeing you near the building this morning."

"What about you, you little shit," the old man said. His voice was tight and strained, the voice of a life-long smoker. "I saw you by the dumpster. I even seen you that night at the cemetery, you and the pretty one there. What's your excuse? How do we know *you* ain't the killer?"

Ben lunged forward, hot anger filling his veins, pulsing through him. Jack shot out a hand and caught him before he could take a second step and hauled him back.

"He's not worth it," Jack whispered to him. Then, to Jasper: "My friend here has more alibis than you have teeth, you drunk. And he's not the one who was caught attacking a woman tonight."

"I was just out on a walk," the woman added through her tears. "He jumped out of the woods and tried to grab me. He's insane. If I hadn't screamed…"

"It's a good thing she did," the young deputy said. "I was driving past, and happened to have my window down. I didn't like the sound of that scream, so I pulled in here."

"You did well, Cranston," the Sheriff added.

"Thank you, sir," he replied. "He was on top of her, sir. God, I thought he was trying to kill her. The way she was thrashing around, and him on top with his hands on her wrists." He noticed the woman flinch at his description. "Sorry, ma'am. It was frightening, is all."

"I understand," Roberts said. "Ma'am, I'm going to have Deputy Cranston take you home. Would that be alright?"

Relief washed over her. "Yes, please." Her voice was desperate. She clearly did not want to walk another foot through Kettering in the dark.

Sheriff Roberts turned to his deputy and spoke a few quiet words. The young man nodded and grunted his agreement, and then he held out the notepad for the Sheriff to take. It was in that moment, when nearly everyone was waiting to see what would happen, that Jasper made a run for it.

"Stop him!" Chase screamed.

Roberts dropped the notepad and fumbled for the switch on the side of his flashlight. By the time he had flicked it to the ON position, all they managed to see was his dark shape disappear into the shadows between the old stone shed and the woods behind it.

"Dammit!" Roberts shouted. "Why'd he have to go and do that."

"Sheriff, there's something going on with that man," Ben said. "I know we've got nothing to tie him to any of the murders, but he's involved somehow. I feel it right in here." He pointed at his chest.

"I wish that were enough to convict him, Mr. Simmons, but whatever he's guilty of, we can't do anything about it if he's running around the woods at night."

"Then we'll go get him and bring him back," Jack said.

He took the black bag from Ben and pulled out three flashlights. He pocketed the first, gave one to Ellen, and then handed Ben the last one along with the shotgun and the box of shells.

"It holds five, and then you have to reload," Jack told him. "Think you can manage that?"

Ben stuffed the ammunition into his coat pocket. "No problem."

"We'll start after him," Jack said to the Sheriff. "Are you coming along?"

Roberts studied the ex-soldier for a moment, and then nodded. Turning to the deputy and the sobbing woman beside him, he handed the man his keys. "Get her home. You can take my car. Then get back to the station and be ready if I call in. And wake up Phillips; he needs to get in uniform and be ready to help out."

"Got it," the younger officer said, and then he and the woman walked quickly back down the gravel path to the cruiser.

"Let's go," Jack said to the others. "He's got a head start on us."

The old stone shed was bigger than Ben had first thought. Maybe it was a trick of the shadows or just that most of the building's rear was now covered in shrubs and small saplings, but it seemed too large to simply be a storage place for the lawn mower and digging tools.

There was a path worn through the undergrowth that led from the short-cropped grass of the cemetery lawn to the edge of the woods. It was dark, but their flashlights were strong enough to show them it was an often-used trail. It was through this opening that everyone agreed the old man had run.

They stopped after entering the woods. The darkness felt oppressive around them, and Ben had begun to wonder if the batteries in his flashlight were going dead because the beam of light barely cut through the shadows.

"What's the plan?" he asked, hoping one of the others had some idea of what they needed to do.

"The woods aren't too deep," Jack replied. "But they run for miles to the east and west. I think we should split up and see what we can find in each direction."

"Split up?" Ellen repeated from behind them. "Are you insane?"

"There've been four murders in this town in the last two weeks, and we're standing in the woods in the dark," Ben said. "Are you really asking me if we're insane? I thought that was crystal clear already."

"I agree with Jack," Roberts said. He turned back to Ellen. "I think you should go with him and head west. He's better armed than I am, and he has the benefit of advanced military training. You'll be safest with him. Ben and Chase can come along with me."

"Got it," Jack said, reaching into the bag again and pulling out a large handgun. "It's loaded. You alright with that?"

Ellen nodded, but her expression hinted at the fear she was holding back. The gun in her hand had somehow made everything seem so real, so dangerous.

"Alright then," Jack said. "Let's go."

Ellen glanced at Ben for a fleeting moment, and then reached out to him, touching his hand. She opened her mouth to speak, but he stopped her.

"You don't have to say it," he told her. "I already know. And I feel the same."

She smiled then, like a light in the shadows. "Thank you."

———

Ben followed Roberts deeper into the darkness. Chase stumbled along behind them, the sound of his breathing barely covered by the rustle of leaves on the ground beneath their feet. Every shadow seemed to move, and the flashlights failed to penetrate farther than a few yards.

"What are we hoping to find?" Chase asked quietly.

"Old Man Levett," the Sheriff replied. "I'm holding onto hope that we're fast enough to catch up to a skinny drunk man in his seventies."

"Yeah, but he had a head-start," Ben added. "And there's a lot of darkness to hide in out here."

They passed between two thick, ancient trees covered in moss and vines, and then stopped. The sound of a stick snapping caused each of them to glance in the same direction, off to their left.

"What was that?" Chase asked.

Ben nodded and turned his flashlight in the direction they all were facing. Movement fluttered at the very edge of their field of vision. The Sheriff brought his handgun up in a blur and fired off a single shot. In the distance they could hear a small, muffled explosion as the bullet connected with a tree somewhere in the darkness.

"Let's go take a look," Roberts said. Then, glancing back at Chase: "Let's also try to be quieter. I have a feeling Jack and Ellen can still hear you."

Chase frowned at the officer. "Hey man, I'm not an outdoor kind of guy. This might be as good as you're going to get from me."

"Just do your best," Ben said calmly. "The less sound we make, the better our odds will be of catching this guy."

Roberts took off at a brisk pace in the direction of the sound and the others followed quickly. It wasn't clear whether they moved with urgency, or a deep desire to stay close to the law enforcement official. Both just happened to be equally good reasons to move fast.

Another sound, this time to their right, echoed out of the shadows. Ben swung his arm around with the flashlight extended, but before the light could find a target, it was knocked from his arm by a solid, immovable force.

"Damn!" he shouted, grabbing at his wrist. Pain ran up his arm, as if something powerful had slapped his hand.

"You alright?" Roberts asked, pointing his light on Ben.

"Something knocked my flashlight out of my hand," he replied.

"Tree," Chase said quietly, pointing beside him. "I think you just hit the tree."

He was right. The flashlight had rolled to a stop beside a thick oak tree, casting its pale light off into the woods. He bent to pick it up, and then rubbed his wrist again.

"Sorry about that," he said to the others. "I think I'm getting jumpy."

"We *all* are," Roberts said. "But I think I hear something over there."

The Sheriff pointed, but not with his flashlight. Ben followed his hand toward a deeper patch of shadows a few yards away. He nodded when he heard it too.

"Quietly this time," Roberts whispered. "And keep your light off it. Sweep off to the sides if you have to."

"Understood," Ben said, and then the three of them were off again, slowly making their way deeper into the trees and darkness.

As they moved along, it became clear that the sound had come from the direction of a tangle of low shrubs and thorns off to their left. Their indirect flashlight beams didn't illuminate the undergrowth ahead of them, but it did provide enough light to notice whether there was movement or not.

They found an upended tree blocking their path as they approached, and Roberts motioned for them to step around the nest of twisted roots. Ben thought he heard the wind as they moved around the tree, but felt nothing on his skin.

The woods muted everything. Light seemed to vanish into the shadows, like hungry black holes devouring entire stars. Sound fell flat around them. They could only hear the occasional sharp snap of a branch or the crunch of leaves, and it was disorienting.

It was clear, though, that whatever was ahead of them had stopped moving farther into the woods. It was stalking them now, waiting in the darkness for them to get closer. Ben could feel the flesh on the back of his neck prickle with an electrical sensation. Something was tracking them.

"It's close," Ben whispered. Roberts nodded soundlessly.

Chase tripped over one of the exposed roots as he passed by the tree, and went sprawling onto the ground. The sound of rustling leaves rang out like an explosion as he hit the ground. He grunted with pain, and then fell silent.

"You alright?" Ben asked quietly as he turned around.

Chase looked up at him from where he lay and nodded. Shame was painted across his face, and he began to pick himself up again, being careful not to make more noise than was necessary.

As Ben turned back around to face Roberts, something huge moved through the shadows. For a moment, Chase was kneeling in the leaves and lifting a hand to grab hold of a nearby tree. Then, with a flash of movement that seemed unnatural, he was pulled out of their dim field of vision.

"Chase!" Ben shouted.

Roberts joined him, bringing his gun up to shoulder height and sweeping the dark trees for movement with his light. Ben heard a muffled cry a yard or two away, and the skittering of something on the leaves, but he couldn't seem to find the source with his flashlight.

Then there was nothing. No sound, no movement, and no sign of Chase.

CHAPTER SEVENTEEN

JACK AND ELLEN MOVED westward as fast as they could. Jack was nearly silent as he pushed between the trees and bushes that tangled around them, and Ellen did her best to follow his lead.

She had walked beside her father through woods much like these as a teenager, although it had never been in the dark. She quickly found a stride that helped her avoid making too much noise, and had managed to keep up with Jack so far. But he was moving very fast.

Jack walked quickly with his knees slightly bent, bringing his body low to the ground. He held the carbine rifle up, locked against his shoulder, keeping one hand on the trigger and the other holding his flashlight against the stock. His movements were quick, almost feline.

She had begun to believe that, without the light he was holding, she might lose sight of him. A ball of tension had taken root in her gut, and she kept her eyes locked on him despite the rugged terrain underfoot. She was willing to risk tripping over an random branch if it meant keeping up with him.

They had seen nothing since leaving the vicinity of the old stone shed. Jack had communicated very little with her as he led them deeper into the trees, but it was clear he was tracking something. Every few minutes he would stop and touch a branch, examining it for signs that Ellen couldn't read. When he was done, he would begin again, guiding them in a new direction.

They had paused for another of those moments, his fingers barely touching the broken branch of a young sapling, but this examination was taking far longer than normal. Ellen stepped closer to him and gently placed a hand on his shoulder, cocking her head to the side questioningly.

Jack turned slowly and locked eyes with her. There was a fierce intensity in his gaze, and a confidence that gave her peace of mind while also frightening her. Without lowering his weapon, he silently mouthed two words at her. In the dim light, Ellen barely managed to make them out.

"Over there," he had said. Then, with a quick nod, he motioned off toward their right.

Ellen looked in that direction but only saw a tangle of branches, undergrowth, and shadows. She could see nothing but varying degrees of blackness among the thick tree trunks and dangling branches, but she had faith in Jack's ability to navigate through the darkness.

Finally, he moved forward, bearing slightly off to the right, and she followed after him. Her hand gripped the gun that Jack had given to her. Her fingers settled into the curves of the metal grip. She could feel her heart beating in the palm of her hand as she squeezed it tighter.

Ahead of them, in the beam of the flashlight, was a tangled knot of thorns and creeping vines. It resembled an enormous nest, but nothing was visible inside it, only the ever-present shadow. Jack led them closer, and then began to move off to the right side of the chaotic jumble of ground cover.

Ellen wanted nothing more than to leave. The darkness was overwhelming, and it felt as if the air itself were thickening around her. Against all common sense, she had allowed herself to be led into the woods. She was deep in a dark realm that was clearly haunted by some evil force.

Suddenly, something burst out from within the nest. There was no sound, only the sensation of something large in their presence. Whatever it was, it was too fast for Jack's light to track, and all Ellen was able to see was a patch of deep black move against the already dark forest background.

Jack took an instinctive step backward, but Ellen's reflexes weren't as trained and ready. The shape connected with her shoulder, and sent her spinning back. The gun slipped from her hand, helped along by the sweat that lined her palm, and she heard it skitter into a pile of dry leaves a few feet away. And then she landed.

Her head managed to find one of the few large stones in the forest, or perhaps it was only a very flat, very firm tree root. Whatever it was, pain exploded behind her eyes as she collided with it, and she let out a sharp cry.

"Ellen!" Jack shouted, bringing the light around to find her.

Reality began to grow fuzzy. Her vision blurred. Pain pulsed from the left side of her head. Leaves crunched beneath her ear, and the sound of Jack's voice seemed to be calling from a great distance away.

A light flashed across her face. A shot rang out, piercing the muddled echo of Jack's voice. She felt her body move, lifted to what seemed like a soaring height, and then unconsciousness washed over her with the gentleness of an incoming tide.

———— ⤫ ————

Ben and Sheriff Roberts backed toward each other. The darkness had swallowed Chase. At least, that was how it looked. Ben had turned to help him, saw the young man's face, and froze.

For an instant, light glittered off of the three small golden rings piercing his lower lip. Fear welled up in his eyes—the kind of fear that comes with the horrible realization that, yes, you *are* in danger—and he had opened his mouth to speak.

Maybe Chase was going to beg for help. Maybe he knew something that he needed to share before it was too late. Chase might have even just wanted to cry out in horror.

Ben would never know. For one brief moment the man had been laying face-down in the leaves, and then he was gone. It was if he had been pulled away with incredible force. His mind drifted to visions of the tablecloth parlor trick, where the dishes were set and prepared for a meal. Someone, typically a magician, would pull the tablecloth out. If done correctly, no dish or utensil would move.

This time it had been done correctly. Chase was gone.

Now, standing with his back to the Sheriff, he felt a fear unlike any he had experienced before. He adjusted his grip on the shotgun and began to sweep the area around him with the flashlight, hoping to find some sign of the young man.

"Did you see him?" Roberts whispered harshly. "Something took him. Did you get a look at what it was?"

Ben shook his head, and then realized the Sheriff wouldn't be able to see that. "No," he replied. "Nothing but shadows. And I don't hear a thing. Not even…" he paused, looking for the right words. "Not even screaming."

"I don't think he's still alive," the Sheriff said. "Nothing that's encountered that thing so far has lived to talk about it, so why should Chase be any different?"

"I hope you're wrong," Ben said, still watching the dark woods around him with a panicked intensity. "I know what you're saying, but I still hope you're wrong."

"Me too."

The silence was pierced by gunfire. Gunfire rang out in the distance, and Ben turned to look at the Sheriff's face. The man looked as frightened and concerned as he himself felt.

"Maybe we should make our way west and see if we can find the others," Ben suggested. "They might need our help."

"Alright," Roberts agreed. "But we move carefully. Whatever this thing is, it's fast. It was just here and took Chase, and now the others are firing at it. It's quick, and it clearly has no trouble seeing in the dark. We're at a disadvantage."

"That might just be the understatement of the night," Ben said.

The two men began to slowly, cautiously pick their way through the trees and shadows. They made their way toward the area the gunshot had come from, lacking all other guides to navigate through the woods.

It helped that both men had flashlights, but neither of them was willing to point them at their feet. It seemed almost essential—core to their very chance of survival—that they train their lights on the areas ahead and around them. This meant tripping over the occasional tree root or stone, but Ben thought it was a fair tradeoff.

"I don't hear anything up ahead anymore," Roberts said from ahead of him. "No gunshots, no screams. I'm not even sure I'm headed in the right direction. Dammit, I think we're lost."

"No, we're on the right path," Ben replied. "It's hard to believe, but I think I recognize some of these trees and bushes."

"Good," the Sheriff said, stepping over another fallen tree. "We're screwed if we get—"

His voice went silent, and Ben swung his light at the man in a panic.

"What?" he asked. "What is it?"

Roberts was looking down at the ground on the other side of the log. Ben let his light fall, following the man's gaze. In a crumpled heap—half covered in orange, yellow, and green leaves—was Chase. He lay facing upward, his mouth a horrible gaping hole of a scream. His eyes wide and glassy, and there was no doubt that the young man was dead.

"No blood," Roberts pointed out.

Ben looked again. He was right. Chase's body didn't look the way all the other victims had. It was intact, as far as he could tell.

"Why?" he asked. He wasn't sure that the question was intended for the Sheriff, though. Maybe it was for the wendigo, or God, or himself.

Why would a creature, one that has been so violent and brutal so far, not do the same to Chase? Why would it kill him but not eat him, as it had done so many times before? Was it a warning? Did the beast know they were hunting it now?

"Maybe it's giving us a chance to leave," Ben wondered out loud. "Like a sign, a warning that death is the only option if we keep following it."

Roberts checked the chamber on his handgun and then flicked the safety off. "Fat chance," he spat. "Let's go find this thing."

They managed to walk a few more yards over stones and leaves and fallen branches when the sound of wind filled their ears. Ben froze and listened, noticing that he felt no breeze on his skin. Still, a shiver ran up his spine. That was when the night erupted around them.

A dark shape came out of the shadows ahead, moving with the speed of a car on the highway. Ben saw it first and jumped out of the way, but Roberts took the full force of the impact. Whatever had collided with him knocked both his gun and flashlight free, and sent the Sheriff's body rolling into a thick oak tree.

There was a cracking sound that reminded Ben of breaking the wishbone from the family turkey after Thanksgiving, and Roberts cried out in pain.

"My arm," he moaned. "My gun. Where's my gun!"

Ben rolled to his feet and swept the area with his light, staying low to the ground this time. Metal glinted from beneath a leaf a few feet away, and he moved toward it. That was when the shape emerged again.

It moved slowly this time, stepping into the dim circle of light as if entering a room full of party guests. Shadows still covered most of it's form, like a fuliginous cloak, but Ben could see long, thin legs. The skin was bare of clothing or hair, and in the light of the flashlight it seemed pallid and waxy and somehow gray.

Like a corpse, he thought.

The creature hissed—Ben knew in his gut that it was a hiss and nothing more—and that sound of dry, rasping wind rose around them again. And then it lunged forward. Not at Ben. The monster seemed focused on Roberts, and he selfishly thanked God for that.

Roberts had managed to crawl to his weapon, despite an arm that looked horribly broken. Bone protruded from the area on the back of his arm between the elbow and shoulder, and it was dark with blood. Still, the Sheriff had found the gun and rolled onto his back, holding it up toward the creature.

When it leaped toward him, he fired. Roberts pulled the trigger over and over until the gunshots were replaced by a metallic clicking sound. And then it was upon him, like a wolf on a fallen antelope.

Ben heard a wet ripping sound, and the Sheriff cried out. There was a gurgling sound, followed by silence, and then Ben knew that the man was gone. Whatever decision the creature had made about Chase, it gave no quarter to Gil Roberts.

Ben's flashlight had fallen into the leaves during his attempt to dodge the monster, and it lay a yard or two away, beaming its pale yellow light into the woods behind them. He had no chance of reaching it now. Not with the creature there, feeding on the Sheriff's body. He was trapped.

He could sense the tug of the shotgun dangling in his numb hands, and it felt heavy and unwieldy. It was loaded; Jack had seen to that. But Jack wasn't here to help him aim it or pull the trigger. He was alone, in the dark, with a monster that was hungry for human flesh.

Ben closed his eyes. He wanted to run and hide, but running would only bring on his death that much more quickly. So he shut his eyes—squeezed them closed with tremendous force—and wished it all away.

He saw Ellen's face in his mind's eye and she smiled. He wished all of this could have ended differently. In some ways, being stuck in Kettering had been horrible —having to lean on the help of strangers, the intense scrutiny of the Sheriff, and of course this creature from the woods—but in others ways it had been a blessing.

Oh well, he thought. *It wasn't meant to be.*

It was the silence that finally caused him to open his eyes.

The woods were empty. The two flashlights, laying among the leaves like fallen branches, cast their pale glow into the trees. It was enough light to clearly see that he was now alone.

The creature was gone.

Where it had been—where the *Sheriff* had been, as well—was now nothing but a tangle of broken leaves, torn clothing, and gore-covered bones. Ben turned his head away, afraid to remember that those remains were once a man.

He felt his gorge rise, and the gun dropped from his hands as he bent and fell to his knees. Bile and the remnants of his last meal rushed from his mouth and splashed on the crisp autumn leaves. It stank and burned.

And then he stood back up.

He grabbed the shotgun and walked toward one of the flashlights. He was free now. He could run, or he could help the others. Ben knew what he wanted to do now. He just hoped he could get out alive.

After glancing around at the terrain for a moment or two, he found his bearings and set off.

———∞———

Jack was running through the trees. Low branches whipped at his arms and face like small weapons. Each of these cat-o'-nine-tails struck his cheek and left a fresh line of red, but Jack didn't feel them. He was tracking something.

It had taken Ellen. He hadn't seen it, but he knew what had happened. Shadows had moved around them, and then something had plowed between them, sending her sprawling to the ground.

Jack had fired his rifle into the shadows, hoping to hit something. He shouted for Ellen to get up, to crawl or drag herself to his feet, but she hadn't responded. He didn't want to take his eyes off the shadows. It was moving too fast for him to do that.

He knew she was alive and awake, though. She moaned in the darkness. Jack could hear her moving among the leaves and tried to inch himself closer to that sound while he kept his eyes on the trees around them. It was fast. Damn, it was fast.

And then it struck. He remembered seeing a shadow move directly in front of him, so being hit from behind was something he hadn't expected. When the creature collided with the middle of his back, he nearly dropped his weapon. It was only his years of military training that helped him hold on, and he had rolled with the force while tucking his shoulder.

Jack tumbled through the leaves and into a small tree. It hurt, but he wasn't injured, and he managed to stand back up as quickly as he could. In the shadows in front of him, a darker shape moved with a fluid stealth. He brought his rifle up, ready to fire.

It was gone before he could pull the trigger.

What he didn't know—not then, at least—was that Ellen was gone with it. He came to that realization moments later after having swept the entire area for any sign of her.

He found the rock she had cracked her head on. It was a flat piece of granite, the bones beneath so much of New England's soil. The dark, wet shine told him that she was indeed wounded. There was no other sign of her, though. No mangled corpse, no torn limbs, and no hunched creature, feasting on her body.

But there was blood, and that's all he needed.

He ran now, stopping every dozen yards or so to check for fresh signs. Each time he did, the blood was where he expected it to be. The creature had picked her up and was taking her somewhere. Why, he did not know. Where, though…oh yes, that much was clear.

Knowing the destination, Jack was free to run. The only reason he stopped at all was to make sure his vector was on target. He was nearly positive where he *needed* to go, but the blood helped confirm it. The infrequent stops did slow him down, but he would rather that than wind up in the wrong spot.

He hadn't failed; Jack was positive that he had done everything he could. The creature, this wendigo or whatever it was, had simply moved too quickly for his human reflexes. Was he older now? Sure, but the reflexes he had honed as an Army Ranger weren't the kind that faded with age. Not at forty, at least. He was still as sharp as ever.

Even at his best—in the prime of his youth and in the midst of the most intense missions of his career—he wouldn't have stood a chance against this creature in combat. It was a natural predator, hunting *as* a shadow *from* the shadows. It moved silently, and with speed that was almost impossible to comprehend.

He jumped over a rotting tree that lay prone across his path. His flashlight, the kind with a flexible neck, was now clipped to his jacket and pointing ahead, allowing him to pick his way quickly. The rifle was slung over his shoulder, but he knew it could be out and ready in a matter of seconds.

He wished he could have found the handgun he had given to Ellen, but it seemed to be lost to the shadows and ground cover. It didn't help that it had been black, making it very easy to mistake for shadows. Jack wondered if someone might stumble upon it in the future and take it home, like a souvenir. That wouldn't be good; he would have to return in daylight to find it. If he survived the night, that is.

Jack stepped around a tall thicket that blocked his way, and then quickly stopped. He had reached his destination and wanted to make sure that he covered the last couple of yards with as much caution as possible.

The back side of the stone shed was shrouded in creeper vines and the heavy boughs of the surrounding trees. An enormous cluster of thistle had grown along the base of the structure, which was roughly ten feet wide, nearly enclosing the stone foundation.

Nearly.

A path was visible to the trained eye, but Jack doubted if anyone had ever ventured back here to even have a chance at noticing it. Surely Jasper Levett had, but Jack was beginning to understand why. It was clear now that the old man was the caretaker of more than just the cemetery.

Set into the rear of the stone building, and almost as dark and featureless as the shadows that enclosed it, was a large metal door. As Jack stepped closer he could see the rusty patina that years in the harsh elements had created. The bent remains of a handle were mounted on the left side like the tail of an ancient metal rat.

He reached for the door, ready to pull it open and step inside, but stopped. Something moved to his left, rustling a low branch still heavy with dry leaves.

When he moved, it was with the speed of a coiled spring being released. He swiveled on his feet while pulling the rifle over his head. The stock and grip fell into his hands like an old lover, and he wrapped his finger around the trigger.

"Stop!" called a hushed whisper from the bushes. "It's me!"

Jack lifted the rifle up to point away, and Ben stepped out of the shadows. His face was painted in fear.

"God, Ben," Jack said. "I nearly killed you. Wait, where are the others?"

Ben didn't answer. He slowly shook his head and grimaced.

"Both of them?" Jack asked. "Dead?"

"Yeah," he muttered. "I left them. There was nothing I could do for now."

Ben's eyes shifted and glanced around at the area behind Jack. At first they were narrow, and then they grew steadily wider.

"Jack, where's Ellen?" His voice was laced with dread, and he stepped forward, nearly pushing the soldier out of his way.

"Gone," Jack replied. "In there." He pointed toward the dark iron door hidden among the thicket of branches and leaves.

"Alive, though?" Ben wanted to be hopeful. He had survived this far, although he wasn't sure how or why. He couldn't fathom making it out alive, only to have lost her now.

"Yeah," Jack replied. "But she's hurt. And the wendigo has her. I think it went in there."

Ben lifted his shotgun. "What are we waiting for, then?"

Jack forced a smile. "This thing is fast, Ben. We're going to be stepping into a small space. It's suicide. You understand that, right?"

"I don't care," Ben replied. "I'm not leaving Ellen in there. You're welcome to leave, but I'm going in."

"Oh, no," Jack said. "There's no way I'm going to let you do this alone. And you'll follow *my* lead, understood?"

"Whatever you want," Ben replied with a nod.

Jack moved back to the door and leaned over the thistles to grab at the handle. For a moment, it didn't appear that the door was going to swing, but with a grunt Jack was able to pull it open.

It was dark inside, but they could both clearly see by the glow of Jack's flashlight that the door didn't open up on the interior of the shed. Someone—how long ago was anyone's guess—had built a wall of old clay bricks across the opening about three feet inside. To the right, though, was a deeper darkness.

Stairs.

CHAPTER EIGHTEEN

BEN GLADLY LET JACK step into the small space first, and then followed close behind. It smelled of mildew, rot, and death inside, and he fought the urge to gag as the first wave of stale air washed over him. The sound of dripping water echoed up from the space below. And there was light.

It was dim at first, but a small light slowly brightened as they descended the wet, rough-hewn stairs. With no other sound, Ben could hear Jack's slow, even breaths as he led the way down. As the light grew, Ben noticed that the walls of the stairway were narrow and covered in a thin, glossy film. He ran a fingertip across one of the stones, scooping up a small droplet of something green and congealed, which caused him to recoil.

Ahead, Jack had reached the bottom and stepped aside to allow Ben to exit the stairs. They had entered a large room—much bigger than the ancient stone shed above—which was spanned by three large wooden beams about seven feet above the floor. Ben assumed that they held up the storage shed above.

The light came from a flashlight that had been discarded on the rough dirt floor a few yards away. Ben pushed the switch on his own light instinctively, and swept the walls for a sign of Ellen.

"There's a doorway over there," Jack said, aiming his light at the far wall of the chamber. Ben looked to see a wide, black opening in the fieldstone wall, like a gaping mouth ready to devour them.

"I suppose we have to go that way," Ben said reluctantly, and then followed close behind as Jack proceeded without reply.

The floor of the chamber was cluttered with wooden crates and rusty tools and digging implements. Everything appeared dry here, and Ben wondered where the dripping sounds he could hear were coming from. Most likely, they originated from the dark hole in the wall ahead. He assumed he would soon find out.

Had this been part of the original stone building? Judging by the items scattered across the floor, it seemed to have been used as a storage area. But that would have been a very long time ago, long before the wall upstairs was built, cutting off the stairs from the front portion of the shed. Ben wondered how many people knew that the iron door and the stairs behind it even existed.

No one alive, at least, he thought. *But no, that wasn't right. Jasper Levett knew, didn't he?*

Ben wondered what happened to the old man. He was fast, as evidenced by his escape into the woods, but surely the five of them—when there *was* five, that is—would have had no trouble tracking him down, even in the dark. Instead, he seemed to have melted into the shadows and slipped through their grasp.

Whatever part Jasper Levett had played in this mystery was doomed to remain unknown as long as he eluded capture. With Sheriff Roberts dead, Ben had doubts that the old man would be found and questioned. Still, he could hope. The greater threat was obviously the creature, and whether or not it waited for them in the darkness ahead.

Toward the end of the room, off to the left side of the opening in the wall, Ben noticed that the floor was covered in a matted pile of dry grass and straw. An impression had been worn into the debris, larger than any human being he had ever known.

Jack saw it too, and pointed. "Bedding?" he asked quietly.

Bedding? Ben thought. The logic of it didn't seem to connect for a moment, but he quickly realized that, yes, even a monster needed to rest. And judging by the condition of the straw, this creature had slept a long time in that dark space.

He immediately remembered what Chase had told them earlier that evening, about long periods of hibernation followed by feeding sessions. Could it be that it was here, in this corner, that the wendigo had slept undisturbed for thirty years, only to awake and hunt the people of Kettering? The more they learned, the more likely this scenario seemed.

Jack stopped at the opening and glanced at Ben.

"Ready?" he whispered.

"No," Ben replied, swallowing hard. "But I doubt I have a choice, do I?"

"Not really."

Ben let Jack step through the jagged opening in the cellar wall and then followed him. The air inside was humid and heavy with the scent of mildew. He could feel the closeness, as if the ceiling were lower and the walls more confining. And the darkness seemed to devour the glow of their flashlights, much as it had in the woods earlier. It was oppressive.

Ahead of them, the space appeared to bend to the right. Echoes of the rhythmic dripping were louder in that direction, and Jack moved toward it. He seemed fearless, but that confidence failed to rub off on Ben this time. All he could feel was an overwhelming sense that he was losing control of his own safety, that he was walking head-first into true, lethal danger.

The ground beneath their feet began to feel unusual, and every step resulted in a faint crackling sound. Ben pointed his light at a space in front of his feet and almost instantly recoiled.

Bones.

Thousands of small, fragile bones. They littered the ground, sometimes creating a layer as thick as an inch. He was certain that most of them were the remains of small animals, but some—longer slivers of white that protruded from the twisted mass of bones—seemed very human in origin.

Every step was accompanied by that sickening crunch. Ben tried to step as lightly as he could, but it was no use. Not even Jack, who had trained for stealth, could walk across the room silently. They had no choice but to move forward, but Ben's heart sank with the realization that any element of surprise they might have had was now gone.

Something shuffled up ahead, around the bend in the room. Both of the men stopped and waited, certain that something was about to round the corner and attack. A long moment of silence was followed by a feminine moan.

"Ellen," Ben whispered harshly to Jack.

The other man didn't turn, instead keeping his eyes on the corner, rifle trained at chest-level. Ben stepped forward—another crunching sound announcing his movement—and passed Jack.

"Ben!" Jack hissed. "Get behind me."

But Ben was driven beyond fear. Someone he cared about was still alive and waiting for him nearby. He could hear her. She moaned again and his heartbeat raced faster in response. She was in trouble and Ben was going to save her.

He froze at the corner. His flashlight cast an eerie luminesce over the passageway ahead, and what he saw nearly stopped his heart completely. Ellen's familiar form was spread out on the bone-littered floor ahead, one hand rubbing at her face. Beyond her, a shape darker than the shadows was slowly moving away from her deeper into the underground space.

Jack rounded the corner and stood beside Ben for a moment. Then, after studying the space and thinking through their options, he turned to Ben and spoke quietly.

"We'll walk forward to where she's laying," he whispered. "I'll keep watch on the back of the tunnel while you pick her up and retreat the way we came. Understood?"

Ben understood. He understood that the creature most likely already knew they were there. It was walking away from them, but that didn't mean it was oblivious to their presence. Judging by how fast it had moved through the woods earlier, there was no chance of racing against it. They were there, alive and armed, purely because the wendigo had allowed it.

The sane choice would be to run. In fact, he was fairly certain that the creature was giving them that chance. To escape and live, to flee the woods and never return. But that meant leaving Ellen here, where she would most certainly become the thing's next meal. Ben was frightened—more so than he had ever been in his life, for sure—but he wasn't willing to leave her here.

He nodded to Jack, and then both men started the slow, painfully noisy walk forward. Each step filled Ben's gut with hot, bitter worry that the creature would finally turn and face them. Jack's footsteps were now as loud as Ben's, and together they filled the small space with a cacophony of crackling sounds.

Finally, they reached her. Ben dropped to one knee and leaned over her.

"Ellen," he said softly, shaking her shoulder with his free hand. He was reluctant to set down the shotgun, whether or not Jack was standing guard over him. "Ellen, you need to wake up."

She moaned and rolled toward the sound of his voice. "Ben?" Her mouth sounded muffled, as it it were full of cotton.

He reached out, took one of her hands in his, and gave it a gentle squeeze. "Ellen, you need to wake up and stand. Can you stand up?"

Another moan, and then she turned her head toward him. "You're alive," she said to him. "Thank God, you're alive."

"There's no time right now, Ellen. We need to leave. Now." His voice trembled with fear as he continued tugging at her. "Get up!"

She leaned into him this time and then slowly sat up. Ben's light flashed across her face and he caught a glimpse of the slash of red that covered the left side of her forehead.

Oh God, she's hurt, he thought. *I hope she can walk. I can't carry her out of this place on my own.*

He hooked his arm under one of her's and gripped her side. Then, with a slowness that was almost painful, he stood, bringing her up with him. She wobbled in his grip and he nearly dropped her, but finally she was on both feet standing beside him.

Jack stepped forward and shifted to be directly in front of them.

"It's coming back," he said, gesturing toward the darkness ahead of them. "You need to go, Ben. Take her and run."

"But—" he began, but Jack cut him off.

"Get the hell out of here," he hissed at them. "I'll be right behind you."

Ben did as he was told. He lifted Ellen as much as he could, and helped her move back the way they had come. At first her feet were barely more than support, but slowly they began to help drive her forward. Ben assumed the change in orientation was helping her regain her senses.

At the bend in the passageway he glanced back over his shoulder. Jack was frozen in place, the light from his flashlight pooling around his feet, and poised for whatever it was that approached from the distant shadows. Ben paused for a brief moment to adjust his grip around Ellen's ribcage, and watched in horror as the wendigo stepped out from the darkness.

At first, all he could see where the legs. They were the same long, gray legs he had seen in the woods before the Sheriff was slaughtered. Ben thought of the shambling zombies that the movies of the last few years portrayed, but he knew this thing was swift and agile. The only common feature it shared with the undead of Hollywood was the corpse-like color of its flesh.

It stepped closer to Jack and the light revealed more of its form. Long, sinuous arms hung limp at its sides. Their waxy, hairless flesh ending with broad, clawed hands. The shadows still hid most of the creature's torso and head, but Ben was certain he saw something that resembled antlers or horns atop its head.

Jack turned one last time, panic washing over his face as he realized Ben and Ellen hadn't yet slipped from view.

"Go!" he shouted before whipping himself back around to meet the beast.

Ben nearly threw Ellen forward and together they stumbled through the piles of animal bones and torn cloth. She was more awake now, and her legs had begun to contribute to their escape. When they had passed through the hole in the foundation wall, he let go and they both moved as fast as possible through the crates and supplies toward the stairs.

"Faster," Ben grunted at her. "We don't have much time now. Climb!"

Gunfire erupted from behind them, filling the confining space with a crashing din. That's when Ben heard Jack utter a deep, guttural shout.

"Go!" he shouted at the others.

Dammit, why aren't they gone yet? he thought as he watched them finally slip around the corner of the tunnel. *I don't even know if I can hold this thing back, let alone buy them the time they need to get out of here.*

Then what?

He ignored his own question and spun back around. The thing, this wendigo or whatever it was, had continued to advance. Now he could see its chest and shoulders. And its face.

Some of the flesh on the creature's torso was peeling away in chunks, as if the body were decaying. There were a few small, round holes as well. Perfectly round holes, he realized. Bullet holes.

But no blood.

His heart sank.

Would this rifle in my hands even make a difference? he thought. *I don't know enough. I'm not strong enough. Do I even have a chance at all? How can I kill something that won't bleed? That won't die?*

But Chase had said it *could* be killed. Fire, he had told them. The burning heat of a flame would end this creature's reign of terror.

It stepped closer. Wide, twisted antlers protruded from the pale skull of a face atop broad, decaying shoulders. Jack could smell it now, its fetid, rotten breath. There was an earthy scent as well, musky and animalistic. It was the thing's mouth, however, that was beyond his imagination.

The lower jaw hung slack, like some cheap Halloween mask, and nearly rested on its chest. The gaping blackness seemed immense, ready to engulf everything—the rifle, his body, even the stones and carnage around them. The eyes were sunken and set within deep wells of bruised, rotting skin, a skin that was drawn taught over the skull, like dry parchment over stone.

Most frightening of all, it looked hungry, as if it had never eaten a meal in its entire existence. Of course, Jack knew that wasn't true. It had eaten well this week. It had feasted on the people of Kettering. On their safety. On their youth. On their fear.

It was eternally hungry, and it was ready to feast again.

Jack pulled the trigger on the carbine rifle. For a moment it felt foreign and awkward in his hands. Hands that should be so experienced, so intimately aware of the weapon's weight and presence. He pulled the trigger with one rigid, frozen finger, feeding round after round into the hungry creature.

He was aware of shouting. It must have been Ben, or maybe Ellen. The gunfire would have frightened them. But they should be gone now. No, perhaps it was he who was yelling, his voice bellowing out in a primitive battle cry.

The wendigo staggered backward for a moment and Jack did the same, purchasing more space between them with the care and diligence of a frugal New Englander. Every inch counted. Every step farther apart was another heartbeat, another chance that he might live long enough to escape.

He brought the rifle up and aimed at the thing's face. It swung large arms up reflexively and backed farther into the shadows. Jack no longer heard his own cry of rage, but now the space filled with another, more alien scream. The beast was hurt and angry, and yet still so very, very hungry.

It howled and reeled under the barrage of bullets while Jack slowly inched backward toward the bend in the tunnel. His heart beat with a steady, rapid thumping that he could hear in his ears. And then he saw the curve in the wall with his peripheral vision, just to his right.

As if on cue, the rifle went silent. It was spent. For an instant—the briefest of heartbeats was all his trained mind needed—he weighed the options. He could try to reload, or he could run. Neither seemed like options that would end well, but at least running would get him closer to the stairs, closer to escape. It seemed more hopeful to run.

He didn't think; he just bolted. The creature howled again and dropped its arms from its face. The gaunt, skeletal features twisted in an expression of curiosity, perhaps wondering if more pain was on its way. But Jack did not see that expression. Jack was running.

He rushed through the break in the wall and into the dimly-lit basement of the shed. He could hear the bones crunching beneath the wendigo's feet as it pursued him. His heartbeat thrummed in his ears, ears that still buzzed from the noise of the rifle. He knew he didn't have much time.

He reached into his pocket while racing through the storage area and found what he was looking for. He was almost at the end of the room, with the stairway only a few feet away, when he stopped and turned around.

The creature was emerging from the opening in the wall. The elongated limbs slipped through before the torso, like some grotesque birthing sequence. The wendigo bent and twisted its neck to fit both skull and antlers through the opening, followed quickly by the shoulders.

And then it was through.

Jack quickly backpedaled toward the far wall, pulling the handful of matches out from his pocket. He eyed a pile of broken wooden crates and the scattering of dry grass and straw around it, and freed one of the matchedsfrom the elastic band that held them together.

Whether the creature understood what he intended to do or not, Jack did not know. It howled, though, throwing its head back and opening the already impossibly-wide mouth still wider. It was a cry of anger, a declaration that it was done toying with him. The room shook with the sound of it, and then silence returned. That was when it charged.

Jack looked for a surface to strike the match on and reached for the wall. If it was too wet it wouldn't work, but he did not have many options. He had to try something. He was scratching the match along the surface of one of the old stones when the creature reached him.

It swung out with one of its long corpse-like arms, vicious claws extended. Jack tried to dodge the blow, and brought the rifle up as a shield. The force was unlike anything he had ever experienced before, and although the claws didn't find his flesh, he felt his arm shudder painfully and his body was thrown against the ancient wall.

Jack crumpled to the ground with a grunt. He kicked out with his feet instinctively and brought his arms up to protect his face. The wendigo was advancing slowly toward him now, almost with caution. Perhaps he had frightened it before. Maybe the beast expected more gunfire.

Jack knew that wasn't possible now, though. The rifle had been wrenched from his hand and lay somewhere across the room. Even if he were able to retrieve it, he would still have to load a new magazine before it would be useful to him. It was too late for that. His time was up.

The creature stood over him, its hulking shape like the branches of some twisted, long-dead tree. Both arms were extended and each clawed finger was splayed wide, ready to rake across his fragile body and shred his flesh and muscle. It was a hunter and a killer, and it had him cornered.

Jack looked up at it, straight into its eyes, and noticed for the first time that they were the only feature that seemed human. Yet they were hungry and dark, like an abandoned well that one might board up and warn the children about.

The creature lunged for him, and then an explosion of sound fill the room. One of the creature's long, narrow arms nearly separated from the shoulder as a shotgun shell tore through the waxy flesh. It howled again and stumbled to the side, trying to turn toward the source of the attack.

That's when Jack glanced toward the stairway door.

CHAPTER NINETEEN

IT WAS ELLEN.

She stood at the bottom of the stairs, shotgun leveled at the monster while smoke spilled from the wide muzzle.

"Just like hunting deer," she said with her jaw clenched. "Want more?"

She pulled the trigger a second time, and a large chunk of the wendigo's torso exploded, splattering gray flesh and something thick and black across the wall. The creature howled in pain and then staggered back deeper into the room.

Ellen didn't flinch. Instead, she stepped into the room, gaining ground on it. As she did, Ben moved out from behind her and rushed over to Jack.

"Get up, man," he said. "I sure hope you can run."

Jack gripped Ben's arm and rose to his feet. "Hold on. I have one more thing to do before we go," he told him.

The matches were still in his hand. Some of the heads had snapped off in his grip when the creature struck him, but there were enough left to try again. He pulled one free and then stooped to strike it against one of the crates.

There was a scratching sound, and then a flame bloomed around the head of the match. Ellen stepped closer to the reeling creature and pulled the trigger a third time. The noise was deafening, but she hit her target again, obliterating one of its clawed hands.

"Let's go, gentlemen," she shouted at them. "This party's over."

Jack held the flame against the side of the crate, close to the debris of straw and dry leaves, and watched the fire jump and catch. He repeated it one more time on a second crate, and then held the dying flame to the rest of the bundled matches.

They sputtered and then flashed to life violently. Jack looked across the room to the makeshift bed that he and Ben had noticed earlier and then tossed the matches toward it. They landed in the center, and the matted patch of bedding exploded in flames almost immediately.

"Go!" Jack yelled, pushing Ben ahead of him.

Ellen pulled the trigger one final time before turning to join them. Jack stepped aside and let her follow Ben, and then he fell in behind them. As he did, a wave of warm air rushed across his skin, and he heard the crackle of flames as they devoured the dry boxes and tinder.

Ben had opened the door at the top of the stairs, and all three of them spilled out into the cold, dark night. Ellen stumbled on a branch, and Ben tripped over her, followed by Jack. For a brief moment they all lay on the leave-covered ground, breathing hard and letting their eyes grow accustomed to the darkness.

A sound from somewhere inside the staircase caught their attention. It sounded like a wild animal trying to run on stone. Jack panicked when he realized what it meant. The creature was coming. It was trying to get out.

"The door!" he shouted at Ben. "Shut it!"

Both men jumped to their feet and together they managed to swing the heavy iron door closed with a thunderous crash. Barely a heartbeat later, something heavy threw itself against the other side, shaking their arms to the bone.

Jack grunted aloud against the strain. The creature desperately wanted out, that much was clear, but he was damned if that was going to happen. He caught Ben's eye and nodded grimly. Ben returned the gesture, and then leaned harder into the door.

They could both feel the metal getting hotter. The flames had grown enough that the space below was now most likely an inferno. If Chase was correct, all they needed to do now was hold on just a little longer. The flames inside the creature's lair would eventually burn it alive, ending the nightmare once and for all.

A powerful blow suddenly collided with the barrier from inside, and it was all Ben could do to keep from toppling over. In his struggle to maintain his balance he took pressure off the door, and it opened slightly. Thick smoke and intense heat bellowed out through the opening, stinging his eyes.

The small gap was all the creature needed, however. A clawed hand quickly slipped around the edge of the door, its pale fingers twitching and searching for purchase. Ben strained to push the door closed again, leaning into the rusty metal with his shoulder while his feet dug into the ground, but it was clear they were fighting a losing battle.

It was Ellen who finally turned the tide. She had grabbed a fallen branch from somewhere nearby, and clubbed at the creature's hand as if she were chopping firewood. A howl rang out as the hand disappeared inside, and then the door slammed back against the frame. More pounding, desperate and erratic, rocked the door before giving way to what sounded like slapping, growing weaker with each blow. Then, after a few tense moments, it stopped.

"Can we find something to bolt this closed?" he asked, turning to Ellen. "Some rocks or a big log? Anything will help."

"Take this," she replied, handing him the branch she had used to beat at the creature. "Let me see what else I can find." With that, she unclipped Jack's flashlight and hurried off into the woods.

"I can see the headline now," Ben said with a grin. "ARMY RANGER'S LIFE SAVED BY LOCAL LIBRARIAN."

"Not a word," Jack replied with an expression of mock anger. "I have a reputation to keep up."

Ellen soon returned, dragging a heavy log about three feet long. She managed to get it close to the door, and then Ben lifted one end and wedged it against the rusted iron crossbeam. They dug the other end into the hard soil, kicking away small rocks and piles of dirt to make room for it. When it seemed secure, both men stepped away and brushed off their hands.

They sat down a few feet away, backs against a large tree, and Ellen joined them. They were silent for a while, watching the barricaded door for signs of renewed struggle, but nothing happened. After the tension of the last hour, it felt almost unnatural to sit still in the silence.

Finally it was Ben who spoke.

"Chase's body is out there somewhere," he said without taking his eyes off the door.

"Chase is dead?" Ellen asked with shock.

Ben nodded. "It's so odd, though," he continued. "The creature didn't rip him apart. It just killed him and left his body. Not like…"

"Not like who?" Ellen asked. Their group was much smaller now, and she had noticed that. "Gil?"

Ben nodded again, unable to find the words to continue. Ellen sighed and lowered her head. He watched silvery lines appear as tears ran down her face. She was quiet, but her chest heaved visibly. Ben couldn't seem to hate her for that. Everyone feels loss at some point in their life, and it's never easy.

"We dated, you know," she said to Jack. "Before college. I couldn't handle the distance, so we split up. When he finally came back to Kettering, he brought a wife with him."

"I'm sorry," Jack said. "I don't think I knew that."

"He died protecting me from that thing," Ben added. "I wouldn't be here without him."

"It's alright," She said, rubbing a hand at the corners of her eyes. "I stopped needing him years ago." Then, turning to Ben and reaching out for his hand: "Sounds like I have one last thing to thank him for, though."

Ben understood what she meant, and he smiled at her as warmly as possible. His body was tired and spent, but now that it was over—now that the creature was dead and the threat removed—he felt that he could allow himself to accept it. They were safe and together.

"We'll have to wait until morning before we go looking for Chase," Jack added. "It's too dark right now, and I think it might be good if we let someone know that Gil is dead."

"Good call," Ben said, rising to his feet. He reached out a hand to help Ellen stand, which she took with a smile.

"Hey, what about me?" Jack mockingly said from the ground.

"What about you?" Ben replied with a grin before offering a hand. "Wimp," he declared.

They set off silently through the dark, moving with slow, exhausted steps.

———

Ben and Jack dropped Ellen off at her home after leaving the cemetery, and then went straight to the Country Sheriff's office. Someone needed to know what had happened, no matter how difficult it might be to believe.

The young deputy on duty, Jim Cranston, was nearly overwhelmed by the weight of the news, and he slumped over the tall counter as they told him what had happened. He had apparently been a part of some of the final conversations between Roberts and the County Medical Examiner, and though nothing could have prepared him for their news, he knew enough to believe what they told him.

In the end, they agreed to meet Cranston at the cemetery in the morning to search for what remained of the bodies of Chase Abington and Sheriff Roberts, and to hopefully explore the shed's lower level. It wasn't a decision either of them were excited about, but they knew it needed to be done and so they had reluctantly agreed to it.

As the men drove home, they passed the cemetery one last time that night. Both of them studied the shadows inside with wary eyes before turning left and heading back to Jack's house for rest.

Unfortunately, however, Ben slept fitfully and awoke more tired than he thought possible. Jack was already up and had cooked them both some eggs and bacon, which they ate in silence while drinking coffee. Once they were finished, the two men headed out to meet

Cranston, who as of the night before was the acting Sheriff of Kettering County.

They arrived at Maple Hill Cemetery to discover that Cranston had called in a favor, and a number of State Police Officers were on hand to assist in the search and cleanup. After a briefing in the center of the cemetery—a meeting that Jack found himself leading, rather than Cranston—the group split into pairs and began to scour the surrounding woods.

Jack partnered with Ben, and the two men began their search at the old shed. Despite being the ones who placed it there, they had a difficult time removing the log that they had used to barricade the door. After a bit of digging around the base, and some hard pulling, they finally managed to dislodge it and wrench the door open.

The heavy scent of decay and charred organic matter greeted them on the other side of the rusty door. Ben pulled his shirt up over his mouth and nose, but Jack simply winced and stepped inside. Both men had brought powerful lights, and they switched them on and pointed them down into the darkness below. They could see no movement from where they stood, but that would not be enough to ease their minds. They needed to go down and see for themselves that the creature was dead.

Jack descended first, keeping his light trained on the foot of the stairs while reaching inside his jacket to pull out a large handgun he had brought for protection. Ben was sure that the State Troopers wandering the woods outside wouldn't approve, but none of them had been willing to step inside the shed. This was a task for Jack and Ben alone, and they got to play by their own rules.

Once inside the lower chamber, the two men found the stone floor littered with charred debris. The walls were painted with soot and ash, and small piles covered the floor in patches. Some had clearly been wooden crates, while others were less distinct.

"Do you see anything that might be the creature?" he asked Jack as they walked slowly and carefully through the chamber.

"That pile over there could be it," Jack replied, pointing to one of the corners. "Then again, so could either of those two over there, near the stairs. And any of them could very well just be old boxes, too."

Ben frowned. "So basically, we don't know for sure."

"Basically? Yeah," Jack replied. "I don't know what else could have happened to it, though. If it wasn't down here, crouched in a corner and waiting for us to return, then my gut tells me it's dead."

"I sure hope you're right," Ben said. "I think I'll sleep better knowing it's not out there in the dark, hunting more innocent people."

"What do you care, Mr. Fancy Writer," Jack said with a grin. "You'll be leaving town soon and heading back to the safety of your condo in Hollesley."

"Perhaps," Ben replied. "I have some decisions to make, for sure. But that doesn't mean I can't be concerned about what happens to the people here. I like Kettering, and even though it's only been a few days, I feel at home here. Cannibalistic demonic monster aside, of course."

"Naturally," Jack agreed. "Alright, this place is clear. Let's head up and help out the Troopers."

They ascended the blackened stone steps and stepped out into the fresh air. Ben sniffed at his shirt and decided it would take at least three spins through the washer before the smell would come out. In the crisp morning air, however, it was easy to breath deep and feel clean again.

"Over this way," he told Jack. "I think I remember where Chase went down. We might even find what remains of Roberts on our way there."

"Lead the way," Jack told him.

They walked east for fifteen minutes or more, occasionally crossing paths with one of the others involved in the search. No one had found a body yet, but they all mentioned finding things that seemed unnatural to them.

Ben and Jack listened to at least four of the State Police Officers mention unusual slash marks on some of the tree trunks. One said that he found the impression of a very large foot in a patch of mud. All around them were signs of the previous night's events, and even though the evidence was concrete and tangible, many of the volunteers simply refused to believe what they were seeing.

About an hour into their search of the woods, a shout went up from one of the State Troopers. Ben and Jack hurried toward him, assuming the man had managed to find Chase's body before they could, but it wasn't who they expected. Instead of the young college student, they saw the body of Jasper Levitt sprawled out among the leaves.

He was dead, though no one there could find a visible cause of death. Their best guess was that he had run himself too hard and suffered cardiac arrest. Jasper had been old, although the man's many years enslaved to the bottle hadn't made it easy to guess *how* old. Ben was simply grateful that they had found him, dead or alive.

After another hour of searching, however, Ben began to worry about what he *hadn't* found: the body of Chase Abington. He knew the general area where the he had seen the body, but he couldn't seem to find the exact spot now that it was a new day. Sure, it had been dark the night before, and the thing hunting them from the shadows had made it very difficult to keep to any sort of trail, but Ben had expected to locate the body over the course of a two-hour search.

In the end, the search was called off just before noon with little success. One of the State Police volunteers did manage to find some scraps of Sheriff Roberts' uniform, along with a few bone fragments, his firearm, and his badge, but little else of the man could be found. Deputy Cranston received the small bag of remains with a somber silence.

Back at the old white Chevy truck, the two men paused to watch the State Troopers climb back into their cars and slowly exit the cemetery. Cranston followed after them, nodding to them as he drove his cruiser past their truck. Ben didn't know how long the deputy would be in charge of filling Sheriff Roberts' shoes, but given the difficult events of the past twelve hours or so, he thought the young officer was going to do just fine.

Ben sighed as the last cruiser left the cemetery, and then jumped when the sound of a phone ringing broke the silence. He turned at Jack with an expression of bewilderment, but the man only pointed down at Ben's pants pocket.

"Don't look at me, city boy," the man said. "I don't carry a cell phone."

Ben felt for the phone and pulled it free. He didn't recognize the number on the small display, but he flipped it open anyway.

"Hello?" he said questioningly.

"Mr. Simmons, this is Buster," came a loud voice. Music blared in the background, and Ben was certain it was Bon Jovi. "I've got your car all patched up and ready to go. I'm real sorry about how long that took. Real sorry."

"No, your timing was perfect, Mr. Moynahan," Ben replied. "Absolutely perfect."

Jack guided the old pickup truck into Buster's crowded parking lot. Ben scanned the collection of vehicles beside the building, searching for his own. The lot was a mess, and he wondered how long some of the vehicles had been there. None of them seemed to have moved since Saturday, at least.

"There it is," he said, pointing toward the far end of the line of cars.

He and Jack had gone home after the call from Buster so Ben could pack up what few belongings he had brought into the house. Those items had been loaded into the back of the truck in a matter of minutes, and then they sat down to eat a quick lunch.

Ben also called the library and told Ellen that he would be picking up the car around 1:00 PM. She was subdued, but claimed to be happy for him. She also asked if she could meet him at Buster's garage. Ben, of course, agreed enthusiastically, telling her he had hoped she might offer to do that.

He spent the entire five minute drive from the Brooder homestead to Buster's in a daze. He wasn't ready to say goodbye to her. In fact, he had seriously begun to believe that he needed to make some life-changing decisions regarding Ellen.

Jack had also been a good friend during his short stay in Kettering, and that friendship was something he would sorely miss. Friends were a rare thing for Ben, and since his move to Hollesley he had met very few people that he would consider to be more than an acquaintance. Perhaps it was the events of the past few days that helped him bond with Jack, as if they had gone to battle together. In some ways Ben supposed they had.

"That should do it for you, I suppose," Jack said as he pulled the emergency break and shifted out of gear. "Let me help you with your things."

"I can handle it," Ben said instinctively, not wanting to be an imposition. "I've been too much of a burden already."

But real friends are the people we're allowed to impose ourselves upon, he thought.

"Nonsense," Jack said, climbing out of the truck.

He grabbed the box of research paperwork and followed Ben to the small Volkswagen. Ben popped the trunk and tossed his overnight bag in beside the box of papers.

"You've been a fantastic host, Jack," he told him. "I know I've said it a hundred times already this morning, but thank you so much for giving me a place to stay while Buster got me up and running. I never guessed it would've taken this long."

"There was a lot about the past few days that caught us off guard," Jack replied. "But I know this: without your little visit, that monster would have gone on killing just as it always had, and then gone back to sleep for another thirty years. Hell, for all I know, you saved my son, or a grandchild."

Ben shook Jack's extended hand and slapped him on the shoulder. "I wouldn't get that dramatic," he said, "but I'm happy I was able to contribute something. Kettering is much safer now, I'd say."

"I sure hope so," Jack replied. "Visit again sometime, alright? You're welcome at our house any time you're in town."

"Thanks, I plan on it," Ben said with a smile. "Now get out of here. Your family will be back in a while, and I need to settle up with Buster. He doesn't look like the kind of guy who gives away hard work for free."

"Will do," Jack replied, returning the grin. "I'll see you when I see you."

Ben watched as the white truck thundered to life and then slowly turned out of the lot, heading back to the Brooder homestead. Jack waved one last time and then he was gone.

Ben turned and walked over to the small office connected to the garage and slipped through the open door. Buster wasn't behind the old desk—Ben wondered if the man even knew this room existed—and he knew well enough to walk straight into the garage and shout for him.

"Good as new," the mountain of a man told him moments later as they walked back out to Ben's car. "A bugger of a part to get ahold of, I'll tell you, but she's purring like a kitten now."

"And what do I owe you," Ben asked, pulling out his wallet.

Buster handed him a piece of paper that itemized the part and labor in a collection of barely legible chicken scratch. The total due was clear enough at the bottom, and Ben realized he didn't have enough cash on him to pay it.

"You take plastic?" he asked hopefully.

"Nope," Buster replied. "But you can mail me a check when you get home. I heard what you did out there last night. It was brave of you; I'm not sure I'd have the guts to do the same. I think I can give you some grace and wait for the check to arrive."

"That's really generous of you," Ben replied. "Word's already spreading, eh?"

Buster nodded emphatically. "Whole town was scared witless the last couple of weeks, and you went and put a stop to it. Damn right the word spread, and fast."

Ben offered his hand, and then immediately regretted it. Buster grinned and returned the gesture. It was a lot like getting your hand caught in a block of cement, only this cement got tighter with every shake.

He was rescued by Ellen, who came walking up from the direction of the library. She had wrapped herself in a coat and scarf against the chill air, and her cheeks had a rosy flush to them.

Either that, or she's been crying, he thought.

"Gentlemen," she greeted them from a few paces away. "I hate to interrupt, but I have some business with Mr. Simmons."

"Sure thing, Ms. Hornsby," Buster said, releasing Ben's hand from the vice and stepping back. "Lots of work to be done, and not a lot of time." Then, to Ben: "You drive safe, and thanks again."

"Thanks to you as well, Buster," Ben replied.

The mountainous shape of the man vanished once more into the garage as Ben turned toward Ellen. She walked straight toward him and wrapped her arms around his neck, planting her lips on his. The kiss lasted much longer than Ben expected—not something he would complain about—and he kept her close after she released him.

"You're really leaving?" she asked. Ben could now tell that her eyes were clearly red, and the frown on her face highlighted her feelings about his departure. "I guess this is what I get for falling for some drifter passing through town."

Ben smiled and feigned offense. "Drifter? I'd like to think I'm more of a hobo with a purpose."

She sighed and bent her head, resting it on his chest. "So this is goodbye?"

"Actually," he said, making the decision as the words formed on his lips. "I was thinking of selling my mother's condo. I've got a feeling I could get a much larger place here in Kettering for my money. And I've heard they have a fantastic public library here."

Ellen beamed. "I don't know what to say. I approve, of course. And yes we *do* have a great library."

"It still means I need to drive back today," he told her. "There's going to be a lot to do in order to make that idea happen. It could be weeks, or even months."

"That's better than never," she smiled up at him. "I'll take it. And I'll do whatever I can to help you. But you're going to visit often."

"I'm counting on that," he replied. "Listen, you need to get back to work, and I need to get home. I have a cat that's sorely in need of some food and companionship. And a realtor to hire."

"One more kiss for the road, then?" she asked. She didn't wait for him to answer, however, and wrapped her arms around his neck, pulling him down one last time.

Ben thought about that kiss the entire way home.

EPILOGUE

SHERIFF JOHN EKLUND MADE the turn from Exeter Road onto Main Street, and then slowed his cruiser. Something had caught his eye inside Maple Hill Cemetery.

The street was wet and glossy from the rapidly melting snow. Spring had arrived with strength the day before, ending what had been a cold but pleasant winter. He was glad for that. He wasn't sure his back could withstand one more pass down his sidewalk with the shovel.

John had settled into his new role slowly since his election in early November. Election might be too strong of a term, though the town certainly did vote. He had been lulled out of retirement by a request from the town government that ended up being too tempting to pass up.

They needed a Sheriff, they had told him, and quickly. Apparently Fred Hamilton, the ancient Constable over in Exeter, had spoken highly of him, and suggested they get in touch before Florida lured him away. But John wasn't about to leave Rhode Island. His family had been in the Providence area for centuries.

They offered him a good salary and a staff of experienced deputies. After an emergency election, he was officially hired and on the job. Getting back in the saddle wasn't as easy as he had thought, though. The hours were long and there were hundreds of new faces and locations to commit to memory. It was tough work, for sure, but deep down it was what he loved to do. Retirement hadn't suited him much anyway.

So here he was, just shy of his seventieth birthday, riding patrol through what had begun to seem to him as the perfect little New England town. His back hurt and it was nearly lunch time, but before he could head back to the courthouse he wanted to check on what he had seen.

John steered the cruiser between the ancient stone pillars that guarded the gap in the cemetery wall, and then slowly drove down the muddy rut in the snow that he took to be a road. The trees were still bare, but the sky had that hopeful blue color that whispered about the approaching warmth.

About halfway into the cemetery the path curved gently off to the left, where he could see it spilled out onto Exeter Road through another gap in the wall. He pulled over to the side of the path just at the start of that curve, shut off the motor, and got out.

The air was cool but had that invigorating crispness that came with the melting snow. A few feet away, along the edge of the property where the leafless trees tangled with smaller underbrush, sat what looked like a small stone work shed. It was old, by the look of it, but it looked well-kept.

In front of the small structure stood a figure who was working at a pile of snow with a rusty shovel. It was this figure that had caught John's attention as he drove past, and he approached with a cordial wave.

"Afternoon," he said cheerfully. "I'm still getting to know folk around these parts, and thought I'd swing in and introduce myself. Sheriff John Eklund."

He extended a gloved hand, and the man reached out and gave it a shake. His hand was icy cold.

"Good to meet you," the man said flatly. He pushed his hood back and gave a forced smile. "Charlie Lockwood," he said.

John studied the man for a moment, struggling to remember if he had seen him before. The man wore dark coveralls, that kind one might expect on someone who works outdoors in cold weather. He had a slight build, and though he seemed to be in his mid-twenties, in many other ways he appeared much older.

It was possibly the overgrown beard and matted hair that stuck out from the knitted cap on his head, but there was also something in his eyes. They weren't the eyes of a young man. Instead, they had a dark and haunted look to them. He didn't know why, but John thought they looked hungry.

Alcoholic, he thought immediately. *Same vacant stare my father used to look at me with, the old bastard.*

"Son, can I ask what you're up to out here?" he asked, motioning to the shovel.

"Just trying to get caught up and ready for spring, Sheriff," the man replied coldly. "Jasper Levett hired me last summer, but work has been stacking up since he passed away a few months ago."

Levett. Now there's a name that rings a bell. That's the old man who up and got himself killed on the same night as my predecessor. Poor kid.

"Well, now," he began. "I'd have to say a lot of folk around here would be mighty glad to know someone is picking up the slack and making sure this place is ready if we need it. I hope that's not too soon, God willing, but you know what I mean."

"Of course," the younger man replied. His face remained cold and expressionless.

"Well, then," John continued, "I'll leave you to it. It was good to meet you, Mr. Lockwood. And if you ever need anything, you be sure to give me a call."

"Thank you," the man replied.

John reached out and shook the man's hand one last time, wondering again at how cold it felt. He turned to leave, but as he did he glanced one last time at the man's face and saw something he hadn't noticed before. There were holes in his lip—three of them, in fact—and another on the side of his nose.

Being a father and grandfather, John knew what they were from, of course. Removing a piercing always left a small temporary hole, but it would eventually heal over. This man apparently had a few of those, but had recently taken them all out.

It encouraged him that this young man, however sullen and shy he might be, had the maturity to do that, given the nature of the job. The last person a grieving family needed to see standing over their loved-one's grave is a man covered in facial piercings.

He'll do alright around here, John thought as he walked back over to his cruiser. *Yessir, he'll do just fine.*